The Con Man

THE CON MAN

A NOVEL BY KEN MITCHELL

Talonbooks   .   Vancouver   .   Los Angeles   .   1979 published with assistance from the Canada Council

Talonbooks
201 1019 East Cordova
Vancouver
British Columbia V6A 1M8
Canada

Talonbooks
P.O. Box 42720
Los Angeles
California 90042
U.S.A.

This book was typeset by Linda Gilbert, designed by
David Robinson and printed by Hemlock Printers for
Talonbooks.

First printing: October 1979

Acknowledgements: Chapters from *The Con Man* have first
appeared in *periodics* and *Canadian Fiction Magazine*.

The author wishes to acknowledge the assistance of the
Canada Council, the Yaddo Foundation and the University
of Regina during the writing of this book.

Canadian Cataloguing in Publication Data

Mitchell, Ken, 1940—
    The con man

    ISBN 0-88922-168-5 pa.

    I. Title.
PS8576.I73C6   C813'.54   C70-091215-5
PR9199.3.M58C6

for Gerry, Colin and Andrew

All of us have taken advantage at times, in one manner or another — one, of the forests belonging to the crown; another, of someone's savings; one man will steal from his children for the sake of some itinerant actress; another, from his peasants, for the sake of buying furniture or equipages. What can one do, when so many enticements exist in the world — expensive restaurants with mad prices, and masquerades, and drives and dances with the gypsies? Surely, one cannot always restrain one's self: man is not God.

Nikolai Gogol,
Dead Souls

ONE
WILLSON

Shall we indict one man for making a fool of another?

> Lord Chief Justice Holt
> of England in 1703,
> before fraud was a crime.

1

Willson appeared in the distance as a long grey line against the white. Gilly watched it through the small oval circle he had thawed with his breath in the frost of the window. As the dayliner rocked and buffeted down the track, the line grew darker and heavier, and streetlights appeared, looking pale blue and frozen.

When the dayliner slowed, the town's buildings flicked past: a few shacks, two or three large crumbling houses, garages, outhouses. There was a single flash of neon from somewhere in the distance, and the train stopped.

"Willson!" the conductor bawled, sticking his head into the car. "All ashore that's going ashore, mister!"

Gilly sighed; it was time to start all over again. He reached to the luggage rack and lifted his club bag down. The five remaining passengers watched him idly, slightly more curious than if he had been a coat rack. He turned up his collar and stepped down the aisle to the passage between the two cars.

"Travelling light?" The conductor gestured at his leather club bag.

Gilly sneered toward it. There was a pair of underwear inside, three socks, a shaving kit and his map. He could have carried them all in his pocket, but the bag was considerably more dignified. On the side of the bag, GOV'T OF CANADA had been impressed in gold letters. "Business," he said.

The train chugged idly as he stepped off. It's horn blatted into the snowy darkness, and it began rolling again. Gilly peered around the platform. The door on the deserted platform was locked. The final grey light of day suddenly expired.

Gilly had hoped for a better reception. Willson was the furthest his money would take him by rail. Now he must either stop in Willson or hitchhike on to Regina, where he might find a warmer welcome.

In the darkness, he could see a couple of mercury vapour lights and a slip of orange neon. A snowflake settled on his eyelashes and blotted out this short vision of civilization. When it had melted, a man appeared, trotting out of the darkness. He was blowing long plumes of steam as he jogged; from where he stood, Gilly could detect the spoor of yeasty draft beer. It was the station agent, who had run out from the beer parlour to pick up the mail sack lying beside Gilly's feet.

"Howdo?" the agent said cheerfully. "Train?"

"Yeah. Hotel?"

"Over there." The man gestured toward the neon, then turned and pointed out into the darkness. "Sunset Inn, too. Highway. No beer parlour."

With only a light overcoat, and the temperature already near zero, Gilly turned and followed the man, now gradually fading into a cloud of falling snow, toward the hotel. Not far from the station, the cinder path became a boardwalk, which took them past the White Rose gas station. It became a concrete sidewalk as they walked by the Willson Community Hall, the locker plant, the pool hall and the barbershop.

The hotel stood in isolation, a tall three-storey building waiting for a town to happen around it. "Terminal Hotel," the neon said. The station agent disappeared through the second door, inscribed "Licenced Premises." When Gilly stepped inside, he discovered immediately why the village was deserted; the beer parlour contained every adult male in Willson. It was November of 1959, and against the law for the women of Saskatchewan to drink an alcoholic beverage in public. Men were allowed beer, but only under strictly enforced regulations. He was suddenly back in the beer parlour at Meadow Lake: dense clouds of smoke, heavy laughter, clash of glasses, the heavy reek of draft beer. He shook off a hint of nausea and sat down.

Near Gilly's table, a pair of farmers watched him. One was an older Slavic-looking man with a fur hat pulled down over his brow, Ukrainian style. The other was a ruddy-faced youth with a Stetson hat and a set of inflamed frostbitten ears.

"Have a Boh, Buddy!" the young man called to Gilly, holding aloft an empty bottle of Bohemian beer.

"Thanks," Gilly said, before remembering he only had a handful of change in his pocket. "I'm only staying for a minute."

"Come over here and be sociable, goddammit," the fur-hatted one snarled.

When the waiter brought the beer, an argument ensued over who would pay for it. Gilly put his hand in his pocket as though pulling out change, but the red-eared youth finally paid. He turned to Gillly. "How about that goddam Rocket, eh? Still skatin' like a rookie! He's gonna get thirty goals again this season!"

"Greatest player of all time," Gilly agreed.

"Goddam pea-souper," the old man snorted. There was a silence as they all took a pull on their beer.

"Betcha I know what *you're* doin' in town," the youth said.

Gilly thought for a moment; maybe the kid might know something he didn't. "What?"

"You're a travellin' salesman!"

Gilly smiled. He glanced down at his clothes: white shirt and narrow tie, business suit, a light beige topcoat. He gave the boy his best salesman's sincere gaze. "You would have lost your money, friend. I'm not a salesman."

The old man laughed. "Don't hand us that bullshit, sonny. I kin spot 'em a mile off."

"I'm not selling anything."

"Sonny, everybody's sellin' something. If it ain't watered whiskey, it's somebody else's ideas."

"Then I'm sorry to disappoint you. I'm just a traveller, checking out the countryside. Headed for Regina."

"Well, what are you doin' *here*?" the youth smiled, as

though he had caught Gilly in a trap.

"Actually," Gilly said, "I've been interested in Willson for quite a while. I got interested while I was studying a map."

The boy pointed a finger at Gilly. "Oil!" he hooted. "Oil!" "Oil?"

"Lotsa oil talk in these parts, sonny. Friend a mine, Harold MacKechnie, had a guy over to his place in July, wantin' tuh buy the oil rights on his land. Offered him four thousand bucks. Wasn't you, was it?"

Gilly shook his head.

"Harold told him where to go quick enough. Figgered if the guy was offerin' that much, it must be worth a lot more, yuh see? Nobody else come around, though. No oil drillers, nuthin'. Guy must have been a con man."

"Country's full of them," Gilly agreed. "I had a brother in oil for a while, though. Up north."

"I knew it," the old man cackled. "I kin tell every time."

Gilly sucked the dregs of Bohemian foam from his bottle and said, "I better get moving." This kind of talk was going nowhere, he knew from long experience. He had just come from nowhere and had no great ambition to go back.

"Siddown, siddown!" the two farmers chorused, their enthusiasm only whetted. "Jimmy, bring this fella another Boh!"

"Sorry," Gilly said. "I don't have a bit of cash on me. I can't afford to reciprocate —"

They burst into uproarious laugher. The old man pointed out Gilly to the rest of the beer parlour, shouting, "*Reciprocate!*" Gilly sat down again.

"That Durelle was really something', eh?" the young man said. "Knocking Archie Moore down — what was it? — three times!"

"Durelle is a dumbo! He threw the goddam fight!"

"They probably brought him on too quick," Gilly said, "He wasn't ready for Moore."

"But to get that close, eh? Middleweight champ of the world! A Canadian!"

"He was another goddam frog," the man in the fur hat snapped. "Didden have the juice to lick a coon!"

Gilly studied the label on his bottle and said, "Well, there's one thing they'll never beat us at and that's curling. Much curling around here?"

They stared, then exploded into laughter again, falling off their chairs. The men around them laughed, too, and someone ordered another beer for Gilly.

"Hell, Mister — you know who lives here? The Bentleys!"

"The *Briar* Bentleys? In this town?"

"You said it! Prob'ly over at the curling rink this minnit. We just got the ice into her yesterday, and they're already slappin' broom."

"You think we could go and have a look?"

"Sure 'nuff! Let's have another couple a beer, and we'll head over to the rink."

It had been four years since the Bentley brothers had taken their rock-curling talent to the national Briar championships and demolished the opposition, becoming an instant legend. Since then, they had turned semi-pro, curling for money and winning nearly every bonspiel in North America. Gilly had followed their career for years, and here he was, in the town where their family had farmed for two generations.

"Do you recall?" Gilly said, "in the '55 Briar when Clayton Bentley drew for one in the tenth, with the other rink holding the shot rock?" It was the skip's most famous shot.

Gilly Savard, in one instant, became the most popular man in Willson. He knew — or seemed to know — more about the Bentleys than anyone else in town. His cup ran over with Bohemian for another hour, before the bar finally closed for the supper hour. Then the entire crowd headed for the curling rink, four blocks distant. Everyone wanted to walk beside Gilly, and they were tripping over each other, stumbling to keep up. On his left, the fur-hatted old man was saying, "Aluminum siding. That's what you're sellin' eh? Aluminum siding!"

The Bentleys were interrupted in the middle of their practising to be introduced to Gilly. Somebody said he was an executive from an oil company, which he tried to deny, but no one heard him. The Bentleys went back to their practice and Gilly watched them laying down take-outs, slinging the heavy granite stones across the pebbled ice, their farm-muscled bodies stretched, sliding down the rink like

Chinese dancers. He watched the sweepers take Clayton Bentley's rock into the centre of the house, beating the ice with their brooms and pulling the heavy stone to rest — dead centre on the red button of the bullseye.

Gilly turned to look for his drinking companions, but they had disappeared to the beer parlour. The only one left was a man with greased-down hair parted in the middle, and a nose like a purple cucumber. "Stan Parnell," he said, extending his hand.

Gilly shook his hand. "Gillman Savard. Mighty fine rink you have here."

"Yeah. Never woulda got it if the Bentleys didn't curl here — but you gotta take the advantages. I run the hotel."

"Oh — the hotel," Gilly said. "Nice place."

"Glad you think so. I hear you're in oil."

"No, no. I'm not in anything. Just — looking around."

"That's what I mean. I own the café, too."

"The — café, Mr. Parnell?"

"Please. *Stan.*"

There was a pause as Gilly turned to watch a perfect double take-out on the ice.

"You haven't heard anything — *bad* about the hotel, have you?"

"No. No."

"Good. You know what farmers are like around here."

"Yep."

"Why don't you come back and join me at the hotel? I'll treat you to a smash of rye and Seven-Up. Got a proposition that might interest you."

The proposition didn't, but the whiskey did, so Gilly walked back to the hotel with Parnell, wondering what kind of trouble this would lead to. Parnell led the way to a small office behind the counter in the hotel lobby. Through the wall, they could hear the sounds of revelry in the beer parlour. Parnell dialled the combination on his big steel safe, flung the door open and pulled out an unopened bottle of Three Feathers and two dirty glasses. There was nothing else in the safe.

"Not often we get oil men stopping to look around," he said, filling the glasses three-quarters full of whiskey. "How'd you like to bunk down in our Deluxe Suite during your stay in Willson?" He topped the glasses from a bottle of Seven-Up on his desk.

"That's very tempting — Stan. But I'm looking around uh, independently. I'm not in oil."

"Think nothing of it!" Parnell cried in protest. "We like to think we enjoy the confidence of our guests, Mr. Savard!"

"Well — that's good," Gilly said. "Cheers."

"Yes, yes, cheers. And don't worry about cash. We can make easy credit arrangements." Parnell gazed with pride as Gilly savoured the sharp bite of rye whiskey, his first now in nearly two years. Easy credit, he thought.

"Let me come directly to the point, Gilly. You don't mind if I call you Gilly?"

Gilly waved his objections away.

"I don't know how you found I was thinking of selling the hotel — but it's fair to say that your opportunity has finally knocked!"

Gilly coughed and a jet of liquor shot across the room, narrowly missing the shoulder of Parnell's grey-checked jacket. "*Opportunity?*"

"Never mind how I figured it out," Parnell said, laying a finger on the end of his purple nose. "How much were you thinking of investing?"

"I'm flat broke!" Gilly cried.

"I understand you, Gilly. Really, I do! I know you can't come right out and haggle prices on the first round. But here in Willson, we like to be — open with each other." He whacked Gilly on the shoulder, sending another stream of Three Feathers toward the wall. "And *honest*, by God!"

"Mr. Parnell. Stan. I'm really sorry to say this, but I'm not especially interested in your hotel."

"What?" Parnell's carbuncled forehead broke out in sweat; his eyes grew desperate. "That's only because you haven't looked it over from top to bottom! Wait till you check it out! Right now, just on the basis of what you've seen, how much would you say the place is worth?"

Gilly looked around, shrugged, and bolted his whiskey. "A hundred thousand dollars?"

Parnell's eyes fluttered crazily and he sat down, tilting sideways.

"Are you okay, Stan?"

The man's face was flushed, and his bulbous nose had swelled to an indigo. "Cigarette," he gasped.

Gilly looked at his empty pack, although he knew he had exhausted his last cigarette in the bar. "Sorry, I'm out."

Parnell leaped to his feet. "Wait right here. I'll go get some for you. What do you smoke?"

"Craven A," Gilly said. "Cork-tips."

Parnell ran out. Gilly listened wistfully to the laughter from the beer parlour next door and fingered the forty-two cents in his pocket. It was getting near closing time. Parnell ran back into the room, shredding the cellophane from a cigarette pack. "I'll tell you what," he gasped. "I'll let you have the whole operation for a hundred and twenty thousand!"

There was only one way to put a stop to this, Gilly knew. He took the cigarettes and headed toward the door. "I'm sorry, Stan. It isn't worth a penny over a hundred thousand."

"You're not going?"

"I left my bag in the beer parlour. I have to get on the road. Important business in Regina."

Parnell poured the glass full of rye again. "Listen, there's nothing in Regina, Gilly! Nothing! A lot of car exhaust and lousy restaurants. We got real home cooking in our restaurant. Tell you what. Stay here overnight and check around the hotel. I've got a real surprise for you — in the morning."

Gilly wavered. It was too cold to be standing out on the highway, hitchhiking at this time of night. It would be easier in the morning. "I am a bit hungry," he said. "Anything to eat in the beer parlour?"

"Just potato chips and pepperonis. I'll order you something from the café, if you like."

"No, that's okay. A beer is all I want. And some time to think. I'll see you in the morning."

"Whatever you say, Gilly. Here's the key to the Deluxe Suite. First right at the top of the stairs. Sure you wouldn't like a nice hamburger?"

But Gilly was already moving toward the door of the beer parlour, where he could hear the sound of laughter and arguments over wheat and hockey and politics. "See you later, Stan."

"Nighty-night," Parnell said. "See you bright and early in the morning."

* * * * *

2

Gilly Savard was not lying when he said he had a brother in the oil business. Gilly abhorred lies and never knowingly uttered a falsehood. However, like all artists and story-tellers, he had a peculiar knack for reshaping the symmetry of a fact to bring his listeners closer to the truth. It is a gift which readers of novels will appreciate.

In fact, Gilly's elder brother, Porter, had once held a part-time job in 1941, selling oil and gasoline at the Red and White general store in the hamlet of Brochet, in the far north of Saskatchewan. The position lasted for three months, before Porter volunteered for the Royal Canadian Army and "went away to war."

Porter's patriotism was a proud moment for the Savard family. Everyone else in Brochet secretly thought him a fool, but no one would have suggested it to M. and Mme. Savard. Porter had always been a romantic; it was his yearning for automobile travel which had got him the job at Caplette's store, pumping gushers of amber gasoline from the glass tank beside the door. He was pumping gas the day the news arrived about the disaster at Dunkirk. He responded immediately to the drums of wartime propaganda.

Enlistment was not possible in Brochet. With the help of the mail carrier from Meadow Lake, Porter addressed a letter to "The Army, Government Office, Ottawa," and within two weeks was told to report to Prince Albert. As this required an overland trek of sixty miles to the railhead at Meadow Lake, the whole family decided to accompany him. It was their first trip away from Brochet.

The Savards made a heart-stirring tableau as they passed in front of Henry Caplette's store. The only store in Brochet, it was really a latter-day fur-trading post, and lay across the trail from the one-room Brochet school, where half a dozen families had gathered to wish farewell to the brave lad. They stood among their buggies and horses, the Union Jack flapping above them at the top of a peeled poplar sapling, and shouted hearty encouragements in French, Cree and English as the Savards' wagon disappeared into the dense bush.

Driving the wagon, seated high on a seat over the horses' tails, was André Savard, the patriarch. Normally, Papa drove alone; but today, Porter was beside him, rigid with pride.

Mme. Savard and the baby, Louise, sat behind them on a blanket spread in the wagon box. Further back, wedged among the boxes, harness, water jug, rifle, broken machinery parts and Porter's suitcase, were Gilly's two elder sisters, Marie and Hélène. At the rear, Gilly and his little brother Wilfred dangled their legs out the open tailgate, watching the tiny settlement disappear behind the fir trees. Occasionally, the bush would thin into poplar bluffs and they would roll past swampy sloughs full of muskrats and mallard ducks.

Gilly's appetite for discovery sharpened; the unending drama of a northern spring dazzled his eyes. The creaking wagon roused everything to life as it passed. All around, the land buzzed and murmured as it thawed from its long winter sleep. It was hard to imagine a war going on somewhere, far from the green willow buds and the flocks of ducks swarming around their new nests. War must happen in a special house, like a hockey rink, Gilly thought, where people roared in thousands and grown men clubbed each other with sticks.

King, one of the two horses, farted suddenly, and Gilly's sisters burst into fits of giggling. Gilly gave them a hard scowl. From the front, phrases drifted back on the spring breeze as Papa delivered an eleventh-hour lecture to Porter on how to survive in the big world: "Teach you hard work . . . man who minds his own business . . . horrible diseases from certain ladies . . . rot your brains out. . . ."

They halted for lunch at the ford over Beaver River, halfway to Meadow Lake. Mme. Savard took a bundle of jam sandwiches from the syrup pail, dealing them around like a deck of cards. There was an intense melancholy expression on her face. Ever since they had left home, her hand had fluttered across her breast, signing the cross. When the sandwiches were eaten, everyone took a long drink from the water jug and they set off to reach town before dark.

When the grain elevators of Meadow Lake appeared

through the bush, it was late afternoon, but still three hours before Porter's train was due to leave. Gilly stared, fascinated, as civilization hove into view. This was where Papa went every few weeks for supplies and machinery repairs. After three or four days, Papa would return from here with a pair of brilliant red eyes and breath that smelled like a turkey-roost.

The wagon crossed the railway tracks, past the elevators to the centre of town. Along the street, buildings grew more magnificent, from the Imperial Esso bulk dealer at the western edge of town to the palatial Canadian Pacific Railway station, dominating the main intersection. The station gazed haughtily down on Main Street to the Great War Memorial at the far end of the street. Across from the station stood the Royal Bank and the King George Hotel.

There were so many things to see that Gilly's head kept revolving to catch anything he might have missed. Dozens of cars and trucks drove by in all directions. People bustled along the busy sidewalks, carrying shopping bags and parcels. Boys smaller than Porter pedalled bicycles, long licorice whips drooling from their teeth.

André Savard drove past the station to a vacant lot behind the blacksmith's shop and tied up the team in the shade of a thicket of willows. He put oats in the feedbags for King and May and handing the water jug to his wife to be filled at the town pump, he led Porter to the back door of the hotel. Porter was seventeen and already shaving, but he had never been initiated into the adult world of beer drinking.

The beer parlour of the King George Hotel was the centre of attraction for fifty miles in each direction and every business in town depended on it for survival. The farmers and trappers would come to town on an errand, perhaps to have a broken binder knife welded. They would leave it at the blacksmith's for repair and step into the hospitable comfort of the "Licenced Premises," where much of their day's business would be done. For example, the town's only solicitor instructed his secretary to direct clients there during his lunch break, from eleven to four. The postmaster carried stamps of varying denominations in his jacket pocket, to save his customers a trek to the post office. Relatives and old friends could always be found in the beer parlour.

Gilly grew restless waiting beside the wagon. There was still an hour of daylight left and many exotic sights to be seen. Mme. Savard was weeping softly by herself and attracting attention from passersby, so Gilly wandered into the willow trees.

Within a few yards, he found a large pond of water covered with thick green scum. It must have been an abandoned cellar or dugout. As he gazed at the pond, a rock suddenly *whizzed* out of the trees and splashed through the green carpet of water. Gilly whirled in time to see some boys duck behind the trees, laughing.

"I saw yez!" he shouted.

Another rock rose in an arc from the trees and *kaplunged* into the water, going off like a depth charge and drenching Gilly from his felt boots to the bib of his denim overalls.

"Saw yez that time!" He edged backward toward the wagon.

In a burst of yells, three boys ran to cut off his retreat. They were town kids of his own age. They wore bright streaks of paint across their faces and had clumps of feathers tied to their baseball caps. The smallest one carried a pole which was whittled to a sharp point. The second carried a bow carved from an old hockey stick and strung with binder twine. The biggest one advanced on Gilly with his fists bunched, and growled, "What you doin' here, white man?"

"*Maaawww!*" Gilly roared.

"Shut up, kid," the little one said, "else we'll cut yer nuts off."

The third one peered into Gilly's terrified eyes. "Hey!" This kid's an Indian!"

"Bullshit! Indians don't wear overalls! He's a farmer!"

"Hey, kid, yer an Indian, aincha?"

Gilly shook his head, frantically looking for an escape.

"No lip, redskin, or you get a big fat kick in the arse. Where's all yer beads and stuff?"

"His old man swapped it for firewater! Eh, kid?" They all laughed.

"I haven't got no beads," Gilly said. "I ain't an Indian."

"Zatso?" the little one snarled, pointing his spear at Gilly's navel. "How come yer skin's so dark? Y'a nigger?"

"Ain't a nigger, either!"

"If yer an Indian, kid, we're gonna cut yer nuts off!"

"*Maaa!*"

"Shut up! We ain't gonna hurt ya, we'll just pertend. Fer cripes sake, Billy, shut up about cuttin' him!"

"Hey, you guys! We're all Commanches and this kid's a Kickapoo. Do we scalp him?"

"Yeah! Let's tie him up and scalp him."

Gilly yelled and took off, running for his life. They grabbed him before he got ten steps and tied him, struggling fiercely, to a tree with their bow string. Then they danced around the tree, yodelling war whoops. With the tip of the spear, they traced a line around the edge of Gilly's dark brushcut hair.

Mme. Savard, who had heard his shrieks, came puffing through the willows to his rescue and the boys ran off, taunting and laughing. "What a problem you are," she sighed. "What were you doing to them?"

"Nothing."

She untied the string and checked him over. "Did they hurt you?"

"Naw. We were only playin'."

"You got to watch town kids," she said.

It was nearly dark when they reached the wagon. Wilfred and the girls were growing frightened. Mme. Savard sent Gilly to the café with a dime to buy some chocolate bars to eat with the pieces of bannock she had brought. When they had eaten, Papa and Porter still had not come out of the hotel. The train was due in a few minutes. Mme. Savard began crying loudly, so Gilly went on his own to find Porter.

The reek of yeast was so powerful inside the beer parlour it nearly knocked him off his feet. It left an impression on him so deep that forever he would see the dozens of bleary eyes peering through the dense clouds of tobacco smoke. "Pa!!" he yelled, closing his eyes and throwing his head back. "Porter! Where are you?"

"Go git'im, kid!" someone laughed.

"Whoopee!" several voices shouted.

Gilly yelled until a man took his hand and led him through a maze of tables and broken chairs, up three steps to a small alcove at one side of the room. It was quieter than the rest of the beer parlour, but it was also very dark and it stank.

His eyes could make out a body in Porter's clothes lying on the floor, its face in a pool of beery vomit. Then he saw Papa, laid out on a bench against the wall, his head rolling from side to side.

"The train's coming," Gilly said.

Papa blinked a few times, then staggered to his feet and kicked Porter. When he could not kick him back to life, Gilly and a couple of men dragged Porter out the back door. The cold night air seemed to revive him and he got to his knees. "Where's'a train?" he moaned, squinting into the darkness.

The train howled a mournful reply from the level crossing at the edge of town.

Mme. Savard appeared beside Gilly. "You take him," she said, "I'll bring the suitcase." She heaved the big leather case onto her shoulders. The commotion had drawn several men outside. They were treated to the sight of Mme. Savard lurching down the street, lugging Porter's suitcase while he staggered behind, leaning on Gilly. When Porter started to cry, Papa returned to the beer parlour in disgust.

'I don't wanna go, Ma!" Porter blubbered, falling all over Gilly. "I don't wanna get shot!"

"Get her, boy! She's runnin' off with your suitcase!" somebody hooted from the crowd.

"That squaw's got a big headstart!"

"Don't give up, kid! She's running outa gas!"

The train rumbled into the station, hissing steam. Passengers stared out their windows at the drama in the street. A few stepped onto the station platform for a better view.

"I'll be good, Ma!" Porter cried. "I won't backtalk any more!"

It was more than Gilly could stand. Despite the Commanches and the darkness, he ran and hid in the willow trees until the train had left. When he returned to the wagon, his mother was showing the men from the beer parlour where to place Papa in the back of the wagon.

Gilly was allowed to sit on the front seat beside his mother to make him feel better, but it was a meaningless gesture. Papa cursed and rolled around in the back of the wagon. He pulled the horse blanket off the children and made them cry. Several times Gilly went back and covered them again. He watched the frosty stars wink through the forest, but over and over, his mind relived the scene in Meadow Lake. When they passed through Brochet again and reached the final trail home, the eastern sky was gleaming with the first grey of early light. He saw the dim, low outline of the barn and the tiny house where he had been born.

"Ma," Gilly said. "Are we Indians?"

She clucked at the horses.

"Ma?"

She looked at him, her dark eyes silvered by the morning sky. "No."

"What are we then?"

"We're halfbreeds. Like everybody at Brochet."

"What do you mean, halfbreeds?"

"Not one or the other. Like right now — not night or day. My mother was a halfbreed from Green Lake. My father was a Scotsman. My mother sent me to the mission school at Ile à la Crosse. Your father came along from Batoche, so we married. That's how it goes. You are a halfbreed, too."

"What was I like when I was born?"

"Like an angel, Gilly. You was born with a smile on your face. Don't never lose it, even when the town kids get after you." She chucked him under the chin. "Well — here we are."

He helped unload the wagon in silence. It was the most he'd ever heard her talk. Then he went into the two-room house and climbed the ladder to the attic above the main room where he and Porter had slept every year from March to December. He crawled under the horsehide robe and watched specks of dust circulate in the shafts of light stabbing through the roof. He thought of the boys in town. But how come they played Indians if they hated them? Did people ever play halfbreeds? How was a halfbreed different?

He sat up in sudden shock: Porter was a halfbreed, too! He was going to be a soldier and a hero, and there he was, a halfbreed! Was it possible? He finally fell asleep in the shafts of light, smiling and moaning in turn. Halfbreed, halfbreed, halfbreed.

In the morning, Gilly woke up in a state of shock. It was not his attic room in Brochet. It was not his cell in the P.Λ. Pen. In fact, to his stunned eyes, it looked like the set from a Fred Astaire musical, with white rococo furniture and elaborate gilt mirrors. Somehow the stench of stale beer rising through the floor was mixed into it. Gilly crawled out of bed and explored the two-room suite, his mouth a raw mélange of plaque and pepperoni. Looking out the window, he was cruelly struck back to reality. The main street of Willson was being lashed by an icy wind; he shivered and turned away from the window. On the writing desk, he found a couple of postcards featuring the hotel restaurant. A waitress stood beside the cash register holding a Terminal Hotel menu, smiling saucily at the camera. He decided on the spur of the moment to send a funny message to his friend Clint Malach, but before he began, there was a tap at the door.

Gilly walked to the door in his underwear and opened it. He blinked in amazement. It was the waitress from the postcard, smiling the same smile; the same little green cap perched atop her honey blonde hair. Her delicately sculptured jaw was punishing a wad of bubble gum, he noticed. His gaze descended down the bursting bodice of her clean white dress, past the exquisitely narrow waist, to the most pefectly dimpled pair of knees he had ever seen. Or could ever remember seeing.

"You," he breathed.

She laughed, a tiny pink tongue showing through her bright teeth. "Seen the pitcher, ay?" she said in an adenoidal grate which sobered Gilly instantly. She handed him a menu, the one she was holding in the postcard. "Stan says it's gonna make me famous, but I think he's pullin' my leg, so's he don't hafta pay me a model's fee. Whutcha like fer breakfast?"

"Fried eggs and coffee."

"Okay. You better get dressed before yuh freeze yer toes off," she said, backing down the hallway.

"And juice," Gilly said, closing the door as she disappeared. By the time he had shaved and dressed, she was back with his breakfast tray. She sat down on the bed to watch as he ate.

"Whatcher name?"

"Gillman Savard."

"Mine's Georgia, but everybody calls me Marilyn. Know why?" she said, her cheeks dimpling as her jaw cranked on the wad of gum like a hammermill.

"No. Why?"

"You dummy! Cuz I look like Marilyn Munroe! Know why?"

This was dangerous territory. Gilly concentrated on his eggs, keeping his eyes averted from the long curve of thigh that disappeared under the white dress. He stuffed his mouth to capacity.

"Stan sez you're buying the hotel, so I thought I should interduce myself. I sorta go with it. I mean, along with the rest of the staff. Stan sez you're a bigshot."

"Maybe so, maybe not." He started on the toast and jam. "Anyway, I'm leaving for Regina today."

She gazed at him and sighed. "Ya know, that's why I kinda like you? You're cute and modest. Most guys try to play the bigshot. I don't even give 'em the time of day."

"That's very wise," Gilly agreed.

"I only been working here since I left school in March. It's a stepping stone on the road of life."

"I see."

"Well, I gotta get back to work before Stan flips his lid. See ya." She bounced out of the room, her firm young body springing as she walked, her blonde curls bouncing on her shoulders, her thighs winking at him through her white uniform. Gilly turned to his coffee. He was perspiring freely, despite the cold.

Stan was waiting for him at the bottom of the stairs a half hour later. "Well, what do you think?"

"Nice room."

"No! The broad! Nice little country girl, eh? She goes with the hotel."

"She's something, okay."

"Well, you ready to inspect the hotel? We have a little while before Mom gets here."

"Mom?"

"My mother, Mrs. Parnell. She has a half-interest in the property."

"Oh — well, I really should be ——"

"Come on." Parnell showed him into the restaurant, an expanse of chrome and vinyl, where Georgia bustled from the milkshake machine to the coffee counter and back before an admiring row of farmers and truck drivers who were perched on stools.

"The reason I'm selling now," Parnell was explaining, "is for reasons of health. I haven't been well for years. And now business is so heavy, I have to find something less strenuous."

Gilly looked out the window. The main street of Willson ran for half a mile, parallel to the railway and the inevitable row of grain elevators. There was not a tree to be seen, except for a ragged fringe of caragana bushes near the railway station. Icy grit whirled through the air, blasting everything it struck. There was not a pedestrian in sight, although several large dumptrucks rumbled past in both directions.

"See that?" Parnell cried triumphantly. "All those trucks are working on the South Saskatchewan Dam — about twenty miles down the road. Know what happens when *that's* finished? Willson becomes the tourist capital of Saskatchewan!"

A white Cadillac with a set of enormous tailfins suddenly pulled up in front of the hotel. Its horn blared. At the wheel of the car was a stylish-looking woman with marcelled silver hair, a cigarette dangling from her lips.

"There's Mom," Parnell said, pulling Gilly outside. He placed him in the front seat of the car and climbed into the back. "Mom, this is Mr. Savard."

Mrs. Parnell power-turned in front of the hotel, spraying gravel and snow in a circle before rocketing down the street in the opposite direction. She turned to Gilly with a cruel grin that somehow contradicted her swirling blue-rinsed hair and flashy spectacles.

"Delighted to make your acquaintance, ma'am," he said, smiling his most charming smile.

Her lips pulled back to show a set of brilliant white false teeth. They barely moved when she spoke. "So you're the son of a bitch who thinks he's got us by the short and curlies,

28

eh? Well, we'll see about that!"

Gilly sat the rest of the way in reflective silence, completely unnerved. The car pulled up in front of a large brown house, one of Willson's most impressive mansions. It was buttressed with sunporches all around and crowned with a network of lightning rods. Mrs. Parnell made Gilly wipe his shoes before entering the hall. The front parlour was an extravaganza of paisley curtains and Gainsborough prints. Mom Parnell placed a straight-backed chair squarely in front of her old rocker and gestured Gilly into the chair for interrogation.

"Now," she said, her false teeth clattering over every consonant, "What's all this bullshit about a hundred grand for the hotel?"

"Well — I'm really not in the market for a hotel. We were just engaged in idle conversation."

"Oh yeah? Idle converstation, eh? You must think you got a couple of smalltown hicks to fleece out of their life's savings! Well let me tell you something, you smarmy-faced swindler, I've had this hotel appraised independently at a hundred and thirty thousand!"

"Hm," Gilly said. This was getting serious. He had to find a means of escape.

"Well?" she snapped. "Are you going to just sit there like a pile of chicken-shit?"

"Now, Mom," Stan said.

"Stay out of this, Stanley. You've already buggered up enough."

Mrs. Parnell held Gilly captive for two hours, insulting, exhorting and threatening him, not once listening to his pleas of innocence. He finally agreed to buy not only the hotel and café with all their furnishings, but also the Avalon movie theatre, the Willson Arms apartment block and an anonymous building mysteriously leased to the government. He was then allowed to leave. They did not agree on a price, although Mom Parnell's final figure was $190,000.00.

Stan walked him back to the hotel. "There she is!" he cried ecstatically, pointing to the neon sign. "This time tomorrow, she'll be all yours."

"We'll see," Gilly said, thinking he had to be far away by this time tomorrow. "Is Georgia still at work?"

Parnell leered at him knowingly. "Naw. She works the early shift and goes out to her dad's farm for the rest of the day. But I got something what'll take your mind off that. There's a big Liberal meeting tonight in the town hall!" Parnell's nose glowed with enthusiasm. "Boss Morgan's giving a speech!"

"Gee, I don't have any good clothes with me, Stan. You know how it is when you're travelling." Gilly preferred the beer parlour to politics.

"No problem! Come on, it's not six o'clock yet. I'll introduce you to my friend Huppe at the Clothes Rack, just down the street."

"I don't have enough money with me, Stan."

"Quit worrying. He's a friend of mine."

As it turned out, any friend of Parnell's was a friend of Huppe's; credit wouldn't cost a dime. If Gilly admired that new narrow-lapelled suitjacket, it was his. So was a handful of button-down shirts and a rich assortment of the needle-thin ties that were just going out of fashion.

"By God, you even look like a politician," Parnell cried, as Gilly stood before the mirror.

As they approached the town hall after supper, Gilly could sense the growing rumble of politics. There would be a provincial election in a few months and Boss Morgan was determined to lick the Socialists this time. The entrance to the hall was emblazoned with slogans: "Time for a Change!" and "Save Us All from Socialism!"

Inside the door, a large beefy man was pumping the hand of all who entered. He was Boston Morgan, a man who had spent ten years fighting his way to the top of the Liberal party. He had been a Socialist before that and had been converted after losing out in a power struggle. Now his crusade was to rally the soldiers of private enterprise.

"Hiya, Boss," Parnell said. "This is the new owner of the Terminal Hotel, Gillman Savard."

"Good to see you again!" Morgan boomed.

"I don't think we've met before," Gilly murmured.

"Well, well — but I've heard of you, of course!"

"Of course," Gilly admitted.

"News travels fast in these parts when you keep your ear to the ground like I do. Anyway, I'm pleased to hear you're a Liberal!"

"Actually," Gilly pointed out, "I'm not."

Morgan's eyes narrowed to suspicious slits behind his glasses. He turned to Parnell, questioning him.

"He's going to join, Boss. Gilly has great plans for Willson."

"Well, that's what we need, Gary. Men of action! It's guys like you who will halt the tide of creeping Communism. Take Medicare, now."

"Gilly's in oil, Boss."

"Ah — a man with the nation's economy in his grasp! Are you aware of the secret Socialist plan to expropriate every drop of oil, every gallon of gasoline in this province?"

"No," Gilly admitted.

"But we are going to smash this totalitarian regime, if they ever dare to announce the date of a general election. You and me and every other ordinary working joe in the province — we'll crush them!"

The crowd standing around them went wild. Boss Morgan knew that in politics, rhetoric was everything. If Boss Morgan could restore decency and free enterprise to this bastion of North American Socialism, he was a god and benefits would accrue to all who kept the faith.

"I think you made an impression, Gilly," Parnell said, as they hurried to find seats. The hall was filling rapidly. The chill of the unheated building had disappeared.

"My fellow sufferers under Socialism!" Morgan began. "I come to you tonight with a message. We in this *great* Liberal party are about to lift the heavy yoke from your shoulders!" The crowd roared. "The task we face is not an easy task. Nor is it a simple one. It is nothing less than the total pulverization of creeping Socialism!" The crowd surged to its feet and cheered mightily.

For an hour and a half, Morgan ripped apart public transportation, free school texts, the failure of the Socialist cheese factory and the sinister designs of every Bolshevik in the government. He promised to cut taxes, liberate business and provide untaxed purple gasoline to farmers. When Boss Morgan rode the wave of approval to his conclusion, the whole audience pressed toward the stage to congratulate the politician.

Later, Morgan and his aides somehow ended up in Gilly's Deluxe Suite. Parnell had invited them back to the hotel for a few drinks and Gilly's was the only decent room he had to offer.

"Well, we really had 'em moving tonight, eh?" Morgan said, a glass in one hand and a cigar in the other.

"You can say that again, Boss," Parnell cried.

"Great speech, Boss," said one of his young sidekicks, manoeuvering Gilly out of the way.

"Whuddaya mean — *great speech*? It was the same goddam speech!"

"I mean, great delivery," the assistant said, thinking fast.

"Thanks," Morgan said, reaching for his rye and Seven-Up. "Well, Gary, what do you think? Ready to join the forces of free enterprise now?"

"I'm thinking about it."

"Don't think too long, my boy. There's going to be a nominating convention in this constituency before Easter. I want you to think about it."

"But I don't have any experience."

"Experience!" Morgan laughed. "You don't need experience! You got the greatest face for politics I ever seen." He leaned close and jabbed him with one blunt finger. "You got a sincere face, Gary. I don't know where you got it from, but I'll tell you it's worth a million bucks in this game! As long as you believe!"

"In what?"

"Anything you like! The party! Money! Taxes, freedom. Even Socialism! I can never remember all the stuff I'm supposed to believe in. That's why I hire these assholes." He jerked his thumb at his assistants who were milling around the liquor bottles in their Ivy League suits.

"Let's look at your assets. You got a wife and family, eh?"

"No, I'm afraid not," Gilly admitted.

"Hm. Let's see. How about a war record? You ever in the armed services?"

"No-o-o-o — but my brother was a hero in the Second World War."

"That's it! Play it for all you can get. And one word of advice. Honest exaggeration! That is the art of politics.

I'll look for you at the nominating meeting." With that, Boss Morgan swept out of the hotel with his flock of aides to return to the capital and the arena of bigger politics.

* * * * *

4

In fact, Gilly had already learned the art of exaggeration. By embellishing Porter's war record during the war, he had become a hero by association.

The Monday after Porter's hysterical departure from Meadow Lake, Gilly had gone to school with his sisters prepared to alter history as determinedly as any Nazi propaganda minister. He had to play it big or shame would forever haunt the Savard name in the tiny Brochet school.

The Brochet pupils surrounded the buggy as soon as Gilly whipped old King into the schoolyard. "What was it like?" they yelled. "Did they give him a gun? Was there a parade?"

Gilly maintained an aloof silence as his sisters climbed out of the buggy. He took King to the stable, ignoring the crowd. "What happened in Meadow Lake, Gilly?" Marny Desjarlais said.

"Not much. Had a chocolate bar. Played with some town kids. Porter's gonna be a hero. He went on a train."

"Was Porter brave when he went on the train?"

Gilly hesitated and looked around to see if his sisters were listening. "He was braver than anything. Braver than Churchill!"

"Let's play war till the bell goes!" Wayne Desjarlais shouted. "I get to be Porter."

"No, you don't," Gilly said. "I'm the only one who can be Porter." Porter was a hero. He was safely somewhere else and Gilly could make him anything he wanted, even an Englishman. Anything but the snivelling halfbreed Porter had become in the streets of Meadow Lake, an image which Gilly suppressed. His fantasy was made easier by Porter's legend. Before he had quit school, Porter had championed the smaller boys and charmed all the girls. He had never been clever, but he was liked by the teachers, so he had been encouraged to stay in school longer than most boys in the district. Miss McIvor had made Porter "rules monitor" to keep the older boys in line. He had captained every sports team from baseball to steal-the-stick. The school teams rallied to his leadership. He would always drive in three runs in the last half of the ninth inning, or deke through a whole hockey team to score the winning goal. He had made caragana-pod whistles for the Grade Ones and had developed a skill for tickling the Grade Eight girls so deftly that they never complained. Now Gilly was expected to step into his shoes.

The Savard children attended school because Mme. Savard believed in education; she had bitterly opposed Porter's quitting to work a gasoline pump. She had wanted Porter to be a priest, which was why he had been allowed to stay in school, even after failing two grades.

Later that spring, Mme. Savard walked the two miles to Brochet to speak to Miss McIvor about Gilly. She sat on one of the tiny benches in front of the teacher's desk while Gilly and the girls waited outside in the buggy.

"Gillman is an above-average student," Miss McIvor said. "He shows promise. And he has a lot of personal charm."

"Someday he will become a priest, so I want him to stay in school and get a good education. My mother said one of my sons should be a priest."

Miss McIvor frowned; she had been through this before with Porter. She herself was a Roman Catholic, but she had little time for priests. They meddled in the schools. Father LaCasse, who ran the parish from Dorintosh, was always dropping by to snoop.

"Gilly could do anything he puts his mind to," she said cautiously. "The priesthood is a possibility."

"He will be a priest," Mme. Savard said in a firm voice as she rose to leave.

Mme. Savard dreamed of the future as Gilly drove her home in the buggy. She had read books at the mission school which said there was more to life than grubbing tree stumps for a living. She no longer sought it for herself, but if one of her children could rise to enjoy a spiritual relationship with the world, she would be happy. She did not disdain her husband's small farm; twenty acres of cleared land was more than most of their neighbours had, and they had homesteaded it themselves. As husbands went, André was not the worst. He beat her and the children only when he lost his temper. But her mother had hoped for more and she intended to give her more.

The division of labour on the farm was equitable. André took the burden of the field operations. Mme. Savard was responsible for the house. The children did all the daily chores, such as splitting wood, milking the cows, slopping the pigs, hoeing the garden and hauling manure out of the barn. Their house was too small, of course. André had often promised to enlarge the house for his growing family, but every time he worked up enough enthusiasm to tack on another room, Mme. Savard delivered herself of one more baby and so demoralized him that he would put it off for another winter. So the family lived in a two-room poplar pole cabin. In the kitchen-parlour, they ate, fought, did homework and, on Saturday nights, bathed. Here, the two girls slept on a couch beside the stove. In the "Other Room," the parents slept, as well as the two little ones. There, the clothing and good furniture was stored. When tidied, this room served as the parlour for guests like Father LaCasse. Above it was Gilly's loft.

It was a sparse life, but endurable. For entertainment, they had the radio and *The Farmer's Advocate*. Except for school books and catechisms, the weekly farm newspaper was the only literature that entered the household. But it was a veritable library: barley prices and news of the Australian wheat crop for Papa; recipes and rural etiquette for Mme. Savard; coloured funny papers for the children. Then when the paper was completely digested, Papa would fill the blank margins of the pages, "figuring" his projected annual profits. When all the white space had been filled with numbers, adding, multiplying and dividing into the thousands, the newspaper concluded its usefulness in the backhouse.

The Farmer's Advocate was the springboard for Gilly's leaps into heroic fantasy. Every Monday evening after finishing his chores and supper, he turned to the *Advocate* funnies. Monday nights were his turn now that Porter was gone. All the heroes, Smilin' Jack, Terry and the Pirates and a dozen others, were fighting the war. Gilly used the cartoons to spice the tales of combat he told at school, tales which he claimed had been sent to him by his brother. It was not long before Porter had been promoted to a wily commando who left a trail of slit Kraut throats across the North African desert. A month later, the pupils of Brochet sat entranced beside the school step as Gilly told them how Porter terrified the Italian armies, plummetting out of the Greek skies with his paratroop brigade. By the fall, he had been transferred to the Pacific theatre for a secret operation against the Japs in China.

The sad truth was that Porter only wrote one letter home in his first six months of absence. He was stationed "somewhere" in the south of England and didn't seem to do much but make his bed, polish his brass and try to sneak out to pubs with the other soldiers. Mme. Savard wept with relief, but Gilly was disgusted. Porter was turning into a yellow-bellied halfbreed. Well, Gilly wasn't going to let Porter ruin everything. He threw himself into frenzies of creation, making up stories in his head while he drove his sisters to school in the buggy.

His innocent fantasizing ended several months later when Porter was unlucky enough to be sent across the English Channel with the Second Infantry Division. A letter from the Minister of Defence announced in doleful tones that Porter had been killed in action at Dieppe; his bravery was praised at length. The following week, Porter's name even appeared in the black box of dead heroes in *The Advocate*. Gilly's efforts had paid off; Porter had become a real hero.

* * * * *

5

It was morning again. Gilly was blasted from his sleep by a wild banging at the door. He had a hangover that enclosed him like a sulphurous aura. Thinking of Porter and the war, he had drowned his brain in Parnell's whiskey. Now, without so much as a glass of milk for his burning throat, he was being forcemarched down the stairs by Mom Parnell, with Stan trotting behind. She was yelling at him through her clacking teeth: "You're celebrating too soon, Savard! You haven't pulled it off yet!"

Retching all the way, Gilly was driven to her house and trudged inside, creaking at every painful joint. She sat in the parlour like a centrepiece in a tableau, rocking back and forth in front of him. "Stanley," she said, "make some tea. And bring me my Tums."

"I have a confession to make," Gilly began.

"*Oh?*" she said, going rigid.

"I cannot possibly buy your hotel. I'm only travelling through and I'm dead broke!"

"And what happened to the hundred and fifty thousand you had yesterday, you lousy crook?"

"Hundred and twenty," Gilly said, sidestepping one trap only to plunge headlong into another. He clapped his hand over his mouth.

"Well?"

"I was lying! It was *all* a lie!"

"Don't try to weasel out of it now, you goddam shark! He made a firm offer, didn't he, Stanley?"

Parnell was staring at him, tea-tray in hand, his eyes popping. "Yes! I heard you!"

Mom Parnell sugared her tea. "I'll tell you what we'll do. What this discussion needs is the spirit of compromise. Give and take. Goodwill." She drew a paper from the bosom of her dress. "Stanley and I have agreed to accept your offer for our entire holdings in Willson." She handed him a bill of sale for $185,000.00.

Gilly shook his head. "You don't understand."

Mom rose, quivering with indignity. "You *stinking son of a bitch*!" she hissed. "You live off my idiot son for two days and try to cheat us on *top of it*?"

"Mom," Parnell said. "Compromise, remember?"

"Just tell me what you want, you fucking crook!"

Gilly thought for a long moment. "Do you think we could have some scrambled eggs?"

Then it began in earnest. The eggs so revitalized Gilly that once more he entered into the spirit of bargaining. It was like a big Monopoly game, scribbling down figures, calculating dividends. If this was the only way to get out of town, he might as well enjoy it. He would be gone in a flash and the Parnells would suffer a temporary disappointment. He couldn't feel sorry for them.

At four o'clock, after a rest break for chicken sandwiches and pickled beets, Mom Parnell put a blank cheque in front of Gilly. He signed it for $165,000.00, against his bank account in Prince Albert. He flourished his name across the bottom. Gillman T. Savard. He looked at it, admiring the opening G. Then he looked again, numb with horror. He stared at his signature on the monstrous cheque, disbelieving his eyes. He had done it again!

"I gotta go," he said, standing up.

"So soon? I suppose now you want to check out the inventory, to make sure we haven't hidden anything. Stan, drive him back."

A light snow had begun to slash out of the sky again as Parnell eased his mother's Cadillac down the street. All Gilly had to do was grab his bag, as he should have done the first night, and get out on the highway.

But Gilly had not reckoned on the electrifying effect of the news in Willson. When he and Parnell walked in the front door of the hotel, the staff was waiting in the lobby. In a demonstration of loyalty, they yelled three cheers for the new boss. Gilly looked around for Georgia, but she had already gone home for the day.

The same enthusiasm exploded in the beer parlour when Stan led Gilly to the only profitable operation in the hotel. The male populace of Willson surged to its feet and cheered. The new hôtelier paled. "Do I have to make a speech?"

"No. They're waiting for you to open her up."

"Her?"

"The free beer."

The celebration had been gathering steam for most of the afternoon. The official moment of inauguration had arrived. It had been seventeen years since the last change of ownership. The place was crowded with veterans from that memorable two-day occasion. With a modest grin, Gilly waved to the bartender and the flood of amber foam gushed forth.

By the legal closing-time of ten-thirty, the party had barely begun. Not even the two off-duty Mounties from the local detachment noticed as the hour passed. Every few minutes, someone would stand on a table and offer another toast to the new innkeeper. Gilly expired at about four a.m., before the kegs had emptied, but after the stock of bottled beer was exhausted. Some of the last revellers carried him to the Deluxe Suite and laid him out on his bed. He slept.

If Wednesday's hangover had been painful, Thursday's was like the aftermath of a train wreck. His mind throbbed to the surface in a fog of blinding light. *It's morning*, he thought, *and I'm still here*! He sat up with a jerk and flopped down again on the bed. There was an orange light sputtering inside his head, like an electric arc leaping from ear to ear. He cranked himself erect and slid edgeways off the bed, then looked outside. The sun blazed off the fresh snow, blinding him. It seemed to be at least ten o'clock. He stumbed down the stairs, jamming his arms into his overcoat. His leather bag was still in the beer parlour, which now was locked. He staggered into the restaurant to find a key.

"Mr. *Savard*!" Georgia squealed, running to him from behind the cash register. Before he could retreat, she was hugging him tightly against her stretched, starched uniform. "Congratulations! It's just wonderful!"

Gilly turned white, his eyes popping through his clenched eyelids. He pried his tongue from the roof of his mouth. "What?" he gasped.

"The hotel! You bought it!"

"Lemme sit down."

"And you came in here last night from the beer parlour looking for me! For me!"

"I did?"

"Hollering at the top of your lungs, they said. Around eleven o'clock. 'Marilyn!' you shouted, 'Marilyn!' So romantic!"

"Chair. Sit down."

"Oh you poor guy, you look *awful*! I'll get you a coffee."

"Yes. An' a glass of water."

As she bustled to fetch the fluids, Gilly looked around. The rest of his staff, waitresses, cook and dishwasher, were staring at him. "Get the key to the bar," he muttered. "I gotta go."

Georgia halted in mid-bounce. "Go? Go where?"

"I uh, business. Regina. Few days. Don't worry."

"Aw, you poor guy. How are you going?"

"Don't know. Train."

"Train doesn't go till five o'clock."

He shook his head. "Water. Now."

She gave him the water and coffee, which he drained in quick succession. Then he stood up. "Seen Parnell this morning?"

"Him and Mom just left for Regina. On business."

Georgia got the key to the bar from the cash register and opened the beer parlour. She stood at the door surveying the shamble of broken furniture and glass. Gilly collected his bag from behind the bar.

"Well — so long," he said, shuffling toward the door.

"Wait!" she said. "Mr. Savard, you really look like you need a helping hand today. Do you want me to go with you? They don't hardly need me here."

"No thanks, Marilyn — I mean uh, Georgia. It's nice of you, but —"

Before he could open the door and escape from the accursed hotel, a fat man in an Imperial Esso uniform barged in and whacked him on the back with an enormous hand.

"Hiya, Gilly!" It was Phil Bendiak, the local car dealer. He vaguely recalled him from the night before. "Boy, that was some wing-ding last night, eh? How ya feelin' today?"

"Fine," Gilly whispered.

"Say, I brotcher car down! Wanta take her for a little spin?"

"Car?"

"Haw, haw, haw," Phil laughed to the hotel staff who had crowded around. "Giss he don't remember. Look!" He stepped to the window and pointed outside. Sparkling in the sun, a two-toned white and gold Chevrolet sat parked at the curb. In 1959, the year of the tailfins, GM had gone overboard and designed a Canada Goose on wheels. "Ya bought it last night. Thirty-two hundred and ninety dollars, less tax. Don't remember, eh?"

"I haven't got the money," Gilly groaned.

Phil winked to the girls and jabbed his elbow at Gilly. "Let's just say I trust yuh."

"I don't *want* a car!"

40

"But Mr. Savard!" Georgia cried, her eyes shining. "How will you get to Regina?"

"Gilly, you and me made a deal. This is my last '59! I get a bonus for clearing my lot."

"I don't care!"

"Look, I won't charge for the extras."

"What extras?"

"Well, you know." Phil ticked them off on his fingers. "Radio, whitewalls, tools, spare tire, seat covers, automatic transmission, rear speaker, block heater, seat belts, rear defroster, electric clock, outside mirrors, cigarette lighter, floor carpets and chrome licence plate brackets. All included in the price!"

Gilly looked at the restaurant clock, a kitty-cat clock whose eyes and tail ticked back and forth with the passing seconds. It was nearly ten. The banks in Regina would open for business. "Give me five bucks cash on top of it," he said, "and it's a deal."

"Hooray!" Georgia said. "Kin I sit in it for a minute, Mr. Savard? I promise not to get it dirty."

"No!" he called, but she ran out the door and climbed into the car.

"Plus sixty bucks for the licence plates," Phil said. "I registered it in your name."

"Phil, I don't have my cheque book with me. Can we look after this tomorrow some time?"

"No trouble at all, Gilly — I got the cheque all made out here. Just fill in your bank account and sign your name."

Gilly looked at the clock again. Two minutes. He signed and ran out to the car to remove the excited waitress. Before he reached the car door, however, Gerry Huppe appeared on the sidewalk, puffing and blowing under a mound of parcels. It was the rest of the wardrobe Gilly had ordered.

"In the back," Gilly wheezed, opening the door.

"Oooh, Mr. Savard, it's absolutely bee*you*-chuss!" Georgia said, stroking the red leather seat covers. "Lissen, if you need a secretary, whyncha hire me? We kin stop at my place an' pick up a suitcase of clothes. You kin meet my Mom and Dad."

"I have to go. Please step out."

"*Please*, Mr. Savard. I took typing in school! My talent is stifled here. I have to go to the city — where I can *meet* people." She clung to the door handle and wouldn't let go. "I'll work for a hundred bucks a month."

At the far end of Main Street, an RCMP patrol car appeared driving toward them. "Oh, all right," Gilly sighed. He ran around to the driver's side. Gerry Huppe and Phil Bendiak and several customers from the restaurant watched with wide eyes as he started the engine, flicked the gear shift and spun off up the street. Approaching the RCMP cruiser, he grinned and waved at the two Mounties, who grinned back. He drove past his apartment block, movie theatre, hotel and restaurant. When he had reached the north end of the business district, he turned and roared back along a rear street, past the kingdom which had been his for a few hours. What more could he ask? In less than three days, he had acquired a commercial empire, a dazzling wardrobe, a fancy car and a beautiful girl who was his, all his.

"Savard, you are a stupid bastard!" he said. The Willson town limit sign appeared beside the road and Gilly floored the accelerator. He had perhaps an hour's headstart on the law, which wasn't long enough, but it was better than nothing. It was better than another term in the penitentiary.

* * * * *

6

Meanwhile, in Regina, "Home of the Royal Canadian Mounted Police," Staff Sergeant Harry Swift was indulging in a favourite pastime — pulling a newspaper reporter's leg. They were in sub-division headquarters, Criminal Investigation Department, of which Staff Sergeant Swift was the head.

Swift was a throwback to the days of the founding of the force a hundred years before. Big, hard-drinking and vulgar, he had no use at all for the faceless pack of technicians that has appeared in modern times. He had risen through the ranks without kissing ass or knifing friends and had been awarded a position he enjoyed. It was also one beyond which he would never be promoted. No matter. Swift loved it so much that he sought out the company of the criminals that he was employed to eradicate. He did not *like* criminals, but he was a criminal detective, so he spent a lot of his off-duty time hunting his quarry in the city's bars and flophouses.

At about 11:15 a.m., according to his later report, while he was discussing the day's crimes with the reporter, he heard a woman shouting from the elevator at the end of the hall. Seconds later, the woman spun through the door of his office, her false teeth making an eerie clatter as she hollered, "Police! Fraud!"

"What's the trouble, ma'am?"

"Police!"

"I am Staff Sergeant Swift. What's the trouble?"

She flung a bank cheque across his desk. "Arrest this man! Throw away the kcy! A bum cheque! Prince Albert! Catch him!"

Swift scrutinized the cheque and whistled. A hundred and sixty-five grand. Then he saw the signature and his scalp tinglcd like a burglar alarm. "Gilly Savard!"

"That's him! I want him hung! Beaten up!"

"Sit down, ma'am. Is this your husband?" Swift gestured to the purple-nosed man behind her.

"That's my son, Stanlcy. The cheque was for his hotel!"

"Ahh — Savard bought the hotel. So you haven't actually *lost* anything?"

"Are you going to waste valuable time talking?"

"Perhaps. Do you know where he is now?"

"Still sleeping it off in our hotel, I expect!"

"Wait here, please." Swift stepped down the hall to the shortwave radio operator in Communications, with the reporter at his heels. "Get the Willson detachment."

When they reached the Corporal in charge at Willson, he sounded vague and confused.

"Has there been a guy called Gillman Savard in town there recently?" Swift asked.

"Gilly Savard? Yeah — I was uh, just talking to him. Last night."

"He gave a bum cheque to the hotel owner for a hundred and sixty-five gees."

"Oh, no."

"You better find him before he writes any more."

Swift signed off and telephoned Superintendent Chernyk, sub-division O.C. "Supe? Savard's back. Showed up in Willson."

"I thought you told me he would go *west*?" Chernyk said.

"That was our information. He was supposed to head back toward Alberta again."

"What's he doing this time?"

"So far, we got one cheque. A fat one. I sent the boys out looking." At the other end of the line there was heavy breathing.

"Maybe you better buzz the other sub-divisions," the Superintendent said.

Willson radioed back to announce that Savard had also obtained a new car and some clothing.

"*Where'd that detective go?*" Mom Parnell yelled, bursting into the radio room.

"Repeat that last part, Corporal," Swift said to the radio.

"I said, he went to the hotel and abducted a girl!"

"Jesus."

"Yeah. Name's Georgia Dreiser."

"*I want him arrested before sundown!*" Mom Parnell shrieked.

"Back off, lady. What do you mean, 'abducted,' Corporal?"

"He took her with him when he skipped town. She was his uh, employee after he bought the uh, hotel . . ."

"Okay. When did he leave?"

"Tanner saw him driving north out of town an hour ago. Toward Saskatoon."

"Okay, we'll put out roadblocks."

Mom Parnell pushed Swift aside and shouted at the radio, "You go *find* him, you lazy sonofabitch!"

"How's that, Staff?"

"Never mind. Slight problem here. Carry on."

"What are you going to do, Staff?" the reporter inquired from the door of the Communications Room.

"Get the goddam press out of here!" Swift roared. "And her, too!"

The reporter and Mrs. Parnell were escorted to the far end of the corridor, away from the investigation. If Swift wanted to halt publicity, this was an error — the first of many that day — because the Parnells filled the reporter's copy pads with anecdotes about Gilly Savard. Within two hours, the reporter had returned to the C.I.D. office with a grin on his face and the afternoon edition of the paper in his hand. Boxed in the centre of Page One was the story that meant his promotion to the City Hall beat:

POLICE CHASING
CONFIDENCE MAN

Saskatchewan RCMP and local police were combing the countryside at noon Thursday for a smooth-talking confidence man and his beautiful teenaged companion.

The man is believed to have "purchased" the Terminal Hotel in Willson, Sask., Wednesday night with a worthless cheque for $165,000.00.

The pair fled from town Thursday morning as the hotel owners, Stanley Parnell and his mother, Ida Parnell, drove to Regina to cash the bogus cheque. The Prince Albert bank account proved to have no funds and the Parnells went to the police.

Roadblocks have been set up on major highways. An RCMP spokesman said, "We'll catch him, even if we have to send out helicopters and bloodhounds."

Mr. Parnell, a life-long native of Willson, said in an exclusive *Leader-Post* interview that the man showed up in town earlier in the week and constructed an elaborate house of cards which flimflammed the whole town.

Acting as a big businessman with oil interests, he claimed to be seeking out good investment property. "Naturally, the hotel and restaurant, one of the best in the province, entered his mind."

The man persuaded Mr. Parnell to give him free room and board while he "observed" the hotel's operation, Mr. Parnell said.

"He also claimed to have political connections and that he was a friend of the politician, Boston Morgan."

Police have issued a stern "no comment" as they

continue to hunt through southern Saskatchewan. They have not indicated whether the young woman accompanying the cheque-artist is an accomplice or an innocent victim. She had been an employee of the hotel restaurant.

Mr. Parnell said that following the "sale" of the hotel, the phoney businessman held a party at the hotel to celebrate and depleted the hotel's entire beer stock. The loss is expected to be about one thousand dollars.

"It is terrible what greed will do to a man," Mr. Parnell observed.

The man also obtained a new car and some clothing by fraudulent means.

The fugitives are believed to be headed north.

* * * * *

7

Travelling east toward the town of Amazon, which he located on the map in his pocket, Gilly had ample time to reflect on that part of his character that had put him in this bind. It was the challenge of acquisition, the game that he had learned from the Go-getter Company of Toronto.

Reading *The Farmer's Advocate* one Monday night about two years after Porter's heroic death, an advertisement he had never seen before seemed to leap off the page, flaunting its possibilities. He had found it on the Young Farmers and Farmerettes Page, tucked among the wheat sheaf poems and letters to Uncle Hank Wheatstraw, the editor. "Boys and Girls!" it exclaimed. "Make $$$$$ in you $pare time! The Go-getter Novelty Co. is recruiting junior salesmen for its line of flavoured fruit drink powders!"

With much care, Gilly invested a couple of evenings writing the letter which outlined his capabilities. He took it to Caplette's store on Friday, the day Wayne Desjarlais, the mail carrier, drove in from Meadow Lake in his Model A.

"Who are *you* sendin' a letter to?" Wayne demanded.

"Company in Toronto," he said. "Gonna be a salesman."

"Aaa — bullshit."

Gilly shrugged. "You'll see."

"Wutcha sellin'?"

"Soft drink powder. Mix it with water and drink it like Orange Crush."

"Bullshit! 'S'no such thing!"

"Sez who? I'm gonna get a camera for sellin' them." There had been a camera shown in the advertisement and the image appealed to him.

Wayne walked away muttering, but as he had two years before, Gilly once again found himself surrounded by an admiring circle of kids. It was the talk of the school. Miss McIvor kept him after class to confront him with the stories she had heard about magic soft drinks and free cameras. "Your schoolwork has been slipping, Gilly. This lying can only make things worse."

He showed her the proof, the advertisement torn from the newspaper.

"Well. Maybe we'd better wait and see what happens. Don't get your hopes up."

Three weeks later, a parcel arrived in Caplette's store. Gilly ran with it to the buggy, chanting at Wilfred and the girls. "I'm gonna be a salesman! I'm gonna be a salesman!" He whipped old King home in a lathered gallop. At the gate, he hauled on the reins and stopped the exhausted plough horse while the others yelled the news. Gilly tore the parcel open and packages of Go-getter Lemon and Orange Drink Powder cascaded to the seat of the buggy. Gilly waved the accompanying letter and read it to his family like a proclamation, his voice tight with pride:

Dear Mr. Savard,

I am delighted to welcome you to the growing army of dedicated Go-getter salesmen. We were most impressed by your qualifications. As a token of our faith in you, we are enclosing twelve (12) packets of our quality drink powders to start you on your *own selling career*.

Each packet sells for five (5) cents. If you choose to work on a cash basis, your commission will be fifteen (15) percent. You have two weeks in which to sell the products, and you must return fifty cents to us to maintain your status within the company.

If you prefer to enjoy the merchandise bonuses like so many of our other salesmen, you may earn two gift coupons by remitting the total of sixty (60) cents and make your selections from the catalogue we have enclosed.

BEST WISHES ON YOUR FUTURE AS A GO-GETTER SALESMAN!

> Sincerely,
> Frank Sterling,
> Sales Manager

"*Tabernac!*" André Savard said, stunned. "They give him sixty cents worth of stuff — just like that? Gilly, how'd you do that?"

"You don't understand, Pa. I have to send the money back. I'm gonna get a pile of coupons and send off for a camera."

"A *what*?"

"A camera. Kind you take pictures with." He flipped through the catalogue until he found the picture of the camera. "Neat, eh?"

André laughed. "Don't be a sucker, Gilly! You ain't gonna send that money back. I'll let you keep two-bits of it!"

Gilly ran into the house with the packages. "I'm gonna send it all, Pa. I want to get a camera!"

André seized a length of cordwood lying near the door and ran after Gilly to beat some sense into him, but Mme. Savard mounted a rare effort at intercession and barred the door with her body. "Don't you dare! He's got to be honest if he's going to go to a seminary. It's good training!"

"I'll give him training! Stand out of the way!"

She closed her eyes in terror. "I'll hide my egg money!"

André hesitated. His wife's egg money tin could be tapped for extra cash when he went to Meadow Lake. This was a serious threat and he knew it. "Awright," he growled. "But if he don't keep the chores done, he's gonna get it good." Then he stomped off to the barn, cursing fate for taking one able-bodied son away for the Germans to kill, and giving the other one fancy notions about himself. If that was what education did, André Savard wanted no more of it.

The new Go-getter salesman was a credit to his profession. Every day between the school bell and milking time at five o'clock, he stopped at farms on the way home and peddled his powders. At five cents a package, it was a real bargain. It made a quart of soft drink, whereas store-bought "pop" offered only ten ounces for the same price. Every night, the girls and Wilfred grew enthused as they studied the merchandise in the Go-getter catalogue, the baseball gloves and large walking dolls. But the page that Gilly always stopped at was the camera: a sixteen-picture "candid" camera with a black case and carrying strap. By the end of the week, Gilly sat down to write to Mr. Sterling:

> Dear Mr. Sterling.
> Here is the money, sixty (60) cents for your Go-getter Drink Powders. I wish to get a Candid Camera, Prize #27 in your catalogue, so I am not taking a commission. Instead, please send my premiums and another bunch of Drink Powders. This time send more Orange than Lemon, which people here like better. I want enough to get one hundred (100) premiums.
>
> Yours sincerely,
Gillman Savard,
Salesman

The second parcel arrived shortly after, six hundred packets, along with his coupons and a flattering letter from Mr. Sterling. Gilly fell to work with a passion, hitting as many as three or four farms a night on his way home, often arriving home late for the milking. But the magic began to disappear. His customers were slow in drinking up their supply. Others were disappointed in the flavour. After two weeks, Gilly had only sold twenty-five (25) packages. He redoubled his efforts, ranging further in the district and coming home long after dark. The nights grew cold and the packets of drink powder went dog-eared and weatherbeaten in his lunchkit, until they were unsellable. He tried to compose a letter to Mr. Sterling begging for more time, but failed to find the words.

Finally, his mother took pity and loaned him eight dollars from her egg money, making him promise her three things: to say nothing to Papa, to order no more drink powders and to pay her back. The next day, he mailed the ten dollar money order to Toronto from Caplette's store. Word spread fast through the school that the camera was coming. A cluster of schoolmates escorted Gilly to the store every Friday to see if it had arrived. He hid the rest of the powders under his bed and told his mother they would sell better in the spring when warm weather returned.

The package arrived in November. His followers stood four deep at Henry's postal wicket as Gilly ripped off the brown paper. But it was not the camera. It was a shipment of six hundred Go-getter Christmas cards, along with a letter from Mr. Sterling and a large scroll-worked "Certificate of Honest Achievement" with Gilly's name emblazoned in Old English script and a big red seal on one corner. He read the letter to Henry and the pupils:

Dear Mr. Savard,

Due to unexpected demand, we are unable to fill your order for a Candid Camera. This will be processed in due course. In the meantime, with the Christmas gift-giving season upon us, you may wish to sell these handsome Christmas cards and earn gifts for the loved ones in your family. If you can return the money by December 15, we will make every effort to have gifts selected from our catalogue delivered in time for the Yuletide Festivities.

Gilly thought a moment. "You wanta buy some Christmas cards, Henry?"

"Sure, I'll take a couple a dozen," Henry said, and Gilly was hooked again. He sent his friends home with the message that he would be taking orders for cards Monday at school.

That weekend, he pored over the catalogue picking out presents for his family. He wanted to keep it a surprise because they had never had a real Christmas. Papa said gift-giving was "blasphemous," although he was merely tight-fisted. Every Christmas Eve, he went through a ritual of assembling a crèche in the kitchen. When it was completed, the children were invited to applaud his arrangement of cut-out shepherds grouped around the plaster Jesus lying in the washbasin. By then, Papa was drunk on the bottle of hootch he had gotten from Victor Samson, the bootlegger, and he would weep nostalgically at the memory of great feasts in Batoche and the great festivities which would never come again. After the children had trooped miserably to bed, Papa would stumble through the Adoration, kicking the angels and wise men in all directions as he stumbled to his bed. Later, Mme. Savard would fill their stockings with peanuts and sometimes, tangerine oranges.

This year, it would be different. Gilly selected his prizes carefully from the catalogue: a new hammer for his father, sets of brushes and mirrors for his sisters, a toy pistol for Wilfred and a rubber duck for Louise. His mother was the most difficult of all; there weren't many gifts suitable for grown-up women. Then, as he gazed at the Red Ryder air rifle, he remembered that his mother had often complained of not having a gun in the house when Papa went on trips and took his thirty-thirty. She felt unprotected. An air rifle would be perfect. And if Gilly could borrow it to shoot a few squirrels or crows, so much the better.

Monday, Gilly began selling. He offered a prize to the classmate who came to school with the biggest order for Christmas cards. At night, he would take King and the sleigh and flog the horse up and down the trails long after the sun had set. He grew frostbitten from one end of his body to the other. But by the end of the third week, he had sold all the cards and a few more Go-getter drink powders to boot. He sent the money off to Mr. Sterling with a letter pleading for a speedy return. He explained that the mail took longer to reach Brochet than it did other places.

On the last Friday before Christmas, Gilly's miracle came to pass. Henry Caplette laid *The Farmer's Advocate* in front of Gilly on the counter. Then, unable to conceal his grin, he reached behind the counter and handed Gilly an enormous parcel of brown wrapping paper which was pasted with stamps and Christmas seals.

Gilly drove home, dazed with his triumph. He would hide the parcel in the barn and open it on Christmas morning when the family was sitting around him.

On Christmas Eve, it took a long time to fall asleep. Wilfred kept poking him and asking if it was morning yet. Hearing his father's mutterings in the other room as the annual tableau was assembled, he finally fell into a deep sleep. Gilly dreamed he was walking down the railway tracks from Meadow Lake to the south, to the cities. He saw a nickel shining among the ties, and when he picked it up, there was a quarter a few feet beyond. Each time he bent down, more coins appeared along the tracks, and the further he went, the more silver he could stuff into his pockets. Presently, he came to a town and inquired the price of a train which sat chugging on the tracks. He reached into his pockets to count out the money. But all the coins had disappeared into thin air! The train engineer grew red in the face and began shouting for the police, as Gilly fled back along the tracks.

He woke up in a cold sweat and laid in bed for a minute, trembling, until he realized he was at home. He got up and tiptoed into the "Other Room," his stomach knotted.

The nativity scene had been kicked apart, as usual, and there was a half-empty gallon jug of bootleg whiskey from Victor Samson's. Papa lay in bed, snoring raucously. His mother was there, too, watching with dark blank eyes as Gilly walked in a daze to the torn-up brown wrapping paper, still festooned with Santa Claus seals. It was just wrapping paper. The gifts were gone. But there was a crumpled letter from Mr. Sterling and a Certificate of Super Salesmanship. They had been of no value to Victor Samson when André Savard had made his barter for the whiskey. Gilly understood in an instant, but said nothing, not even to his mother. He spent Christmas Day by himself in the attic, refusing to speak to anyone.

Two months after New Year's, when he had nearly re-pressed the incident, Gilly's camera arrived from Toronto along with a consignment of eight hundred new valentines. The camera was a gleaming black plastic model with a pointed snout and a viewfinder as streamlined as a Spitfire. It was loaded with film. Gilly practiced all weekend, photo-graphing cows and pigs. Word spread fast. When he rode into the schoolyard Monday, there was a large crowd of kids waiting to get their pictures taken. And while he unharnessed King from the sleigh, Marny Desjarlais sent a message with one of his sisters that he could have a kiss if he took her picture.

The moment of ecstasy was worth the pain. No one else was allowed to handle the camera except Marny, who snapped several pictures before dropping the new camera on the concrete walk, shattering it into a dozen shiny black pieces. The exposed film started curling up in the winter sunlight.

"Look," Marny cried, not knowing what else to say. "It's only plastic!"

Even this did not defeat Gilly, though his smile grew sick. He took the film and the pieces of camera and threw them down one of the holes in the boys' backhouse. A few days later, his mother mailed the valentines back to Mr. Sterling saying that Gilly had given up a sales career in favour of the priesthood.

* * * * *

8

"Say, are you hungry yet?" Georgia made a plaintive face as the Chev pulled away from the Royalite gas station in Amazon.

"Hungry? No." Gilly was preoccupied. Somehow there had to be a way out of this game, he knew, a line of escape leading to Regina. He put the map back in his pocket.

"I haven't had a thing since seven o'clock this morning. I gotta have lotsa protein, ya know. For my skin."

Gilly had just spent the last of his money filling the gas tank and didn't have the price of a bag of peanuts, let alone lunch. Somehow he had to dump the girl, the car and the new clothes and make them all understand it was a mistake.

"Vitamins, too. They're for your liver."

"How much money have you got?" he said. A highway sign announced that they were approaching Holdfast.

She shrugged. "Couple of dollars. Why?"

"I don't have any cash. And my credit cards are no good in little towns like this."

"So? Let's head for a *big* town. Donchuh wanna go tuh Regina?"

"It's hard to explain," he said vaguely.

"Well, I mean — dumpy little places like this! Holdfast? And *Amazon*!"

"Listen, Georgia, I don't ask you a lot of questions about waitressing, do I? So let me look after my own business."

Her eyes brightened. "You mean we're on oil company business? Right now?"

Gilly nodded, hoping to silence her. In fact, all he was doing was wandering the backroads, hoping for gaps in the roadblocks and killing time until something miraculous happened. The direction he took came from the tattered provincial road map at his side. A number of towns were underlined on it in ballpoint pen. Holdfast was one of them. Gilly had a fascination with maps. He never travelled without one.

Holdfast was identical to most other prairie towns. A single main street lay parallel to the railway and the grain elevators; four side streets intersected at precise intervals. On the main street was the usual line-up: gasoline station, general store, machinery dealer, lunch counter, school, community hall, town office, church and pool hall. No trees. Gilly pulled up in front of the Maple Leaf Café.

"You gonna eat in that dump?" Georgia said.

He nodded and pulled her inside. The café had not been renovated since the 1940's. It was sectioned into darkly varnished wooden booths with six-foot backs. Two large electric fans, black with grease, hung motionless from the ceiling. An old Chinaman — or perhaps a Chinawoman — sat on a high stool behind the ornate cash register. Gilly checked the jukebox: Glenn Miller and the Andrews Sisters. The menu offered hamburgers at twenty-five cents, a pork chop special for a dollar. There wasn't a customer in sight.

"Never thought we'd be eating in crummy places like this," Georgia sniffed.

"Get used to it, sweetie. It could get worse."

She gazed at the menu. "All they got is pork chops and veal cutlets."

While eating his veal cutlets, Gilly took out the map and laid it on the table. He studied it for a long time, then folded it to a section west of Highway 11. If there was no roadblock where they crossed the highway, he might get clear. The map showed more empty space on the other side.

"Eyebrow," he said, looking at the map.

"Did you say Eyebrow?"

"Yes. Give me your two bucks, will you?"

They took off west in a cloud of powdered snow, tacking along the grid roads crisscrossing the farmlands. Every mile, a road ran north-south; every two miles, one went east-west. A surveyor could have driven it blindfolded, but to Gilly it had the fascination of a maze.

"What were we doin' at Holdfast?" Georgia said. "I mean, just what's so great about that? No oil wells or *nuthin'!*"

"I liked the name."

Eyebrow had the same features as the others, as he knew it would. Nothing about it suggested an eyebrow at all. He cruised up and down the streets of the nearly-deserted town looking for the answer. Finally, he parked in front of the Office of the Rural Municipality of Eyebrow.

"Couple of minutes," he said.

Inside, a youth in a bright red V-neck sweater sat at a desk behind the counter, combing his hair with a rat-tail comb. He grinned a lopsided grin that he had painstakingly learned from an Elvis Presley photo. "What kin I do yuh for?"

"I'm doing a sort of uh, survey on the names of Saskatchewan towns."

"Yeah?"

"Yeah. How did this place get to be called Eyebrow?"

"Gonna put it in a book?"

"Maybe."

The boy went to a shelf at the far side of the room and retrieved a Chamber of Commerce brochure. "Eyebrow is one of the most progressive towns in eastern West-Central Saskatchewan," he recited. "'Population 782 in the last census. Eyebrow boasts a curling rink, modern sewage plant and a community hall renovated in 1952.' Say, how much are you charging us to get into this book?"

"Nothing," Gilly assured him.

"Near the site of the future South Saskatchewan Dam. Home of the Eyebrow Icers Senior B hockey team. Centre for the best duck hunting in North America."

"But how did it get the name?"

The boy held up a hand. "Eyebrow is named *after nearby Eyebrow Lake*."

Gilly stared at him. "Well? How did Eyebrow Lake get its name?"

The youth put the brochure back and began combing his hair again. "Doesn't say," he shrugged.

Gilly returned to the car and checked the map. Darkness was already falling.

"Where we goin' now?" Georgia sighed.

"Elbow," he said.

"Hey," she said, snuggling up to him. "How about letting me drive for a while?"

"Have you got a licence?"

She pouted. "I got a learner's."

Gilly thought about it. Then he stopped the car, got out and walked around to the passenger's side. "Take over." Perhaps it would keep her quiet and he could study his map in peace.

* * * * *

9

Gilly had always had a fascination for maps. It dated at least as far back as the big map of Canada which hung in front of the entire class at Brochet school. It was a beautifully coloured cloth map which had been supplied by the Neilson's Chocolate Company and it featured four of their candy bars as well as the nine provinces of the Dominion and Newfoundland. To Gilly, travel would be linked forever with knowledge, chocolate bars and Miss McIvor.

Miss McIvor didn't know what to do with Gilly by the time he reached Grade Six. He had spent the entire year daydreaming about something else, and the only interest he seemed to have in school was in sports. His sister Marie often had to drive the buggy or the sleigh home because Gilly would disappear to play baseball or shinny. Miss McIvor did not think he would make it to Grade Seven. Even his mother couldn't make him take an interest. It was too bad; he had shown so much promise earlier.

That summer, a year after the war ended, André Savard was figuring harder than ever down the blank margins of *The Farmer's Advocate*. There was a construction boom across the country and the price of lumber had gone sky-high. Timber was the only thing which grew well on his farm and most of it was only in the way, anyway. The new Socialist government in Regina was giving subsidies to small timber cutters, and a wave of ex-soldiers was fanning across the countryside looking for work at wages even André Savard could afford to pay. He and Gilly threw together a shanty on the back edge of the farm, building some rough bunks in it. Then André declared himself in the logging business.

For the first time, Gilly enjoyed working on the farm. The men who came to work had travelled the world; they were tellers of awesome and frightening tales. One wizened drifter, "Crab" Campbell, hired on as the cook for the outfit. André offered Gilly a job as cook's helper. This offered several advantages at once. He had a good excuse to leave school, to help with the family business. He could earn money. And he could enjoy life for a year. Gilly mollified his mother by saying he could always go back to school in a year's time.

The cookhouse job was menial in itself, much less interesting than bush cutting. It meant pecling potatoes and washing dishes for twelve hours a day, but time passed quickly with "Crab." Campbell was an ex-logger from Duncan, B.C., with two fingers gone from his left hand and a thumb and index finger gone from his right. He was a living legend, having done everything from killing timberwolves to thrashing four men in a street brawl in Port Alberni. He had been all over the world: to San Francisco, New Orleans, Marseilles, Regina, even Hong Kong. He sang the praises of ladies of those cities and told sad tales of the bush loggers and sailors doomed to chase them with a bottle of rum in one hand and a thin roll of sweat-stained dollars in the other. Gilly asked him about the capital, Regina.

"Queen City of the Plains!" Crab declared, raising his soup ladle to the heavens. "I never saw such a bunch a women as what they got there. Hoor-house on every street corner, down behind the market. And a whole raft of amateurs —

four wimmen to every guy! Guvviment town, see?"

"It sounds swell," Gilly said, scrubbing down the long table where the loggers ate.

"The only place to live in the summertime. Long wide streets and a big lake right in the middle of the city, if you feel like just goin' for a swim!"

"Where else, Crab?"

"Ah, now — 'Frisco. Ya gotta go to San Francisco, Gilly. The Golden City with the Golden Gate. The Western City of Gold!"

But the idyll ended in the spring when the rivers broke up and the men deserted the timber operation for the fleshpots of Prince Albert and North Battleford, their denim jackets stuffed with a few of the dollars André Savard had raked in during the season.

"Goin' to Regina?" Gilly asked Crab as he packed.

Campbell looked him over speculatively. "Might. What's it to you?"

"Maybe I could go along. What do you think?"

"Got any dough?"

"I will soon's Pa pays me off. I'll go ask."

Crab waited while Gilly went to the bunkhouse to ask for his salary. He had been promised ten dollars a week.

"Salary!" André roared. "I'll give you a goddam *salary*! Who do you think pays for your clothes and all that dam' food you eat?"

"You mean you're not gonna pay me anything?"

André laughed. "I'll pay you a good kick in the arse!"

Gilly returned to the cookhouse fuming. He asked Crab to stake him till they got to the city. But Crab, who knew answers before questions were asked, said he had changed his mind and was going to visit his mother in Victoria.

After several days of brooding in the vacant camp, Gilly sneaked out of his attic room early one morning with forty cents in his pocket and struck out south for the fabulous cities. Luckily the Mounties, alerted by Papa, found him before he was irretrievably lost in the dense bush, floundering through the muskeg a couple of miles off the Meadow Lake trail.

The policemen conferred with Mme. Savard, then Miss McIvor. They informed André that Gilly had to remain in school until he was sixteen or André could be prosecuted. They pointed out, however, that he could continue to work at home, as long as he attended school. At this, both André and Mme. Savard nodded with satisfaction. Miss McIvor advanced him into Grade Seven. To Gilly, it sounded like a jail sentence.

* * * * *

10

The huge map on the wall of Staff Sergeant Harry Swift's office was a topographical map of the province. It absorbed the complete attention of the newspaper reporter who had been assigned to cover the Willson kidnapping case on a twenty-four hour basis. Swift had marked several points on the map with a red grease pencil. The reporter was trying to figure out what they meant. There was a big circle around the hamlet of Amazon.

"That was the first place," Swift explained finally, irritated with the reporter's obtuseness. "He stopped there for gas and tried to cash a cheque."

"And the others?" the reporter pointed to the red X's marking the communities of Eyebrow, Conquest, Elbow, Thrasher, Wartime and Sanctuary. Swift nodded.

"But there's no pattern or anything! It's like he's running in all directions at once."

"I *know*, dammitall! Why don't you go and peddle papers or do something useful?"

Just then an electrifying report came via telephone from Swift Current. Savard and the girl had checked into the El Dave and Mona Motel. They had stayed long enough to order a meal, fill the car with gas, charge these expenses to their room, commit Lord knows what other illegal acts and check out again. Staff Sergeant Swift was elated.

"He's on the Trans-Canada Highway! Heading west after all!" Swift phoned Superintendent Chernyk with the good news and then ordered three roadblocks between Swift

Current and Medicine Hat, with one more on the east side
of Swift Current, just in case.

It was a good night's work. Now he had his quarry boxed.

* * * * *

11

Keeping one eye on the road, Gilly read the afternoon
newspaper that he had picked up in Swift Current. Biting her
tongue, Georgia wove back and forth across the white line,
concentrating on the task of driving south.

"How'm I doing?"

"Fine, fine." He was reading the paper by the light inside
the glove compartment.

"Any interesting news?"

"Police are chasing some guy. Supposed to be roadblocks
up everywhere.

"Well, I haven't seen any."

"Let me know if you do."

"Mr. Savard?"

He did not answer.

"Gilly?"

"What?"

"I'm gettin' tired. Whenner we gonna stop?"

"Not far. Place up ahead."

"What's the name of this one?"

"Climax."

She stared at him, shocked. The car swerved suddenly
across the road and careened along the gravel shoulder for a
hundred yards, teetering on the brink of total wreckage.
Panicked, Georgia tramped her full weight on the accelerator.
Before he could push her off the controls, the speedometer
hit ninety.

"So where are we gonna stay?" she demanded when he
had brought the car to a stop. His heart was pounding from
the scare. "In a hotel?"

"That's what I'm hoping for."

"There better not be any funny business!"

"Funny business?"

"Yeah, I'm not goin' for anything funny. I'm only fifteen."

Now he really was alarmed. No wonder they were setting up roadblocks. For a moment, he considered turning himself in and begging for mercy. His last stretch was nothing compared to what he could get for this.

* * * * *

12

"*Climax?*" Swift exclaimed, leaping off the campcot in his office the next morning. The constable reported that one Gillman A. Savard, in the company of a girl, had taken two rooms in The Climax Hotel the night before. After breakfast, they had left without paying.

"What the hell is he doing in *Climax?*"

A couple of ribald suggestions came from the policemen and reporters who had assembled to watch the drama unfold. Swift stabbed his finger at the wall. "Look at that! Headed straight for the U.S. border! Why didn't we think of that?" He picked up the telephone and alerted customs officers at all border crossings to watch for the phantom Chevrolet.

The next complaint came from a North Star service station in Limerick.

"East!" Swift said, staring at his map in disbelief.

Over the next few hours, sightings were reported from Old Wives, Mitchellton, Galilee, Willowbunch, Horizon, Wheatstone, Amulet, Forward, Yellowgrass, Forget, Montmartre and Peebles. By eight o'clock Friday night, Swift sat exhausted in his chair, staring at the telephone with baffled outrage and waiting for some new assault on his sanity.

"Do you know something, Staff?" the newspaper reporter said.

"What?"

"He's travelling in a big circle. Look! All around Regina. He's done nearly 270 degrees now."

Swift leaped to his feet and peered at the map.

"See? Spiralling in toward the city."

"Naa."

"Isn't it worth a try?"

Harry Swift sent a general bulletin out to all detachments in the area. Less than an hour later, an excited radio report came in from Indian Head, forty miles east of the city. The golden-winged Chevrolet was parked outside the local hotel.

* * * * *

13

On the other end of the circle's radius, Gilly sat looking out the hotel window at the street, two floors below.

"What's so interesting out there, anyways?" Georgia said, stretched out on her bed with a Coke in one hand and a cigarette in the other.

What interested him was the police car parked a half-block down the street, where it had been for twenty minutes.

"Nothing." He looked at the map. "Thinking I might make it to Regina tomorrow."

"Kin we go to a nightclub?"

"There aren't any nightclubs there. Besides, you're too young."

"How do you know there aren't if you never bin there?"

"There are no nightclubs in Saskatchewan!"

"Gilly?"

"What."

"Gonna give me some dictation tonight?"

"I don't know. Listen, Georgia, I just remembered something. You wait here, I'll be right back."

"Are you *kidding*? We just got here!" She sat up, her young breasts straining angrily against her dress. She stubbed out her cigarette. "What the heck is it this time?"

"I just want to be alone for a few minutes."

"I knew it!" she cried. "You're tired 'a me awready and wanna abandon me in the sticks!"

"Okay, okay. Shut up and get your coat on. We have to leave again."

He took her hand and they tiptoed down the hall to the fire escape. "Hey," she shouted. "You're not gonna sneak out *without payin'*, are ya?"

He seized her and carried her out the door, down the clanging metal steps to the parking lot and the car. Driving with the lights off, he edged the car down the back alley to the next street. Before they reached the first intersection, a Mountie appeared on foot from a side alley, signalling with a flashlight to halt.

There were two alternatives: flee in a blind panic or stop like a mature human being and face the music.

"The fuzz!" Georgia yelled, and Gilly fled in a blind panic. He gunned the engine so hard that the car's windstream blasted the policeman off his feet as they roared past.

"Gilly! That was a *cop*!"

"What?" Gilly said. "Where?" He put the pedal to the floor.

"You nearly hit him! We cheated that hotel! We're in trouble!" She began to cry.

"No, not now! Listen, Georgia. You don't have a driver's licence, *do* you? You wouldn't want me to get pinched for letting you drive!"

"Boy! My Dad'll shoot me if I get into trouble. I mean it!"

They reached the edge of town on a backroad, the car bouncing wildly in the darkness. Behind them, there were faint strains of a police siren opening up. Gilly flicked the lights on.

"Where we goin' now?"

He tossed the map to her. "Fort Qu'Appelle."

Five miles down the road, a red flashing light blinked into action some distance behind them. Gilly cut the lights and swung off the road at the next farm driveway. A long hedgerow led to some unlit farm buildings. At the end of the road, he turned into the trees and stopped the car. The red light flashed past at the end of the drive and disappeared as the cruiser went by.

"That was close," Georgia said, sliding toward him on the seat and clutching him. She laid her head on his shoulder.

"Probably an ambulance." One more exaggeration would not matter, he thought, driving along a set of ruts rambling through the pasture. It looked like an old wagon trail winding among the poplar bluffs and large boulders. They had left the flat prairie and were skirting the moraine along the lip of the Qu'Appelle Valley. Gilly no longer needed the car headlights; the moon was nearly full.

"How can you see in the dark like that?"

"I'm an Indian."

"You know," Georgia said after a moment, "I thought

you were a Frenchman."

The trail suddenly disappeared into nothing. Worse than nothing. There was only a deep black void. Gilly hit the brakes, but it was too late to stop the car from soaring into space like a shot arrow. He clenched the wheel as the car hurtled downward leaving behind it an arc of flying gravel. The wheels bounced off the side of the cliff once and the car plunged with a crash into a pool of water amid flying shards of ice. A few boulders drummed on the car roof.

"Where are we?" Georgia shrieked.

Gilly could see snowflakes through the spattered windshield. At least they weren't underwater. He opened the door and stepped out. He was up to his belly in freezing slush.

"What's happening?"

"Will you quit screaming?" he gasped.

They had plunged into a twenty-foot gravel pit that had been excavated in the middle of the trail, diving headfirst into the slough like a gold and white dart. The back tires were high in the air.

"Thought you said you were an Indian," Georgia said.

It was midnight before Gilly found an occupied farm house and an hour later before the tow truck made its way from Regina to the gravel quarry. The front end was wrecked, but the engine started. Gilly and Georgia could warm themselves in front of the heater as they were towed away. By the time they reached the main highway, Georgia's teeth had stopped chattering and the ice in Gilly's shorts had begun to thaw.

Ahead, he could see the golden lights of the Queen City winking like sparks of warmth along the horizon. At the first roadblock, a Mountie waved them past as Gilly hunched down in the seat. The next roadblock was at the entrance to the city. They passed it with no difficulty. But in the rearview mirror, Gilly could see the constable's look of recognition as he observed the goose-winged car. The policeman ran to his radio.

"Oh no!" Gilly cried. He slammed the car into gear and floored the accelerator, forgetting that the car's front end was suspended. The back tires spun, thrusting the radiator forward into the tow truck. The driver turned and looked.

Gilly waved at him to *go, go*! The driver shrugged and slowed down to fifteen miles an hour.

A more absurd entrance to the capital would have been hard to imagine. At the intersection of Victoria and Hamilton, directly below the windows of the courthouse and the federal building, two squad cars blocked the road completely. City policemen crouched behind them with their guns drawn. From the sidestreets, howling sirens approached. Parked behind the roadblock was Staff Sergeant Harry Swift's baby blue 1950 English Ford Prefect.

The tow truck rolled up to the roadblock and stopped. Swift had got his man.

* * * * *

14

For two years after the Mounties had brought him back from the muskeg, Gilly plodded from farm to school and back to farm. He put his mind to work thinking up good lies so that he could stay behind in Brochet and play baseball or hockey with his friends. He worked up an intensely hypocritical interest in religion which provided solid opportunities for escape on Saturday and Sunday. Gilly became Father LaCasse's altar boy, smiling his angelic smile and wearing his hockey pads under his robe. This paid off far more handsomely than he had imagined possible, for it was Father LaCasse who eventually made the arrangements for him to move into town and study at Meadow Lake High School. Gilly had become so totally rebellious and large for his age that Papa was rather relieved to be rid of him. Mme. Savard was ecstatic. None of their family had ever gone to high school.

Gilly and Father LaCasse rode to Meadow Lake on the first of September in the mail carrier's new '48 Plymouth. As they drove past the railway station, the hotel and the vacant lot by the blacksmith's, Gilly thought of Porter and the night they had both learned that they were different.

Gilly was to live with his Uncle Leo — a cousin of Papa's, who lived in the halfbreed section of town. It was a little frame house with a yard full of junk, but a motorcycle sat in the driveway. Gilly felt a tingling across his scalp.

"Ahh — Father!" Uncle Leo said when he opened the door. "And little Gillman."

Inside, they met Aunt Louise and Cousin Alex, a wild-looking boy of eighteen or nineteen, who owned the motorcycle. Cousin Alex declined to stay in the front room and talk to his cousin or the priest, so he went out. The motorcycle roared down the street. Father LaCasse lifted his eyebrows. An inspection of the house finally arrived at Gilly's room in the basement. It had belonged to an older daughter who was now married; she had left behind her crucifix which pleased Father LaCasse, so a deal was struck. Board and room was $40.00 a month, which would be provided from special parish funds.

"Little Gillman" by then was nearly six feet tall and outweighed his cousin Alex by fifty pounds, but this did not prevent Alex from teasing him unmercifully about his "bush" manners. Alex was finished with school; he worked in the grocery store and occasionally gave Gilly a ride to school on his Harley Davidson. He taught Gilly how to say, "So long, punk," with just the right sneer.

Gilly would remember the year of 1948-49 as a magic time of discovery: Algebra, French, cars, girls, masturbation and movie queen pin-ups. And, he discovered football. He had been at school a week when the coach approached him in the hall and asked him to come out and play. He played tackle at first because of his size, but when they discovered how fast he was, he was moved to the backfield where he played both offence and defence. He was so good he became popular, despite his grinning naïveté. He usually went with the gang to the café after practice. Hardly anyone seemed to notice that he was a halfbreed.

That fall, he travelled to other schools throughout the district to play football. It was the year that the Calgary Stampeders went East to play in the Grey Cup game. Their fans invaded Toronto and rode horses through the lobby of the Royal York Hotel, while the Stampeders trampled the eastern team and returned in glory with the Grey Cup. For months, until the hockey season began, Gilly could think of nothing but football.

As his sixteenth birthday approached in March, Gilly's

interest focussed on the next milestone in his journey to manhood: the acquisition of a driver's licence. Alex demonstrated the superiority of the man with a vehicle over a pedestrian, much like the horseman of older days. To emulate him, Gilly had switched from a music option to Motor Mech during the first week of school.

On March 26, his birthday, he went to the motor vehicle licence office and scored one hundred percent on the written test. He could already feel the grip of a steering wheel in his hands, but there was a problem. He didn't have a car for the driving test. Motorcycles did not qualify and Uncle Leo's ancient Whippet would be impounded as a public menace if he took it to the examination. It was galling. All he could do was wait until he earned money to buy a car. He tried to concentrate on his schoolwork. In May, opportunity finally knocked at the front door of Uncle Leo's house. Gilly was called from his homework to the door where a man in a rumpled khaki uniform stood holding a piece of paper.

"Gillman Savard?"

"Yeah — what is it?"

"There's a forest fire at Green Lake. Government's hiring firefighters of uh, native origin." His eyes measured Gilly's height. "It's a pretty bad fire. Your father signed you on."

"What do I get?" he said thoughtfully.

"Eight bucks a day. Get paid every week."

A vision flashed into Gilly's mind of a shining second-hand car, a 1939 Ford he had seen at the B.A. gas station the day before. Eight dollars a day? He could earn enough in two weeks for a down payment and be back at school before anybody missed him. The hockey season was over; there was little else to do.

"Truck leaves in an hour from the railway station. Make sure ya got a decent pair of boots."

It took him fifteen minutes to throw a bundle of clothes together and run to the station. A one-ton truck waited there, with about a dozen Indians and halfbreeds laughing in the spring sunshine, excited about the adventure. He recognized a couple of Alex's friends. The truck started up and headed east along the marshy shore of the lake into the thick bush.

For two weeks, he choked on the heat and smoke of the roaring blaze, ploughing firebreaks and chopping down trees. He ate on the run, when he got to eat at all. The fire roared through the heavy stands of dead timber along the shore of Green Lake. More and more workers were brought in, white as well as native. They finally pushed the fire to the lake and held it there, just as the rain came and drowned it for good. That same night, they were driven back to town and Gilly was dumped off at Uncle Leo's house. He was asleep on his feet, but already dreaming of cruising up and down Main Street in his new Ford. Uncle Leo was waiting for him in his nightshirt.

"Oh, hi Gilly" he said, avoiding Gilly's eyes. "Your Pa dropped by to pick up your cheques for you. Said you'd only spend the money on something dumb."

There was a twisted feeling in his stomach and the dream vanished. "Where's Alex?" he said.

"Gone to a dance over at Loon Lake with some buddies of his."

"Uncle Leo, I hafta get home tonight. Can I borrow his motorcycle?"

Uncle Leo looked dubious.

"I'll have it back in the driveway before he gets home."

"He's really touchy about the dam' bike, Gilly."

"I'm only gonna be gone a couple of hours. Nothin's gonna happen."

He ran outside and pulled the motorcycle upright. He had never driven it before, but had watched Alex. With Uncle Leo watching anxiously through the screen door, Gilly kicked the motorcycle to life and revved the engine. He wobbled slightly, starting out. At the corner of the driveway, the back wheel skidded sideways on the gravel.

"For Crissakes, be careful!"

"It's okay!" he yelled back, although his right heel had jammed in the spokes and he could feel blood already seeping into his shoe. He roared off into the night, toward Brochet, cursing his father and hoping he had not yet spent all the money.

He was home within an hour, covered with dust. Stomping into the house, he met his mother who was crying. "Quit bawlin'," he said. "I'm only gonna give him a lickin'."

"I'm not worried about him, Gilly! It's you. You dropped out of school and now you'll never become a priest! The man from the school board was out here — and Father LaCasse!"

The girls and Wilfred appeared, rubbing the sleep from their eyes.

"Where is he?" Gilly said, picking up a broken axe handle outside the door.

"*No*, Gilly!"

He turned and ran, crashing through the scrub bush to the logging shanty on the other side of the farm. As he approached, the light in André's office went out. Gilly smashed the door open and caught his Papa scrambling out the back window.

"Hold on!" Gilly yelled, swinging the axe handle over his head. "Did you cash them cheques a' mine?"

"Your cheques?" André said indignantly. "I thought they were *my* cheques. That's why I signed you on. We needed the money to pay the loggers!"

"I'm going to beat the money out of your hide," Gilly cried, shaking his father like a muskrat.

"Why don't you?" André yelled back. "I'll have the cops out here so fast you'll shit your pants."

Gilly hesitated and lowered his club. Papa was right. The law would punish him worse than he could ever hurt his father. "You better give me that money," he said uncertainly.

"It's all spent, I toljuh!"

Gilly looked around the office and his eye fell on André's gold pocket watch which was hanging beside the window. He put it in his pocket. "It's not worth what you owe me, but it'll help — for a while."

"Where are you going?"

"None of your business!" He turned and strode back to the house. His mother was standing at the door, staring at the motorcyle. She was pale with shock.

"What did you do to him?"

"Nothing."

"What is that thing?"

"It's Alex's motorcycle. Ma, can you give me any grub? I'm goin' south."

"South? Where?"

"I dunno where, I'm just going."

Mme. Savard's hnds flew across her breast in the shape of a cross. "She heard my prayers! You're going to the seminary to become a priest! The Blessed Virgin has heard us."

Gilly stepped back, stunned. "Never mind the food," he said and ran to the attic, where he pulled out all his spare clothing. He rolled it into his jacket pockets, along with his Certificate of Honest Achievement. Mme. Savard pushed a cloth-wrapped bundle at him as he ran past her out the door. "Biscuits and jam," she said. "I'll send more when you're settled. Have you got your rosary?"

"Where's Gilly going, Ma?" Wilfred said, poking his head out of the loft.

"Goodbye, Ma. So long, Wilf." Gilly jumped onto the machine and spun its tires out of the yard. As he roared past Henry Caplette's store with its tall glass-crowned gasoline pumps, he revved the engine furiously. That would wake them, he thought, swooping onto the Meadow Lake road. The power of the Harley flowed from the engine through the pedal to his toes, through his crouched knees to his thighs and back. It spun along his spine and exploded off the top of his head like a discharging lightning rod.

The wind clawed at him as he sped through the night. Nothing would slow him down. He swerved and dipped and soared along the dusty road, opening his jacket to catch the wind which slammed against his chest. Nothing would stop him. He was travelling again, much faster than he had on his first journey to Meadow Lake. It was spring and over the stink of the exhaust, he could smell the marshes and the new green buds. Eight years before, the journey had seemed to last a thousand miles. But now, he rode in the Age of the Atom. Jet planes were smashing the sound barrier and before he could even think of time or distance, the lights of Meadow Lake flashed as he rounded a curve in the road. Gilly turned toward the town, to school and to the police, to get his last cheque and to return Alex's motorcycle before he got back from the dance. He swerved along the railroad tracks and headed for his uncle's house. At the station, a freight train waited, hissing quietly to itself. The engineer's

70

face turned toward him, and between them there appeared a faint tableau: an old woman and a young man crying.

Gilly twisted the handle grips, driving the speedometer up to sixty as he blasted down Main Street. He hit the corner by the War Memorial where Porter's name had been inscribed the year before, skidding in a circle on the new green lawn. He paused, saw in his mind's eye the highway heading south and revved the engine once again, flying past the railway station and along the tracks. Stopping at the entrance to the highway, he stroked the machine once and took off into the night, straight as an arrow toward the golden cities of the south, shining on the far side of the dark, forested horizon.

* * * * *

15

A large audience had gathered in the magistrate's court to hear the charges: eight counts of false pretences, four of fraud, one of dangerous driving and one of driving without an operator's licence. Gilly pleaded guilty to all of them.

"Has this man got a criminal record?" the magistrate asked.

Staff Sergeant Swift handed the prosecutor a typed sheet. "Yes, Your Worship. A lengthy record dating back to 1949: theft of a motorcycle. He was released from Prince Albert Penitentiary four days before committing the Willson offences, after an eighteen-month term for fraud. Do you want them all?"

"No, it won't be necessary. Why were charges not laid in the abduction of this young girl? That appears to be the most serious part of this escapade."

"She apparently went willingly, Your Worship. He didn't threaten her or harm her in any way."

"Am I to believe that they spent the better part of two days and nights together and he didn't lay a finger on her?"

"That's right, Your Worship. Our information indicates that they had separate bedrooms in the hotels. The accused hired the girl as his secretary and he dictated company business to her in the evenings."

The magistrate turned to Georgia who was cracking gum in her teeth as she sat wide-eyed and beautiful in the front row of the courtroom. "Is that true? He never propositioned you?"

"Hey, what do you think I am, Judge? We did *dictation* every night."

"What was it about?"

"Eh?"

"The dictation."

"Oh — I never paid much attention. It was all about those goofy little towns we were driving through."

The magistrate motioned with his nose for Gilly to stand up.

"Gillman Savard. You have behaved disgracefully. You went straight from jail to a defenceless little town and practiced your vile trade till you bled the citizens white. You introduced this child," indicating Georgia, "to a life of crime. What have you to say?"

Gilly shook his head. "Nothing, Your Worship."

"You are a foul, vicious hoodlum, Savard. I hereby sentence you to seven years of penal servitude on the first charge specified. The rest will run concurrent."

Mrs. Parnell smiled. Georgia cried a piercing shriek and began to weep. Harry Swift was surprised at the severity of the sentence, but relieved that he wouldn't have to chase Savard again for a while. The reporter wrote it all down. Gilly Savard was led back to his cell. He appeared to be smiling at some private fantasy.

TWO
REGINA

*The swindler is often savagely punished when he
is caught, for our laws are designed to protect
property in the first place. The father who beats
his child with a red-hot poker will almost certainly
receive less punishment than the man who deprives
you by fraud of a hundred pounds. It's a strange
world, but as long as we use money, and worship
it, that incorrigible opportunist and individualist,
the swindler, will be treading his primrose path to
prison.*

Judge Gerald Sparrow,
The Great Swindlers

1

If Gilly Savard's punishment appears excessive — in light of the fact that none of his victims lost much actual cash — it should be pointed out that he was doing something far more outrageous than bilking people of money. He was making fools of them. What was worse, he was making fools of important people, who resent it far more than ordinary folk. The law courts can no more permit anarchy and ridicule than they can permit the destruction of property and life. Possibly, they are the same thing.

When Gilly finally walked out of the P.A. Penitentiary again, in February of 1964, he was wearing a good winter coat. His leather club bag was well-stocked with accessories. After slightly more than four years — his sentence having been reduced somewhat by the usual procedures — he had saved enough money to undertake his quest for self-improvement in better style. He would make one more effort to get to Regina and start his search. Time had allowed him to plan more carefully.

The first thing which jolted him when he stepped off the train was the climate. He had always imagined the capital city of Saskatchewan to be warm, even tropical, in the winter. He had hoped to find a golden city basking in the sun, its citizens sauntering the streets in sunglasses and beach attire. Instead, it was like walking into a wall of frozen bricks — worse than the north, for here the wind whistled across the level plains in a frenzy. It cut through his new duffel coat as if it were cheesecloth. A dense cloud of frozen mist and car exhaust enveloped everything, including the cars growling through the streets. A few pedestrians trotted here and there, wrapped like dark mummies, leaning into the bitter wind. He could hear wires snapping and bricks cracking in the cold.

The first step in Gilly's plan was to find a place to stay, so he stepped into a Chinese restaurant and bought a news-paper. Ordering some egg rolls, he turned to the classified ads and got another shock. The cheapest apartments rented for eighty dollars a month, unfurnished. Rents had sky-rocketed in the ten years since he had last priced the market. He turned to the "Room and Board" section and selected a place on Scarth Street. The woman on the phone said it was only a few minutes from downtown. On the way out, he picked up a pack of cigarettes: they had risen from thirty-five to fifty cents.

The walk to the rooming house occupied twenty of the most painful minutes in Gilly's life. The wind shrieked at him from every direction. Cars speeding through the fog nearly knocked him down twice. Underfoot, the sidewalks were raw ice and buried in foot-deep drifts of snow.

At the address, he found a faded red brick house, two storeys high and crumbling at the foundations. It had the unpainted, neglected face of a true boarding house. He stepped into the glassed-in verandah and rang the doorbell. One of the homeliest women he had ever seen opened the door and peeped around the edge of it.

"You've come about the room?" Perhaps she was not ugly so much as physically deformed. Every feature of her face, from her lopsided hair to her pendulous earlobes, was distorted, as if seen through a bad lens. Her eyes looked in two different directions. Whiskers sprouted from her skin.

"Yes — the room."

"You're not a student, are you?" Her smile turned into a frown, her mouth reversing itself, mirror-like. Her lips, already large, were further exaggerated with bright red lipstick.

"No, I'm not."

"I didn't think so," she said, smiling hideously again. "You look so — responsible."

"Can I see the room?"

"This way." She motioned him to remove his snowcaked shoes at the door, then led him upstairs. The second-floor room was small and turned out in pink. A pink satin comforter buried the small bed. The wallpaper was covered in pink tea-roses climbing to the ceiling in massive columns. There were pink lace curtains on the window; a dresser, a chair. The only non-pink object in sight was the Bible on the dresser.

"You are an abstainer, aren't you?"

Gilly nodded.

"And a non-smoker?"

"Afraid not."

She frowned. "No smoking in the house. Dinner is at six o'clock. We'll give you a key for the front door, to hold in trust, at the end of your first month. Till then, you'll have to be in by ten."

"Bathroom?" he said.

She blushed and nodded toward a door at the end of the hall. "Toothbrushes must be kept in your room. I am Hilda Blackwood. Miss Blackwood. And you are —?"

"Gillman. Gillman D. Savard."

"Well, you've timed your arrival very well. Dinner's in an hour. Perhaps you'd like to meet Mr. Scharf and Mrs. Filsom, your fellow guests."

"No thanks, I think I'll get settled in. Do you have a telephone book?"

"Downstairs hallway. In the drawer of the telephone desk. I hope it's not long distance?"

"No — just looking for an address."

He took the directory to his room and turned immediately to the "S"s. There were several Steffens, but no Maggie Steffen. He wrote their numbers down, planning to call later from an outside phone. Then he unpacked his bag and went to dinner.

Miss Blackwood met him by the double oak doors and ushered him in to the front parlour, which featured thick brown curtains and overstuffed armchairs. There was a middle-aged gentleman with horn-rimmed spectacles, and an old lady with a hearing aid, solemnly gazing into space.

"This is Mr. Savard, everyone!"

"Praise the Lord!" Mrs. Filsom cried. Her companion, Mr. Scharf, said, "Savard? Not a Catholic, are you?"

"Of course he's not," Miss Blackwood retorted. "He is an abstainer. Dinner is served." She flung open a second set of doors that separated the dining room from the parlour. There was a table set for four, from which a fishy odour wafted toward them. Miss Blackwood motioned them in to sit.

"Would you say the grace, Mr. Scharf?"

Mr. Scharf collected his thoughts and began. "Dear God, we ask You to bless us and our simple meal. We are Your humble servants, and try to serve You the best we can, remaining faithful and unwavering in our belief, and expressing our continuing loyalty in the righteousness of Your path and to the only true national flag of Canada, the late and lamented Red Ensign, which along with John Diefenbaker, we still love and respect. We ask Your blessing as humble and devoted servants, even Mr. Savard, as we accept this, Your bountiful harvest, Amen."

"Amen," they repeated. When the salmon casserole reached Gilly, it was cold. The rest of the meal was spent in silence, as the boarders stared at their plates and chewed. Miss Blackwood went to the kitchen and brought in four bowls of tinned plums. After disposing of them, they retired to the parlour again.

"Of what faith *are* you, Mr. Savard?" Miss Blackwood asked.

"I'm a — Person of God," he said after a moment's reflection.

Her eyebrows shot up. "Oh, really? I don't think we've had one of those before."

"We don't get around much."

"Jehovah's Witnesses drink your blood," Mrs. Filsom said.

"One of our rules," Gilly said, "is that we never discuss religion. It upsets the spiritual balance."

Miss Blackwood smiled and turned to Mr. Scharf, who took off on a soaring, fiery assault on the Scarlet Harlot of Rome and its sinister influence on Québec, where the Unholy

Church spewed forth the evil trinity of Separatism, Terrorism and Communism. After a few moments, Gilly stood up. "Well, I could listen to this interesting conversation all night, but I have to go and attend to some unfinished business."

He got the telephone numbers from his room, put on his coat and stepped outside into the icy wind again. A car stopped and gave him a ride to the public library. There, he began dialing the numbers on his list.

None of them had ever heard of Maggie. He tried the *Henderson's City Directory* and found "M. Steffen" listed without a telephone number at an address on Forget Street — 1954 Forget Street. He wrote it down and went to the Reference Section.

"Where is Forget Street?" he asked a young woman behind the desk.

"I'm sorry, I'm new to the city."

"Have you got a map?"

She took out a city map and found it on the index. "Here," she said, pointing to the west side. "But there doesn't seem to be a 1900 block."

It was true, and more than confusing. Where could he try next? It was a long shot, but he smiled at the girl. "Pardon me, but do you know any strange places in Regina?"

The girl scrutinized him. "Strange?"

"Yes — unusual places."

She thought for a moment. "Well, of course, I'm a stranger myself, so the whole city seems pretty unusual to me."

"What do you mean?"

"There's no reason for the city to be here, is there? No river, no natural trees — it's just *here*, in the middle of the bald prairie. There isn't a single hill in the place. And every tree you see was planted. This whole town is manmade."

It wasn't much help, but he thanked her and headed for the exit. It was too cold to wander the streets looking for the two addresses. He would start searching in earnest in the morning. While putting on his gloves and earmuffs at the door, he heard a familiar voice shout, "Savard!"

Gilly turned. A small, flashily-dressed man waved at him and grinned. It was Clint Malach. The deep lines of his face wrinkled in waves. "Gilly, ole buddy! What are you doing here?"

"I'm looking for somebody. What are *you* doing here? I thought you hated libraries."

Malach waved his hand. "Aaah. I hadda do some research. One thing and another. I got a new business, ya know."

"What is it this time?"

"Strictly legal operation. New idea, just came up from the States. Fantastic possibilities." He looked around for eavesdroppers. "You interested?"

"Not really. I'm pretty busy."

"So you're keepin' yer nose clean eh, kid? Well, if ya need any bread, let me know. I'm rollin' in it. Howza bankroll?"

"I got enough to get by."

"But ya haven't got a job?"

"Well — no."

"Then you better hear what I got to say before you turn your nose up at it. Hey, what're we doin' standing here in the windstream? Let's go have a drink!"

"I have to be back at my rooming house by ten. They lock the door."

Clint stared at him, the deep lines of his forehead crinkling to the hairline. "I kin see you're serious. So you just come along with me and watch, while I wet my nose, okay?"

He took Gilly's arm and they waded through the snow-drifts to a big luxury hotel overlooking the park. Gilly blinked in astonishment when they stepped into the beer parlour. There were women everywhere: old ones, young ones, students, housewives. The law had changed while he was doing slow time in the P.A. Pen. Women could now drink legally in Saskatchewan.

"Let me buy y'a beer," Clint said, ordering four glasses of draught. He pulled a wad of bills from his pocket and paid with a ten. "Cheers," he said, and they sucked the foam from two glasses of golden Pilsener. Clint leaned across the table and winked.

"Cosmetics," he said.

"Eh?"

"This stuff is *dynamite*, Savard. Everything from hair cream to female sprays. Organic, see? Concentrated beaver oil."

"You sell it?"

"Sell it? I *give* it away! Vitalife Nail Polish! Vitalife Cleansing Cream! Vitalife Toothpaste! It's all organic shit. The latest thing."

"It doesn't sound like anything I need."

"Don't be dense, Savard. You couldn't afford it, even if you did need it. Anyways, I don't sell the stuff. I sell dealerships. Listen, I want you to come to this meeting I got lined up tomorra night."

"I'm tied up, Clint."

"I'll give y'a hundred bucks just to go there."

"Why me?"

"That baby-faced innocence! Those dark sincere eyes. They'll love ya! We'll sell a hundred dealerships!"

"Hey, Clint — where have you been since I saw you in B Wing?" Gilly tried to change the subject. "I just got out, you know."

They reminisced over their adventures in the penitentiary until Gilly suddenly remembered his curfew.

"Well, you're already five mintues late," Clint pointed out. "If ya gotta wake somebody up, better do it late at night, when they're sound asleep and won't remember in the morning."

After eight glasses of beer, that sounded reasonable. They continued drinking until the beer parlour closed. Clint saw a couple of girls he knew at the far end of the room and they joined them. The conversation flowed so easily they transferred to the cocktail lounge, which stayed open until one a.m. Malach's money ran out, however, so he wrote a cheque to Gilly and Gilly went to the bar to cash it. This was thoughtless, but — what the hell? He was with an old friend; they were in the company of two lovely young women; the night was young. It was the same old story — but how it would end, he did not care to predict.

* * * * *

2

There were several obvious factors contributing to Gilly Savard's self-immolating ways. He was far too innocent for his own good. He had an unfortunate weakness for booze and pretty women. And, he was cursed with an astounding affinity for ill fate. But then, who isn't? Gilly felt that all of these factors arose from the warring genes he carried in him, the twilight mixture of Indian and white, of America and Europe, of new and old.

But when Gilly rode off on his cousin's motorcycle that spring night in 1949, he believed he was escaping from his heritage. He would never go back to the life of the half-breed, though he had no knowledge of what lay ahead. The future was as blank as the curtain of darkness beyond the glare of his motorcycle headlight, but he would ride through the dust of Highway 4 until he at least got to Prince Albert, the frontier city of the north. Periodically, he would see a small cluster of lights approaching, a tiny hamlet asleep at the roadside. Nothing stirred as he roared through Glaslyn, Spiritwood and Mount Nebo. At Shellbrook, a sign announced that Prince Albert was twenty-seven miles away. His heart beat faster as the miles ticked past on the odometer. A pale glow of light appeared in the eastern sky, but he could not be sure if it was the coming dawn or the city — or both.

Then, coming down a long slope through the rough spruce forests, he turned a bend in the highway and, two miles away, the silver lights of Prince Albert dazzled him. Just then, the motorcycle sputtered and died. It was out of gasoline. He began pushing it as the sun rose and the road came to life. Cars and trucks began rattling past. He approached the bridge across the North Saskatchewan River. Across it, the city lay spread out, just as Crab had often described it: six-storey buildings towered to the sky, higher than trees; smoke stacks rose even higher. Everything was in motion. Even the buildings danced in the sun. Cars sped by in all directions. On the river below the bridge, motorboats chugged back and forth. Trucks rumbled past, shaking the bridge violently.

Indecision paralyzed him for a moment. If he could get across the bridge, he would be in the city. He would be in the south. He waited for a pause in the traffic, then rushed across, his heart pounding as the span swayed and trembled under the traffic. He reached the other end of the bridge, rolled the bike into a small park and fell on the grass to recover his thoughts.

Almost immediately, the demands of urban living forced themselves upon him: a place to stay, something to eat, gasoline for the motorcycle, money to pay for these things. A job.

Across the street was a small grocery store; the owner had just opened the front door for the morning's business. Gilly had not eaten since finishing his mother's biscuits on the road. It took him fifteen minutes to get across the street. Each time he started off the curb, a horn-hooting car appeared. The old man in a white apron watched with amusement as Gilly, perspiring and dusty, finally crossed.

"Can I get some bread here?"

"That's what I'm in business for, son."

"And a jar of peanut butter?"

The man showed him the shelves and waited watchfully behind his cash register. "That's forty-three cents, altogether."

Gilly removed his father's old watch from his pocket. "I'll sell you this watch. It's real gold."

The old man examined the watch, rubbed it on his white apron. "Don't really need a watch."

"If you don't buy the watch, then I can't buy the bread."

"Well — I can give you three dollars."

"It's worth a lot more, ya know."

"I know, I know," the storekeeper sighed. He extracted change for three dollars from his till and handed it to Gilly with the groceries. He scooped the watch into his cash register.

"I don't suppose you could give me a job?" Gilly said.

The storekeeper shook his head and gestured at Gilly to move on.

Walking down the street, Gilly began to understand the burden of material possessions. A dead motorcycle can be a very awkward companion for a young man. He walked several blocks with the machine to a gas station and leaned it against the wall while he went to the washroom.

As he sat on the motorcycle eating his bread and peanut butter, one of the young pump attendants noticed him and walked over to him.

"Your motorcycle?"

Gilly hesitated. "My cousin's."

"You gonna start 'er up, or just gonna sit there showing

'er off?"

"It's outa gas."

"Well, you came to the right place for that, bub."

"I don't have enough money. You think I could get a job here?"

The attendant grinned. "Any experience?"

"Doin' what?"

The young man laughed. "Straight outa the bush, eh? Well, good luck, kid. There's only a couple more thousand like you in town. I'll give ya fifty bucks for the Harley, though."

Gilly started out again, pushing the motorcycle. It might be harder to get a job than he thought. How had Crab and the others done it? If he could only find a safe place to leave the bike, he could find a job and pick it up later. He walked toward the centre of town. The tall buildings blocked the sunlight from the street. There was construction going on everywhere; the post-war boom of mineral exploration was on. To the north lay huge deposits of uranium and nickel and cobalt. They were drawing people to the Frontier City like a magnetic core.

A small hotel on Central Avenue, offering "Rooms by the Day or Week" came into view. Inside, a narrow staircase ascended into gloom. At the top of the stairs was a tiny man seated on a stool, reading the *Police Gazette* under a bare lightbulb.

"Can I get a room?"

"Two bucks a day. Advance."

That was all Gilly had left, but he handed it over and wrote his name on the register. "I got a motorcycle downstairs, too. Can you give me a hand to bring it up?"

The dwarf peered at him. "Tryna get rid of a hot bike?"

"No. I want to put it in my room."

Saliva sprayed down from the dwarf's toothless gums as he leaped off his stool and yelled, "Fuck off, you dirty fuckin' clown! You wanna room — go and get one in the Pen! That's where you'll get a fuckin' room!"

Gilly retreated down the stairs as the man reached up and yanked a string, switching off the light and plunging the stairway into darkness. He stumbled down the stairs, hitting the bottom before he remembered the money. He didn't have the nerve to go back and ask for his two dollars.

On the sidewalk, a delivery boy was fingering the ignition switch on the motorcycle. "This yers, kid?" the boy said. "Don't worry, I wasn't gonna hook it. Just lampin' her over."

"That's okay. Listen, I'm lookin' for a room. You know where I could find one?"

The boy broke into shrieks of laughter and staggered around the sidewalk. Two young men in wide fedoras and pegged trousers looked out of an adjacent pool hall.

"Ya hear that?" the boy yelled. "This jerk's lookin' fer a room!"

"What's so funny?" Gilly said.

This set them all to laughing and pointing, as he stood dumbfounded beside his cousin's motorcycle. He fled down the street pushing the machine and the laughter followed behind him. Everywhere he wandered, he got hostile stares and suspicious questions. Finally, he walked back to the riverbank park to lie down and recuperate.

When Gilly fell asleep, his head on the motorcycle seat, a dream came to him. He was pushing a broken-down baby carriage with twisted wheels, trying to force it through a dense forest full of broken stumps and snagging windfalls. Suddenly, his brother Porter appeared in the distance, in a soldier's outfit. He raised a gun and fired. Gilly turned and fled with the baby carriage, jamming it through the broken trees. Porter chased after him, laughing and shooting his gun. As Gilly looked back, Porter became a skeleton with black eyesockets and grinning teeth. He was still laughing and shooting. Gilly screamed and woke up.

An old man in a black cowboy hat was standing over him. "Bad dream, eh?"

"Who are you?"

The old man wore buckskin clothing. His white hair hung in braids below a felt hat. His dark eyes were deep and strangely comforting. "Isidore McKay. You were yelling."

Gilly stood up and stretched. It was after dark and the streetlights were lit. He was hungry. "Guess I had a bad dream."

"Yuh. Where'd you get the motorcycle?"

"It belongs to my cousin Alex. I rode it from Meadow Lake."

"From Meadow Lake, eh? I used to live near dere. What you doin' here?"

"I'm looking for a job. And a place to stay."

"No family?"

Gilly shook his head.

"Well, you come along wit' me. I can fix you up for tonight, anyway. Can we ride on the motorcycle?"

"Naw, it's outa gas."

The old man looked disappointed. He motioned Gilly to follow him east along the river. After a few hundred yards, he turned onto a street and approached a small frame shack which sat in darkness apart from its neighbours. McKay lit a kerosene lamp on the porch and showed him into the kitchen, where there was a small cot for Gilly to sleep on. He lifted a padlock and chain off a nail and chained the motorcycle to the back step.

"How much money you got?" he asked, laying some bacon into a frying pan.

"'Bout fifty cents."

"What the hell you think that's going to buy?"

"I dunno," Gilly shrugged. "Breakfast, I giss. I'll be okay when I get a job."

"A job!" the old man snorted. "What was wrong with farmin', eh? You came from a farm, didden you?"

Gilly nodded. "My old man's. He's a drunk. My Ma wanted me to be a priest."

The old man clicked his tongue and nodded. He served the bread and bacon. "The city, she's a funny place. Can be okay, you know — but takes a while to figger her out. Not easy. People are different here, even de breeds."

"I'm not a halfbreed."

McKay gazed at him. "Gilly, you be whatever you want to be. To me, you look like a halfbreed. It ain't no insult." He stood up with the lamp. "Now, I got some reading to do. I'll fix you breakfast in the morning." He went to his bedroom with the lamp. As he lay awake, thinking about the many things he had to do to start life in the morning, Gilly could see the light flickering long into the night.

When Gilly awoke, he was being strangled by a satin pink comforter. He could hear the sound of a meadowlark chirruping. As he tried through his hungover haze to imagine why a meadowlark was singing in his bedroom in the middle of February, a light tapping came at his door, then Miss Blackwood's voice:

"Mr. Savard?"

"Who is it?"

"It's me — your little meadowlark."

A shiver of fear went up and down his back. He struck himself on the forehead and the evening's events began coming back to him.

"Can I come in now? They've all gone to work."

He tried to think of a reply to stall her, but it was too late. The door creaked open and Miss Blackwood, clad in a pale blue chiffon negligée, slid into the room. "We're in luck!" she exclaimed rapturously.

Gilly tried to duck beneath the covers, but she threw herself onto the bed and clasped him around the neck.

"I thought morning would never come! I told them I was staying home from the office today. Quick, let me under the covers!"

Gilly moaned in protest.

"And just think, if you hadn't tapped on my window, I never would have known how you felt! And last night in my room, oh, it was heaven! Listen! Listen to my little meadowlark song!" Again, she trilled the meadowlark's cheerful riff. Again, he moaned in reply.

He tried to crawl out the other side of the bed, but she clasped him tight, kissing his arms. "Listen, I hear somebody!" he cried in desperation.

She sprang up in alarm, covering her meagre chest with both arms. And, with a timing which nearly made Gilly laugh with relief, the telephone rang.

"It must be Scharf!" she cried. "Don't worry! He's only wondering if I'm all right. It'll stop ringing in a minute."

Gilly jumped out of bed. "I'm expecting a call!" he yelled, running downstairs in his pyjamas to the telephone. "Life or death! Hello?"

"Good morning," a woman's voice said. "This is the city police. We're doing a rooming house checkout. Do you have a Mr. Gillman Savard registered there?"

He held his breath for a minute. "Um, what do you want him for?"

"One moment, please. I'll connect you with Sergeant Hearn."

Gilly hung up the receiver and turned back to the staircase where Miss Blackwood waited, her eyes shining with desire.

"Who was it?" she said.

"The police."

"Really? What did they want?"

"I'm not sure. Me — for some reason."

"Oh, no! You're not going to go, are you?"

"Not if I can help it," he said, trying to slip past her on the stairs. She clutched him.

"I'll hide you in the basement. They'll never find you, Gilly! You'll be safe with me!"

"You don't know anything about me. I'm an ex-con."

"It doesn't matter! I don't want to lose you! We've hardly got to know each other." Her eyes dissolved into tears. She followed him down the hall to his room with deep, heart-rending sobs. "If you leave, we'll never have another chance."

Gilly turned and looked at her in the doorway. The negligée clung to her pathetic frame. What the hell, he thought. Maybe they weren't after him. He couldn't remember committing any crimes the night before. And maybe she was an old boot, but he could remember times when he had been more desperate. He could spare half an hour at least. He'd never see her again.

"All right," he said, taking one hand and drawing her under the covers. As he caressed her, she began to whimper. The whimper soon crescendoed into a series of staccato whinnies, and finally, a full-throated wail like an air-raid siren, which almost obscured the sudden chime of Miss Blackwood's front doorbell. Gilly stopped and listened. He clapped his hand over Miss Blackwood's howling mouth. The bell rang again. He leaped out of bed. "The doorbell!"

"It doesn't matter! It doesn't matter!"

He peered out through the lace curtains. There were two policemen in a squad car; God knows how many of them were at the door.

"It's them! The police."

"Oh, *nooo*!" Miss Blackwood cried.

"Yes. Can you help me get away?"

"No, no, don't go. Not now."

"Listen to me. You have to go down to the front door and tell them a story."

"Like *this*?"

"Say you've been raped."

"But it wasn't! We didn't even —"

"For God's sake, *lie*! Like a decent Christian would!"

Miss Blackwood walked down to the door while Gilly dressed and threw his gear into his leather bag. Before she had opened the front door, he was climbing onto the back porch from the bathroom window. He ran down the alley and across an avenue to a large public building. Directly in front of him was the entrance to the library of the University of Saskatchewan. It seemed an appropriate sanctuary, a place where he could collect his thoughts and try to find out what was going on. He pulled a random book from a shelf and sat down at one of the tables among the students. No one paid any attention to him.

It had to be Clint Malach's cheque, he thought. It was the only possibility. Gilly would go to Clint's sales meeting that night and grab him, have the cheque honoured before the police could find him, and get the law off his back.

In the meantime, he had his own quest to pursue. Gilly took the city map from his pocket and studied it. He had the two addresses, but now they seemed like a remote possibility. As he looked around at the students, he had a sudden inspiration and ran out into the hallway. He looked out the door onto the street. No sign of the police. Miss Blackwood had done her part. He went down the hall to the Registrar's Office.

"Yes?"

"I'm looking for a person who may have been a student here a few years back. Do you keep records?"

"How far back?"

"Could be any time in the last ten years. Eight years."

"Name?"

"Margaret Steffen."

The registrar disappeared into what appeared to be a bank vault and came out smiling a few minutes later. "Here you are. One year of Arts. A good student, by the look of her file."

"Just one year?"

"1960. This was Regina College then. Students usually took one year and finished their degree in Saskatoon."

"No. She'd never go to Saskatoon. Is that all you have?"

"Well, I see she took English. You could try Dr. Tyrone — he was teaching the freshmen that year." He glanced at the clock. "He'll be finishing the Shakespeare class in five minutes."

The registrar directed Gilly to a second-floor classroom from which the professor would emerge. He could hear Dr. Tyrone inside, declaiming lines from a Shakespearean play.

Tyrone was a tall, spare man, who removed his eyeglasses when he spoke. "Yes, I remember Maggie Steffen," he said, looking curiously at Gilly.

"Do you know where she is?"

"I'm afraid not. She was only here for one term. Then —" He shrugged expressively. She had passed into the future, as all his students did. "She was an unusual girl, you know. Very bright, very private. I don't think anybody here got to know her."

"She was interested in — strange places," Gilly said. "Can you remember anything she might have mentioned? Along that line? Where she might have gone?"

Tyrone turned and looked out the classroom window. To the south, the enormous dome of the Legislature loomed over the city. Between it and the university was Wascana Lake, now a wide expanse of windswept ice glistening in the morning sun. "No, nothing helpful, I'm afraid. She was always intrigued by the lake, though."

Gilly thanked him and walked down the hall, pondering. Strange places, strange places. The university was pretty strange itself. Political posters were everywhere; there seemed to be ten different elections going on at once. He wandered into the art gallery, gazing at the large white canvasses covered with balls of colour and streaks of dripping paint. No answers there. He wandered into the lower depths of

90

the main building and found the student council offices, where a hulking young man was typing at a desk.

"Do you keep back copies of the student directories?" Gill inquired.

"Might. Who you represent?"

"Nobody."

"Gotta be a bona fide student club or political party."

Gilly handed him a dollar. "I'd like to have a look at the 1959-60 book."

The behemoth rummaged in a box of old papers in a cupboard until he came out with a tattered, coffee-stained directory. Gilly turned to the S's. There it was: Maggie Steffen. 1954 Forget Street.

He turned to the student, shaking with excitement. "Where's Forget Street?"

The young man laughed. "It isn't For-*get*. It's *For*-jay! It's clear over the other side of town."

Gilly ran out and flagged a taxi. He was hardly able to believe his luck. His mind raced back across the years, remembering her face as the taxi headed across the city. It stopped finally beside an empty expanse of snow-blown prairie, along the railway tracks. The driver pointed. "There's your spot, mister. 1900 block Forget. Only one problem with that address, though. There ain't no houses."

Gilly dismissed him and stood gazing at the empty space, trying to penetrate the puzzle. A set of railway tracks struck out across the snow-blank landscape, glowing red in the glare of the dying sun. It was an abstraction that just kept going on and on. She could have faked the student directory, but not *Henderson's Directory*. 1954 Forget. And what had Tyrone meant about the lake? He began jogging back to the city along the tracks. The ties ticked past, like seconds of his life going by. He was on the same old racetrack again, running into the darkness. But there was immediate business to attend to. He had to find Clint Malach and get the police off his tail.

With Alex's motorcycle safely chained to Isidore McKay's back porch, Gilly set out with a light heart to look for work. At the first place he went to, a construction site, he was told to get lost; the foreman was looking for experienced carpenters and bricklayers. Even labourers had to have experience. Gilly spent five cents on a newspaper and went to the bus depot to read the "Help Wanted" ads. Cooks, barbers, salesmen, truck drivers; they all needed experience.

Coming out of the bus station, Gilly saw a policeman in a car at the curb. He ran around the corner. This was a mistake. He didn't get more than two blocks before the same cruiser intercepted him and he was invited to sit in the back seat.

"Name?" he was asked.

"Gilly Savard."

"Where you live?"

"I uh, don't have a place yet."

"Any identification?"

Gilly took out his wallet. Inside was his high school student's card and the folded Go-getter certificate. The policeman laughed at it. "Well, I could book you for vagrancy, son. But I'm willing to give you a chance. When are you going back to Meadow Lake?"

"Pretty soon. I have to take my cousin's motorcycle back —"

"Motorcycle?" the cop said, his eyes widening. Within an hour, Gilly was sitting in a detective's office, reading the statement a typist had transcribed from his painful explanation.

"Wait a minute," Gilly said. "This says 'stole'! I never *stole* Alex's bike! I told you, I *borrowed* it!"

The detective shrugged and crossed out the word. He wrote in "borrowed." Someone came in and took Gilly away to be photographed and finger-printed. Then they put him in a cell to wait for his appearance in the court the next morning. The cell wasn't bad. In fact, it was the most luxurious room he'd ever slept in. It had a toilet and a wash basin. But he was numb with terror over what would happen to him in the morning. The duty policeman made jokes all night because Gilly kept flushing the toilet. His diarrhea would not stop.

In the morning, Gilly was escorted to the courtroom, a barren hall full of long wooden benches for spectators, on the second floor of the police station. A large picture of King George hung at the front of the chamber above the magistrate who sat in a black gown and shuffled gloomily though a stack of papers.

When Gilly heard his name being spoken, he stood up. He was blinking tears.

"Gillman Savard, you are charged that on the 19th of May, 1949, you did steal property valued at more than fifty dollars, to wit, one Harley Davidson motorcycle. How do you plead?"

"Not guilty," Gilly murmured.

The policeman rose. "We are still investigating, Your Worship. Possible further charges, including assault. I think a remand for one week, in custody."

"Juss a minute!" said a voice from the back of the courtroom. All eyes turned as an old man, his white hair twisted in long braids, suddenly stood up. It was Isidore McKay.

"I juss hear about dis boy last night, Your Worship. I come to speak on his behalf."

"You know this fellow, Mr. McKay?" the magistrate asked.

"He stay at my place two nights ago. He left de motorcycle there. I tink maybe you should hear his story and mebbe we can settle de case dis morning."

The little man in the black gown listened to Isidore with surprising deference. Then he asked Gilly to tell his story in court.

"Well, I don't know what I can do," the magistrate said when he had finished. "The charge was laid in Meadow Lake. We can't just —"

"If he says guilty to de charge, you give him a suspended sentence and make me responsible for him."

The judge looked relieved. "Well, of course, if the accused is willing to plead guilty . . ."

Gilly looked at Isidore. What kind of deal was this? He wasn't guilty. The old man stared directly into his eyes and although he didn't speak, Gilly could hear him saying, "Yes,

Gilly, it *was* stealing. You stole your cousin's motorcycle. Now you got to do something. Don't juss stand dere!"

"Guilty, Your Majesty," Gilly said.

Fifteen minutes later, he was back on the street, walking in freedom beside the man with the white braids. Something magic had happened; he wasn't going to jail after all. "How did you do that?" he said. "You got lots of money?"

The old man laughed. "No, no money. Dey know me from a long time. Once I hit a man in a beer parlour and broke his neck. I spent a long time out there." He pointed west of the city, where the federal penitentiary lay. "But I learn de law. Now, police believe me when I tell dem things. I look after people here."

"What people? Good people?"

"Good people, bad people. Who knows? My people."

Sweating in the damp summer heat, they walked back to the frame shack in the east end. The motorcycle was gone. "Police took it back to your cousin," the old man muttered. "Let him get into trouble."

"Don't you like motorcycles?"

"Sure, I like to ride one sometime. But I also like cigarettes. Deadly poison. Dey kill you. Like motorcycle. Motorcycles not good for a kid. 'Specially one who don't know de city."

"You know the city?"

"I know de city."

"Can I stay with you?"

"You're not ready yet. First you gotta work a while on de farm. Stay out of trouble. Learn a few useful tings. How much schooling you got?"

"Grade Nine. Partly."

"You go to school."

Gilly stopped at the door. This was worse than jail. "Do I hafta?"

The old man did not turn around. "Yah."

"You mean I hafta go back to my Pa's place? To Brochet?"

"No. I get you a job with a friend of mine, Arden Gundarson. He grows cattle at Shellbrook. Can you cook?"

"No."

"Come here. You learn how to fry eggs. Arden can't even boil water."

After supper and long into the night, Gilly watched the flickering reflection of light from McKay's bedroom door. The rustling pages of the old man's book whispered him to sleep.

* * * * *

5

The gold-brocade conference room of the Wascana-Ritz was grander than Gilly had expected. Clint Malach's lifestyle had obviously grown more opulent. He slipped through the double doors of carved oak and found himself in the middle of a crowd of forty people who were all facing a speaker's rostrum at the far end of the room.

Behind a microphone, Malach's cracked voice was working its spell. "Now, ladies and gentlemen, our scientifically computed surveys have identified *you* as the people of drive and influence in the community of Regina!"

Gilly watched as the audience smiled indulgently.

"Now you all know the name of the game in our present-day modern society. It's *money*, right? Don't be fooled by woolly-headed idealists who talk about some never-never land and live off your taxes. No. It's *money* that makes the world go round." He paused. "What makes the world go round?"

"Money?" someone suggested.

Malach cupped one hand to his ear. "Can't hear you."

"Money!" a few voices called.

"That's right. And that is why you are here tonight! So that we can *all* make a lot of —?"

"Money!" the cry came back.

"Right! Now I'm going to pass around these full-colour brochures which explain the details as I've outlined them to you. In them, you will find how you *too* can acquire a dealership in Vitalife — and join the great Vitalife family! But first, I see the star of our organization has arrived! I want to introduce you all to the man who broke all sales records for the month of January — Mr. *Gillman W. Savard!*"

He waved his arm at Gilly, who had reacted too late. He only managed to get one hand on a door handle before the crowd swivelled to hit him with their hypnotized gaze. Malach applauded. They all applauded, standing to deliver an ovation while Gilly tried to gesture modestly.

"Now, tell us what it's all *about*, Mr. Savard!" Malach roared.

Gilly looked at the crowd, a dollar-eyed assembly of citizens waiting to hear the secret of the universe. He wanted to tell them, to warn them before they fell into the same old trap again. But he remained silent. Malach grinned and put a hand to his ear.

"Money," Gilly said.

The crowd burst out in a delirious roar of approval. Straightlaced bank clerks and school teachers clutched each other in delight and danced in joy among the stacked chairs. Visions of Oldsmobiles and Motorolas, Evinrudes and Ski-Doos blossomed in their heads. Gilly looked on, appalled, then turned to find the bar.

He had finished two double ryes before Malach arrived, sliding into the chair beside him. "Well, ya sure earned your pay tonight, Gilly my boy. Those innocent black eyes a yours are worth a fortune. You ready to go into business?"

"Why don't you go piss up a rope?"

"Listen, don't worry about *them*. They'll get their money back selling Vitalife adviserships. It's a pyramid, you see?"

"You know the cops came after me this morning?"

"What for?"

"That cheque you wrote in the bar last night!"

"Not a problem, Gilly. Now we got the cash to cover it. I pulled in at least ten thou tonight. Cash!" He opened his briefcase and showed it to Gilly. "We'll go over there right away and look after it."

"*You* go and look after it!"

Malach peered at him slyly. "Think ya can trust me?"

They walked to the bar where they had been drinking the night before and took the manager aside from his desk to explain the misunderstanding. The man had indeed called the police after he had been in touch with the bank. It was the customary procedure. Malach gave him a hundred dollars to mollify him. The manager promised to call the police station the next day and say that he had been reimbursed. That was the best he could do. In the meantime, if the gentlemen wished to enjoy the service of the bar, they were welcome.

"I have to go home," Gilly said.

"Past your curfew again? And while I think of it, here's the hunnerd bucks I owe ya."

"Thanks."

"Don't mention it. More where that came from. Say, what are you doin' in town anyway? Not lookin' for that little doll from Saskatoon still, are ya? What was her name? Millie?"

"Maggie," Gilly said.

"Never mind, I can tell it's a long story. You and me, a deadly combination. Well, here's to the great and glorious future, Gilly my boy! Drink up. Plenty more where that came from!"

The next thing Gilly knew, he was trying to silence the telephone that was ringing beside the bed in his suite in the Wascana-Ritz. "Hello?" he said.

"This is Mayor Gorius calling," said the telephone. "Welcome to Regina."

* * * * *

6

Arden Gundarson was a Swede who had homesteaded about fifteen miles from Shellbrook, at a district called Wild Rose. He squeezed a living out of a half section of marginal land by raising beef cattle. An old bachelor who had been in the 1914 war with Isidore McKay, he spent most of his evenings playing poker in the Legion Hall at Shellbrook. Any friend of Isidore's was a friend of his, and as long as Gilly would look after his cattle for ten dollars a week plus room and board, Arden didn't care if he was a jailbird or a blackbird.

However, Gundarson had grown weary of drifters who spent more time ransacking the shack for hidden money than forking cow manure; for the last two years, he had tried to do the work himself and now his farm was disintegrating around him. His shack was a rat's nest of broken furniture, tattered quilts and old bacon rinds. The reason none of the drifters had found any money was because he carried it all in his moneybelt.

Gilly liked working there because Arden left him alone and let him get on with the work: putting up fences, repairing buildings, cleaning trash out of the house. Isidore McKay drove out in his truck a couple of times during the summer and the three of them played cards under the hissing lantern while moths fluttered around them in the warm darkness. The two old men told stories from the war. They had both fought at Passchendaele, and Arden had been gassed at Vimy Ridge. Gilly told them of Porter's heroic adventures in the Second World War, which they all knew were lies, but enjoyed hugely. On Saturdays, they went into Shellbrook where the two men got drunk in the Legion. Gilly went to the pool hall and played snooker with the young farmers. They drove home singing in Arden's old blue Plymouth and slept in on Sundays. Later, they would walk out to Arden's pasture to inspect his scrubby Shorthorns and watch the Cooper's hawks circling overhead.

In the fall, Arden took Gilly to meet the teacher at Crystal Plains school, where the vanished hamlet of Wild Rose had once been. Here, he would attend school two evenings a week, until he finished Grade Nine. The teacher, Mr. Pennistone, was a handsome middle-aged Englishman with a sherry-coloured face. Although he carried a torch for humanistic education, he was in fact a failed actor who had memorized a bit of Virgil and a lot of Wordsworth. He too kept a map of the world spread across the wall behind his lectern.

Pennistone saw in Gilly Savard a lump of clay to be formed and polished into a symbol of the new age: an educated savage, a product of the new pedagogy who would put Pennistone and Crystal Plains school in the journals of the nation. The school's enrollment had been declining for three years straight and Pennistone's job — the last in a long line of Canadian appointments — was in danger. He threw his whole effort into Gilly's education, declaiming at the top of his lungs in the empty frame schoolhouse, making it echo on Tuesdays with Lord Tennyson's galloping metre. On Thursday evenings, they pursued geography.

"Travel, my dear Gilly! Liberation of the soul! Until

you've crossed the Himalayas and swum the Hellespont, you will always be an ignorant farmer. You must see the glories of ancient Greece, the Great Wall of China. *That* is education!" He struck a pose:

> Roman Virgil, thou that singest
> Ilion's lofty temples robed in fire,
> Ilion falling, Rome arising,
> wars, and filial faith, and Dido's pyre!

As autumn passed into winter, a new confidence came to Gilly with his management of Gundarson's farm. He got along well with the neighbours in the district, who often called on him to lend a hand. And if he needed a truck for hauling cattle, one was quickly loaned.

On Christmas Day, he and Arden drove around the district treating their neighbours with a bottle of Calvert's Grand Reserve. At the teacherage, Hartley Pennistone extracted a case of port from some private hoard and the two men got roaring drunk well into Boxing Day. Gilly drove them back and forth across the grid roads while they visited friends and neighbours.

After the holidays, winter set in for good. It was an oppressive winter in which the snow never stopped falling and the wind never stopped blowing. The news on the radio was all about the Korean War and the world's frightening progress toward holocaust; the Communists were a menace everywhere. Gilly wondered if he would be expected to serve like Porter. As the snow gradually buried and blocked the roads, Arden's weekly ventures to Shellbrook for poker were abandoned. The car was buried in a snowbank. It even became impossible for Gilly to travel the three miles to Crystal Plains school, except with a team and sleigh. And Arden had sold the last of his horses the year before.

As spring delayed and delayed its arrival, Arden grew increasingly strange. He spent most of his time huddled beside the radio, refusing to go outside, even for firewood. Gilly arranged for their supplies to be transported from Shellbrook to the school. He collected them on foot when weather permitted, packing the groceries in a potato sack across the snowdrifts. One evening, he came back to find the old man scattering the pile of split firewood Gilly had stacked beside the door.

"What are you looking for?" Gilly said.

"Nothing! I vas re-arranging de voodpile."

That night, their favourite programmes were on the radio — *Wayne and Shuster* and *Hockey Night in Canada* — but Arden went to bed early, slamming the door behind him. Gilly was puzzled. What had the old man been up to in the woodpile? He got up early in the morning and looked at the wood where Arden had been fussing. Near the bottom of the stack, a canvas bag was buried. Inside it was a rusted old forty-five calibre revolver which was fully loaded. Gilly put the gun back in its hiding place and returned to the house to fix breakfast. Arden was clearly getting a touch of cabin fever. Crab had told Gilly of a case where a fur-trapper caught his partner cheating at solitaire and split open his head with an axe. He resolved to get the old man into Shell-brook for an evening at the Legion.

The opportunity came a week later when a neighbour was sledding to town with a load of grain. But the old man refused to leave the house, so Gilly himself decided to go. He would ask the doctor for advice. The doctor could only recommend what Gilly already knew — that Arden had to get out and find some entertainment. After buying supplies, Gilly went down to the pool hall where the young men gathered in the evening to smoke cigarettes and tell lies about the district girls. One of them was Perry Lasuisse, a slim youth of twenty, who played snooker with long, elegant fingers and always had a cigarette dangling from the corner of his mouth. Gilly had often practiced the pose in the privacy of his bedroom.

"So old Gundarson's acting kinda spooky, eh?" Perry said, bending low over the table and slipping the cue through his long fingers. There were three or four others standing around.

"Yeah. The doc says I gotta take him out and get him drunk or something."

The boys laughed.

"Didn't know you drank, Savard."

"I've had the odd bottle of beer."

Perry pulled a flask of liquor from his pocket. "Try some of this."

"Naw," Gilly said. "I won't like it."

"How do you know till you try it?"

"It makes you do funny things."

Perry snickered. "Don't knock it, if you won't try it. You'll know yer grown-up when you take this stuff. Puts hair on your chest."

They all drank from the mickey, swearing boisterously.

"You going back tonight, Savard? Better take some of this back for the old man — cool him off before he takes after ya with the gun."

When Gilly returned to the farm the next day, the cattle were standing in the wind shelter behind the barn, bawling at an empty water trough. He went into the house. The fire had gone out. Gundarson was huddled in his bed under a mound of blankets, nearly frozen. He wouldn't come out of his room, even when Gilly started the fire.

The following week, the snowploughs came through and Gilly spent a day digging the car out of the snowbank. He would take the old man to town, even if he had to tie him up in the back seat and carry him. First, they would go to the doctor; then, the Legion Hall.

In the morning when he awoke, Gundarson was standing beside the living room sofa where Gilly slept, pointing the revolver directly between his eyes.

"Get up," he said.

"What's wrong, Arden?"

"You trying to steal my money. Same as rest of dem. Get up and pack your bag."

"What are you going to do?"

"I take you in to the Mounties. You are finished here."

"Okay, Arden. Listen, just — point the gun the other way, will ya?"

"I shouldn't have listened to McKay. You go around sneaking, digging up the woodpile. What you find dere, eh?"

"Hey, Arden, this isn't funny. We'll go to town right now and you can take me to the cops, eh? But point the gun somewhere else, okay?"

They drove to Shellbrook with the old man in the back, his gun levelled at the back of Gilly's head. Gilly's muscles went numb at every snowbank the car shuddered through. At the RCMP office, the constable took the revolver away from

Gundarson and got him to make a statement. Then they bundled him back into the car and drove him to the doctor's office.

"What should I do now?" Gilly asked the policeman after Arden had been sedated and put to bed in a cell.

"You better leave the car at the station and find yourself a job. Keep away from the farm until we get this sorted out. You'll have to appear in court, so you better stay in town."

"Who's going to look after the livestock?"

"I'll ask some of the neighbours."

Gilly's new life had ground to a halt. With this business hanging over his head, he would never be able to get a job in Shellbrook. He couldn't leave until it was cleared up. After, perhaps, he could head south to the golden cities.

In the pool hall, he told Perry and the others about the strange episode. Perry laughed a sardonic laugh. "I toljuh! Nobody gives a shit about you, Savard. You better start lookin' after your*self*! Here, drown your sorrows."

The first swallow of whiskey burned his gullet, but an immediate warm glow bubbled in his stomach. For a few seconds, the whole whirling universe was blanked out of his mind: Gundarson, Isidore, the motorcycle, Porter, Go-getter Drink Powders. When the world swam back into focus, it was all in a slight blur. It wasn't real anymore and there was comfort in the faces grinning around the pool table. They finished the snooker game and Perry's bottle in the same burst of merriment. Gilly laughed and cavorted down the street to the Shellbrook Hotel with Perry and Oscar Burnie. Later, he stumbled, but was held upright by Perry as they went to his room for more booze. All the words echoed in his head twice like double hearing; something about Arden and something about Arden's money. He tried to focus the echoes, but they banged into one another, confusing him. He and Perry laughed and fell, and fell and laughed — and he was still laughing when they reached the cattle loading chutes, trying to remember how he had gotten back to Gundarson's farm and falling out of the truck into the snow — Perry kicking and swearing, cows all around them, wild-eyed in the early morning light, charging back and forth from the watering trough to the loading chute, a truck strangely out of place too, a big green one with a rack; it was warm inside the cab as they lurched down Arden's driveway, and there was good old Arden now too, must have been feeling better, coming down the road in the old blue Plymouth.

"You goddam moron!" Perry was yelling. "You said he'd be in town for a week!" He was hitting Gilly on the head with a pair of pliers while the truck veered back and forth across the road through the snowdrifts, the old man running toward them in the early light; everything was double, then triple, except the road receding into the distance, even Arden leaping sideways toward the ditch in slow motion, right in front of the truck, flying high in the air and back down with a metallic *whump* on the hood of the truck right in front of Gilly's eyes. He stared directly into Arden's accusing face for what seemed like twenty years, but must have been the slightest fraction of a second before the body bounced and slid off the truck, leaving Arden Gundarson's deep blue irises burning into Gilly's retinas like twin halos of the sun, even long after he finally managed to close his eyes.

* * * * *

7

Bart Fester had been in his City Hall office somewhat later than usual that Wednesday, just getting into the juicy parts of *Sex and the Single Girl* while waiting for his wife to pick him up with the car. The outside temperature stood at about thirty below zero Fahrenheit and a raw wind whistled down Hamilton Street that would have frozen the balls off a brass monkey. It was days like this which made Bart curse his decision to leave Toronto for the raw, challenging West. His telephone rang.

"Bart?"

It was Frank Gelowitz, the manager of the Wascana-Ritz.

"Frank! How's the old hammer?"

"Still hanging. Listen to who checked in here last night. Thought you might be interested."

"Shoot."

"George Rizutto."

"Who?"

"George Rizutto Jr., from Chicago!"

"The *beer* Rizutto? The midwest construction Rizutto?"

"Right! Right! That's him." Frank giggled, he was so excited.

"What the hell is he doing here?"

"Don't know — holidays maybe?"

"Holidays — in February? In *Regina*? Christ, Frank!"

"Who knows? He only brought one bag with him."

"Listen, I better give him a call, eh? As Industrial Commissioner. Welcome to the Queen City and all that crap."

Gelowitz hesitated. "Wouldn't it be better if Mayor Gorius phoned him? Top of the totem pole, as it were?"

"Maybe you're right," Bart said after a second's reflection. "If we don't give Deke first shot at it, he'll get his nose out of joint again." He hung up the phone. Frank was absolutely right. Deke Gorius would have a shit hemorrhage if Bart phoned Rizutto first. But the problem with Deke doing it was that he would get the whole thing buggered up with his country-boy style and his free tickets to the hockey game. He'd probably never even heard of Rizutto. The last outburst of Deke's paranoia after Bart had tried to do something on his own had resulted in ten thousand bucks being slashed out of Bart's public relations slush fund. There was no sense in getting the mayor all stirred up again and watching the whole project go down the drain. Rizutto was big money and he had to be handled delicately, in the way Bart had been trained as a professional to do.

Bart telephoned the mayor's home. Sefton Gorius was rarely in his office at City Hall at that time of day. If he wasn't at home, he would be attending a coffee reception in his honour somewhere on the north side of the city; and if he wasn't there, he would be at a big ethnic funeral, weeping and wailing. That afternoon, Mayor Gorius was at home.

"Deke? Bart here. Hold on to your jockstrap. A once-in-a-lifetime opportunity has just checked into the Wascana-Ritz. It might be a good idea for you to go over and give him the royal Regina fanfare."

"Who is it? Bobby Hull?"

"Check this, Deke. We have been visited by none other than George Rizutto, Jr., from Chicago."

"Razooty? What's he, a football player?"

Bart had to put his hand over the telephone while he laughed out loud. "You dumb shit!" he said, and uncovered the speaker again. "No, Deke, *Rizutto*. He's one of the most important industrialists in the United States. Like, he owns the Chicago Cubs!"

"Well, I never heard of him."

"Take my word for it. He's got a dozen companies all over Western Canada. I know for a fact that he's the big money in Saskalt Explorations."

"Eh? Where?"

"Never mind. Listen, I'm going to dig out some background material on the guy. I think you should cancel your social engagements for the next couple of days. Phone him at the hotel and start giving him the treatment. See if ya can get him down to the club for a couple of drinks tonight and I'll get our industrial pitch all prepared. Maybe we can set up a luncheon tomorrow."

"I'd like to, Bart, but I have a wedding reception tonight."

"Couldn't you cancel it?"

"Nothing doing! I'm toasting the bride at the Bulgarian-Canadian Cultural Centre and there's gonna be two hundred Bohunks there! There's an election this fall, you know."

"Yeah, I know. Well, at least phone Rizutto up and introduce yourself. Set up a meeting and I'll go and cover for ya."

Mayor Gorius phoned the hotel and was put through to Mr. Rizutto's number. A voice snarled, "Hello!"

"This is er — Mayor Gorius calling. Welcome to Regina."

"Lissen, Clint!" Gilly growled. "If this is another one of your goddam jokes ——!"

"Is that Mr. Rizutto? George Rizutto of Chicago? This is Mayor Sefton Gorius."

"Oh. Well — how do you do, Mayor? I was uh, just napping."

"I'm delighted that you decided to honour the city by a visit, Mr. Rizutto. It's uncumbent upon me to extend you my official and most heartfelt welcome."

"Well, uh — thanks."

"Tell me, is there anything at all we can place at your service?"

"No, no. Don't go to any trouble."

"Nothing would be any trouble, Mr. Rizutto, Entertainment? Hospitality chits? Um, ladies?"

"Not right now, thanks."

"Say! How about a couple of tickets to the hockey game?"

"Hockey game? Did you say hockey game?"

"I thought so! I'll send Bart over with a couple of tickets."

"Bart?"

"Bart Fester, the Industrial Commissioner! A real cracker-jack. He'll look after all your needs. He's going to meet you later at the Frontier Club for a couple of drinks."

"Oh, well, I'm kind of busy right now. I'm working on a couple of things and uh —"

"Oh, I can smell *development* in the wind. Something big, I'll bet, eh?"

"You could say that."

"Say no more, Mr. Rizutto. Deke Gorius is the last person to snoop into somebody's private enterprise. But, I want you to know we're sympathetic to your plans, whatever they are. There's plenty of opportunity in Regina — and cheap labour! Did you know that we have the lowest average wage of any major city in Canada? Isn't that great?"

"Fantastic, Mr. Mayor."

"Call me Sefton, okay George?"

"All right — Sefton."

"Hell, make that 'Deke.' My friends all call me Deke."

"Sure, Deke."

"I can tell we're gonna get on famously, George. I'm a hockey fan too, y'know. So when are you gonna be finished with your — napping, heh heh? You want to meet Bart around nine or so?"

"Well, maybe later. I'd like to get myself oriented, Deke."

"Okay, ten o'clock. He'll be there at ten with bells on. Bye-bye for now."

Gilly hung up the telephone and leapt to his feet, instinctively pulling the tattered city map from his pocket. But there was nowhere to run. He was *in* the city he had been trying to reach for years. In the centre of the map was the blue patch representing Wascana Lake, surrounded by a wide green swath of parkland. The park in turn was hedged sharply by the square grid of streets and avenues. He searched for a clue, something strange, but the map looked so bland, so ordinary, that he sighed and put it away. The City Hall boys would be arriving in four hours. He would either have to disappear or put the Rizutto act together. He must have signed Rizutto's name on the hotel register when Malach got him the room.

* * * * *

8

The eyes were still there when Gilly became aware of the freezing cold in the cab of the truck. The bellowing of cattle was sending stabs of pain through his head. The truck was buried to the doors in a snow-blocked ditch. He climbed out the window. He was dazed and rigid with cold, trying to make sense of the bawling cattle and the wind whistling past him in long streaming feathers of snow. He could not erase the image of the burning eyes from his retinas. Where was he? Where was Arden? Where was Perry? Suddenly, he remembered his wallet and jammed his hand into his pocket. All his money was gone.

A car appeared a mile down the road with its headlights on, picking its way through the snowdrifts. It stopped at the truck. "Where ya headin'?" It was a farmer, probably going to town. But what town? Gilly had no idea where he was.

"North Battleford," he said, vaguely recalling Perry shouting something about North Battleford and the stockyards there.

"Sure. Hop in. That yer truck fulla beeves?"

"Yeah. No. I was helpin' a guy."

"Funny time a year to ship cattle."

Gilly sat silent as they drove through the storm. He did not hear the farmer's steady chatter. A mile down the road, a man appeared outlined in the snow, standing at the side of the road with a long elegant thumb extended. It was Perry.

"Friend a yers?"

"No," Gilly said, turning his face away as they passed.

The farmer speeded up again. "I never pick up more'n one hitchhiker. Even on a day like this. Never know who you're gettin'."

"That's right," Gilly said.

107

When they reached the next gas station, about a mile later, Gilly asked the driver to stop. He went into the station to warm up and watched the highway. Finally, Perry appeared, limping through the white wind. Gilly stepped out of the gas station toward the highway.

When Perry saw him, he turned and ran into the snowy ditch, cutting across the fields towards the buildings of North Battleford. But he was half-frozen and barely moving. Gilly caught him before he had run a hundred yards. He struck him once on the back of the head, knocking him face first into the snow. He pulled him upright and removed the wallet from his back pocket, then began punching him in the face. When his arm couldn't hold Perry up to smash his face anymore, he kicked him as he lay in the field and was still kicking when the RCMP car stopped on the highway. He was still kicking Perry when the two policemen struggled through the snow and grabbed him.

Garfield Krull, LL.B., Gilly's court-appointed lawyer, was a hopelessly incompetent alcoholic who had already left half a dozen cities in disgrace.

"Well, well, well, what have we here?" he said, breezing into Gilly's cell at the North Battleford lock-up. "Doesn't matter, we'll have you out in nothing flat, just leave it to Garfield Krull. They're all terrified of me, of course. Just *having* me on this case assures that you will be found innocent; at the most, you'll get a mild warning."

Gilly had refused to speak to the police until they'd found him a lawyer. Now, he told Krull the whole story, as much as he could remember. He gestured violently at Perry Lasuisse, who sat in the cell across the corridor, cracking his long fingers and grinning with contempt. Perry planned to plead guilty and get the whole thing finished with. He had his story all prepared.

"Now, as nearly as I can make out, you're both being charged with cattle rustling and manslaughter. The manslaughter's easy to beat, nobody can prove it wasn't an accident — anyway, that's his worry, if he was driving the truck. The cattle rustling looks a little more serious, but I think I've got a line on that. I've been digging through the precedents and we're going to nail them to the wall with the King vs. Grywecjeski."

Perry Lasuisse laughed every time Krull showed up with bulging briefcases full of lawbooks to plan his blazing assault on the Crown case. He had the case delayed several times to prepare his defence, irritating the judge. When the trial finally began in May, Krull whirled, shouted, pointed his finger, pounded the table, sneered and wept, but to no avail. Gilly was found guilty of cattle theft.

Krull then held a brief conference with the judge and the Crown prosecutor, saying he would need more time to prepare an adequate defence on the manslaughter charge. The judge, now violently biased against them, insisted that the second trial proceed immediately, while Perry Lasuisse was still available to testify.

The Crown prosecutor, who had been prepared to drop the manslaughter charge against Gilly, now was ready to go ahead. The choice was clearly presented: Gilly could plead guilty and beg for a reduced sentence; or they could fight it. Krull said that he knew now where the Crown case was weak; he would tear the prosecutor apart. However, he would require more money than the $300.00 Gilly had already given him, so under the circumstances (unless Gilly had more money he had not revealed), it was best to plead guilty and get it over with, as Perry had done two weeks before. Perry had gotten eighteen months.

Gilly admitted guilt to the charge of manslaughter and was sentenced to four years in the Prince Albert Penitentiary. Krull leaped to his feet in outrage. "A travesty of justice!" he yelled. "We'll appeal this case to the Supreme Court!"

He rushed to Gilly's side as he was being led from the courtroom. "Well, that's not so bad," he whispered. "He could have given you five. There'll be some extra expenses for the postage and typing, so I'll send your statement to the Pen. Good luck." Dazed, Gilly shook his hand once and was gone.

Bart Fester was feeling pretty keen when his wife dropped him off at the Wascana-Ritz. For once, the kids hadn't bugged him all through dinner for more money for clothes, records or hockey sticks. Bart was allowing himself to dream about the Rizutto deal. If he pulled this one off, he would be in line for a Vancouver job which was opening up in the fall. It wasn't every day that George Rizutto Jr. fell into your lap with a million bucks.

Waiting by the elevators in the hotel for Rizutto to appear, he checked the hockey tickets in his pocket. Rizutto would probably just throw them in the wastebasket. Deke and his stupid goddam hockey. He hoped the mayor had not promised the guy a broad. If Bart came home stinking of perfume once more, his wife would cut him off for good.

Bart nearly didn't recognize Rizutto when he stepped out of the elevator, dressed in a thirty-dollar sports jacket and cheap flannel pants. But there was something about his face which made Bart look again. He hadn't met too many multi-millionaires, but there was no mistaking that *look* — relaxed and confident. He had the aura of distinction and good breeding which fit with the information Bart had assembled on Rizutto from *Who's Who* and other sources.

"Ah! Mr. Rizutto?" The hearty direct approach. A gamble, but worth it. "Bart Fester." They shook hands. "Have you sampled our famous Canadian rye yet, Mr. Rizutto?"

"Yes, yes, I know it well."

"I was going to take you down to the Frontier Club. We have lots to talk about."

"What did you have in mind?"

Bart looked at Rizutto cautiously. "Oh, you know — one thing and another. Wine, women and song. I'd like to pop a few questions about your uh, plans, if they're not *too* private, heh heh."

"The Mayor said something about a ticket to the hockey game tomorrow night."

"Oh yeah — here. Two of 'em."

"Two?"

"Deke thought you might like to take somebody."

"No, no — I don't think so." He stared oddly at the

tickets. "Say, Bart, I want to do some thinking. I'll take a pass on the Club, if that's okay."

"Well — okay, George. Can I call you George? And I wasn't going to mention this till after we'd hoisted a couple of cocktails, but some of the boys from city council and the Chamber of Commerce are sponsoring a businessmen's luncheon for you tomorrow at the Club — kind of a surprise, like. You'll be able to make that, won't you?"

"We'll see. What's for lunch?"

"Jeeze, I don't know — you got any favourites?"

Rizutto thought for a minute. "Liver and bacon, with baked Alaska."

"Uh-huh. Okay. Well, we'll see ya tomorrow? I'll come round and pick you up around noon. And lissen, I just wanta leave a couple a these brochures and fact-sheets with you. Look 'em over at your leisure, and remember: the business climate here is *very* good. Boss Morgan's government is a big friend of private enterprise."

"Boss Morgan is the Premier now?"

"Yeah. You know him?"

"I'm sure he wouldn't remember me."

"Well, you know what a great guy he is. Always looks after his friends, take it from me."

"Thanks for the tickets," Rizutto said, walking toward the hotel exit. "Goodnight."

Bart didn't know what to think of the situation. This Rizutto was a *real* weirdo, a tough nut to crack. He gave *nothing* away about his plans, which could be *anything*: another branch of his construction industry; some big potash deal with Saskalt; maybe a factory of some kind. Until Bart found out what was going on in Rizutto's head, he might as well take it easy and get drunk. With a glance at his watch, that was what he decided to do. There would be a lot of the boys down at the Club.

Bart lost sixty dollars playing poker that night. Vic Tesko, a city alderman and the chairman of the finance committee of the junior hockey club, was there; so were Gary Giles and Doug Linton, who could be counted on for help. He was up until four a.m., playing cards and coaching them on how to handle George Rizutto at the luncheon.

So Bart Fester was considerably more bleary-eyed than

usual when he appeared at the hotel the next day to collect the industrialist for the luncheon. He had salvaged part of the forenoon to put together figures on property tax exemptions, comparative wage analysis and service allowances on water and power. The weather, at least, had improved. A front of warm air had moved across the plains and the Queen City lay basking under a warm sun. Water dripped from the icicles on the eaves of the Wascana-Ritz.

"Lovely day, isn't it?" Bart said as they walked down the street to the Club.

"Yeah," Rizutto, looking unimpressed. Bart felt a twinge of his ulcer.

Deke was at the Club, shaking hands with everyone in sight and handing out buffalo bone cufflinks. There were about a dozen aldermen and businessmen waiting for Bart and George outside the private dining room.

"Get those hockey tickets okay?" Deke asked, clapping Rizutto on the back.

"I sure did. Thanks a lot. You going to the game?"

"Wouldn't miss it for anything! Most of the boys'll be there. We're kicking off the campaign for the new stadium tonight."

"You a hockey fan, George?" Bart said. "I thought your big interest was in baseball. The Cubs, isn't it?"

"Only for the money," Rizutto replied, accepting a cigarette. "Frankly, baseball bores me. Give me a good hockey game any night of the week."

"Atta boy, George!" Deke cried. "You guys hear that? We got a blueliner here!"

Vic Tesko picked up the cue. "You sure got a hockey player's build, George. Bet you still get out on the old skates once in a while, eh?"

"Not much anymore. I used to play."

"I could tell! You can see it in his shoulders."

Bart went to get some drinks while the others wandered into the dining room. The luncheon didn't go too badly, he thought, considering that Deke complained to Rizutto four or five times about the liver and bacon. Bart and George sat side by side, doodling figures on their napkins and talking about the invigorating business climate in Western Canada. Bart was favourably impressed by George's grasp of profit

112

margins and his concept of corporate responsibilities.

When the baked Alaska arrived, Gary Giles rose and clinked on his wine glass with his spoon.

"Well, I think we've all had a very instructive and worthwhile luncheon," he said, "even though I can't vouch for the liver and bacon." Bart groaned to himself. "And on behalf of all of you, I wish to thank Mr. George Rizutto Jr. of Chicago for sharing his time and interests with us." There was hearty applause. "Now, I turn you over to Mr. Rizutto, who no doubt will favour us with a few choice words of wisdom."

George Rizutto stood up. His handsome face glowed with the importance of the occasion. "Actually, I don't come from Chicago," he said. "I come from De Kalb, Illinois, a town about forty miles outside of Chicago. And De Kalb is famous as the place where barbed wire was invented. That's how my family made its fortune, in fact. They make a lot of barbed wire there. 'Barb City'."

A few of the boys looked around, concerned. What the hell was *this* all about?

"But I don't want to bore you with my personal history. As you can see, I am not dressed for public speaking, but since your diligent mayor dragged me out of seclusion, I wore the work clothes I brought along. I didn't think I'd be meeting this many important people." A flattered chuckle rose spontaneously. "If you're going to be at the hockey game tonight, I'll probably see you at the reception. I'll make a statement at that time about my visit to Regina." Rizutto sat down to the sound of wild applause.

Fred Twamley, vice-president of the Chamber of Commerce and a director of the hockey club, rushed over and shook George's hand. "*Great* speech, George! And I think we can take care of your clothing needs."

"Fred is the owner of Twamley's Top Tailoring," Bart explained.

"We'll get you decked out in the best the city's got to offer. Drop by after lunch."

"Well, I still have some exploring to do in the city."

"It'll only take a few minutes!"

"We'll be there, Fred. I'll bring George around."

Twamley's was an exclusive shop just around the corner from the Club. A visit there would allow time for Bart's wife to hustle downtown with the car. Then Bart could personally take George on an inspection of the potential industrial sites.

"You just pick out whatever looks nice on you, George," Twamley said, slipping off the cheap sportscoat and laying it near the wastebin. "Everything is from this year's fashions."

When Rizutto was led back again to the sunny street where Bart's yellow Oldsmobile was waiting at the curb, he was resplendent in a four hundred dollar gabardine Nehru suit, purple silk shirt, fur-trimmed leather overcoat and polished calfskin boots. His toes nestled inside a pair of ten dollar socks. He looked like a new man.

"Now, I've booked off for the rest of the afternoon to escort you around," Bart said, "in case there's any questions you want to ask or any places you want to see."

It was one of the goofiest afternoons Bart Fester had ever spent in his life. Rizutto paid no attention to all the warehouse section north of the tracks or to the new industrial park, or to the oil refineries. Finally, when Bart asked in exasperation if there was any place special he wanted to see, Rizutto took a map from his pocket.

"Can we drive around the lake?" he asked.

"*Wascana* Lake?"

"Yeah."

"Okay, but it's just a big park. A few government buildings."

They drove by the university campus and the Museum of Natural History, then across the Albert Street Bridge.

"Of course, it isn't really a lake at all, just a big hole they dug when they widened the creek back around the First World War — a make-work project. That's when they built this bridge." The bridge crossed the western edge of the lake. In the centre of the ice on the lake, there were a couple of tiny islands. Children skated around them and an iceboat flashed by in the sun. Bart turned past the Legislature, with its dark dome looking over the lake, through a forest of blue spruce and fir trees. As they turned back to the north shore, approaching the university, a gate appeared and a sign which read, "Regina Yacht Club."

"Stop here," Rizutto said. He got out of the car and walked through the gate. The path led to a narrow wooden foot bridge which went from the shore to one of the small islands.

"Willow Island," Bart announced, stamping his feet beside the car while Rizutto walked across the bridge. The boat club had disappeared and the bare island now lay in the middle of the frozen lake like a beaver lodge hibernating for the winter.

When Bart finally crossed the bridge to see what the hold-up was, Rizutto was gazing at the skyline of white buildings wreathed in winter smoke and mist, gleaming along the northern horizon. "They used to call this place Pile of Bones. Along the creek," he said.

"Yeah, I know. You want some buffalo bone cufflinks?"

"The animals were killed along the banks and the bones left in big piles. Must have looked like all those buildings. Then they rotted back into the ground. Fertilizer."

The sun was going down. Shaking his head, Bart hustled George back to the car. He was having one hell of a time getting an angle on this guy and his ulcer was bothering him. If only he could figure out what the hell he was *looking* for.

* * * * *

10

At the age of seventeen, Gilly was not crushed by the thought of four years in the Pen; he had survived a few weeks in jail without cracking. It was his conscience, haunted by the image of Arden Gundarson's eyes, that was hardest to endure. The caged feeling and the lack of privacy were easy burdens compared to that. But even Arden's eyes gradually faded in P.A. Pen, obscured by the suffocating routine. Every action was regulated by whistles, buzzers and sirens, from eating to shitting to taking a shower. Time was measured not by the cycles of the sun, but by the number of minutes and seconds which divided each assault on his ears. Any diversion was an entertainment. When Gilly was raped in the laundry room by two men he never saw again, ten days after his arrival, he didn't bother to complain. Even rape was commonplace, and like everything else, it had begun and ended on the hour, between the buzzer signalling the end of work and the bell for supper.

Gradually, Gilly accepted the routine and counted off the seconds and hours like everyone else. There were advantages to this life. He never had to wade into a shed three feet deep in chicken shit to shovel it out. He never had to freeze his ears chasing strayed cattle in the snow. When he accepted the fact that he was indeed a criminal, even the future seemed not all that bad. After their brief periods of liberty on the outside, the convicts came back to tell lively stories of big Buicks and buxom women.

B Wing was a veritable academy of technical education. For the fee of an ounce of tobacco, an apt student could learn the secrets of cheque-passing and safe-cracking. The long-termers in the motor shops were pedagogues in the field of ignition wires and altered serial numbers. As in all academies, an attentive and physically attractive student could enjoy tuition in a wide range of subjects.

Gilly's chief tutor was one Clinton Malach, resident of the adjoining cell. Malach was a wiry little character with a maze of remarkable lines charting his face. When he laughed or scowled, his face rearranged itself into a constantly shifting kaleidoscope of patterns, nearly as intriguing as his attitude which was one of amiable contempt. Malach's was a world into which a fool was born every minute, where the people fleeced were the greedy and gullible — the ones who always wanted something for nothing.

"Now you, for example," he said to Savard as they worked on a press, stamping licence plates. "You walked in here like a plucked chicken. All your life, other people been livin' offa you and you *let* 'em. You're a babe in arms, Savard. You've gotta get them first."

The stack of licence plates grew in front of them: 22-312, 22-313, 22-314 — like the seconds going by.

"That may be true," Gilly said. "But I don't want to spend the rest of my life in jail, either."

"All you need is a better con game than everybody else, Savard. You ain't stupid. That mug of yours is worth a million bucks, if you look after it. Sincere as hell! You could

116

go a lot of places."

"And get caught."

Malach shrugged. "There's always bad luck. Like I had last time in Banff."

In Banff, Malach had been promoting a new drive-in restaurant franchise. The great fast food chains had not yet sprung up across North America. Malach was a prophet ahead of his time; it was still only a brilliant idea the day he tried to unload his Tee-Pee Burger House franchise onto a vacationing U.S. Treasury agent from Seattle.

"Remember, Savard, act like ya got money. Money charms money from the air. It doesn't matter if you're a halfbreed, as long as you don't *look* like one. You'll see. They'll beg you to lift the wallets from their hands."

"People aren't that dumb."

"If they weren't, there wouldn't be no con men."

"Okay, why isn't *everybody* a con man?"

"Well, there aren't many who ain't. Maybe a few Yewkeranian stubble-jumpers. The whole society is one big con game! The whole dam' set-up. Schools, government, movies, newspapers! All of it. Look at the legal system, that's somethin' you oughta be familiar with. Know the first thing a lawyer learns? I mean, after his fee schedule? That it doesn't matter a sweet god*dam* if you're guilty! That's irrelevant. The good ones get you off, 'cause they make you *look* innocent — even when you're guilty. That guy in North Battleford, Krull, he made you look twice as guilty as you were!"

"Why doesn't the judge know that?"

Malach sighed with exasperation and punched out a couple of licence plates. "That's the point, dammit! Of course, he knows that! Every judge in the country is an ex-lawyer who couldn't make enough money at play-acting. So he got himself a political party. He doesn't give a shit if you're innocent or guilty, either. If yer lucky and a good actor, you'll win the case."

But Gilly drew the line at sports, which Malach considered the greatest fraud of all. And Gilly was right, because his enthusiasm for sports served him well in prison. Being on a baseball or hockey team was the only trip outside the walls, even for a few hours a month. In no time at all, Gilly was

117

the prized pitcher on the baseball team.

It was the Classifications Officer, Vern Carney, who had pointed out his opportunities in sport. Gilly had been called into his office a few weeks after beginning his sentence. He rudely refused the cup of coffee he was offered. Gilly had been warned that these sessions were a waste of time, useful only for getting extra cigarettes.

"Come on, Gil, that's no way to start. I'm here to help you. Cigarette?" Carney held out a pack of Sweet Caps. He didn't look much older than Gilly himself. He had just graduated from university. "Suit yourself," he said.

They waited in frustrated silence for half an hour till the interview was over. On his way back to his cell, two heavies from C Wing knocked Gilly down and took the cigarettes.

At the next session, Carney said, "I've studied your case, Savard. I think I can get you out."

There was a long silence. "How?"

"You've got a good chance appealing the manslaughter. Especially if you can get some character references. It would mean writing some letters."

"What will it cost?"

Carney shrugged. "Time."

"I'll think about it."

There was another silence.

"I hear you're quite a sportsman."

"A what?"

"You're a good athlete. You should stay at it. It'll keep you sane. And it'll help with the parole board. If you're good enough at it, you can get outside."

It was August and the baseball season was drawing to a close. Froggy Howard, the third baseman and captain of the team, stopped Gilly in the locker room. "You ever play football, Savard?"

"A little."

"How about rugby? English rugby."

"Something like cricket?"

"Why don't you come out tomorrow night and see?"

On the sports field the next evening, Gilly found a group of convicts throwing a football around. They were dressed in makeshift rugby costumes of gym shorts and hockey sweaters. There were no helmets, no shoulder pads, not even stockings.

"What is it, like touch football?" Gilly said.

"Watch."

Froggy blew his whistle and the players formed into two sides. Several from each team then locked their arms together and ran at one another, heads and arms intertwining as they fought for position. Then Froggy threw the ball into one side of the scrum and it erupted into a brawling mêlée. The ball came heeling out one side of the pack and one player leapt to pick it up from the ground. With no more ceremony than if they were stomping an ant, four opposition players smashed into the scrum-half, trampling him to the ground, kicking the ball out of his hands, then booting it down the field.

"No equipment?" Gilly said, impressed by the ferocity.

Froggy laughed. "No fag Yankee games here, Savard. Put on your cleats and try it. You wearin' a can?"

"Yeah."

"Okay. All ya gotta remember — no forward pass, no hittin' from behind and the ball never goes dead. Go and play prop forward for a while."

They played Rugby League rules, a brutal legacy left to civilization by the English coal miners of Lancashire. It was said they ground each other into pulped flesh every Sunday afternoon for beer, a handful of silver and the entertainment of their friends. Gilly loved it.

At the second practice, he asked to play scrum-half, the player who removed the ball from the heels of the deadly scrum.

"Naw. You're a natural centre," Froggy said.

"But our scrum-half takes a beating! He's too small."

"A scrum-half has to be small and really, *really* fast. Size is no good to you there."

"I want to play scrum-half," Gilly insisted.

He had everything else it took: speed, brains, sure hands and a talent for reacting before thinking, muscles anticipating the brain. So it became Gilly's role to heave the oval ball into the slashing maelstrom of boots, elbows, fists and teeth which formed the scrum. While the big forwards tangled for possession of the ball, the opposing scrum-halves waited on the flanks. When the ball finally squirted out, Gilly had to pounce on it, snatching it out of the mud and flying cleats, and fling a perfect spiral pass to begin the run. Or else he could boot it high over the heads of the on-rushing tacklers and fly down the field after it before the stampeding horde descended and kicked him into oblivion, as their boots hacked away at the bouncing leather.

Gilly's life began to revolve around the Saturday afternoon game. He exercised in his cell, doing push-ups and running on the spot, stretching the bruises out of his thighs. The more he played, the more immune he grew to injury. He was never more physically fit in his life; the punishing tackles were a tonic to his body. Every week, there were two matches among the teams from the four wings of the penitentiary. For this sport, no outside teams would play against the convicts.

Clint Malach was indignant. "What's it all prove? Nothing! Knocking yerself out for a second of passing glory! Big deal. Sure, everybody's buddy-buddy now — but what're they gonna do for ya when you bust a leg?"

"I don't play for *them*, Clint. I do it for me. It makes me feel good."

"Don't be a dope, Savard. Take up tiddly-winks before ya get yourself killed."

Finally, as the frost penetrated the ground in October and a couple of players' bones were broken, the inmates' enthusiasm shifted to hockey. Hockey was the *big* sport in P.A. Pen, and this elevated Gilly to star status. At nearly two hundred pounds and in prime condition, he was made right-winger on the first line before the opening practice. This was unusual because the prison hockey team got lots of games outside. Positions on the team, therefore, were a reflection of political power, not athletic ability. They were subject to influence-peddling and outright extortion. Even so, Gilly could not be shaken from the first line. Even Clint Malach was impressed.

In the meantime, Carney had talked to Isidore McKay and had made formal depositions on Gilly's behalf to the court of appeal. "I think we can get the manslaughter conviction overturned," he said. "If so, it means you could be released at any time. You've already served out the cattle theft."

"I'm not sure I want to leave," Gilly said. "I always get into trouble outside."

Carney handed Gilly some cigarettes. "You've got a whole life waiting for you on the outside, Gillman. You're only nineteen! Hell, you got a better chance of surviving than most high school grads. You *know* what life's about!"

"Let's wait till after the rugby season, anyway. I want to play centre this year."

"Good God, man! If it's sports you want, you're a fool to stay in here. You could be a hockey pro! You could play football!"

"I've heard this line before."

"Don't take my word for it. Ask your friends."

Gilly asked his friends. Clint Malach thought he was crazy for not taking every advantage of Carney. "Christ!" he said. "That guy can spring you out of here in two seconds flat and you won't even *co-operate*! What are you, Savard, some kind of dumb john? You could be out there, makin' us *both* a lotta dough!"

But Gilly could not explain his reasons for wanting to stay to either Carney or Malach. He was afraid of becoming a halfbreed again, of succumbing to his own self-doubts. He would always be a loser. He could survive here in this world of losers where at least he got a chance to carry a football or a hockey puck once in a while. In the end, however, they convinced him.

Isidore McKay was at the appeal. He testified that Gilly's character was flawed only by youth. He told the court that Arden Gundarson had gone a bit crazy before his death, that he was prone to bizarre acts, most of them self-destructive. Pennistone was brought in and testified to Gilly's scholarship and intelligence. He was acquitted and told by the warden the next day to pack his bag.

11

It was ten years since Gilly had seen a hockey game, he realized, driving toward the arena. It was odd how time stretched and shrank. He had managed to avoid the police and Clint Malach for nearly two days. Maybe he could carry off this Rizutto routine, which hadn't been too demanding so far. He still didn't know what he would say at the reception after the hockey game. Whatever it was, he would try to get them all off his back for once and for all.

Gilly was looking forward to the game. The evening newspaper was full of glowing accounts of Danny Tuck, the new *wunderkind* of junior hockey. He was a hometown boy who had already scored more goals that season than all his teammates combined. In honour of the warm spring-like evening, the rink was full. On the way to his seat, Gilly met Deke Gorius and Vic Tesko shaking hands with all the citizens they could find.

"Hey, ya got here okay, eh?" Deke said. "Great, great. We're going back to the Directors' Lounge for a couple of snorts before the game. Want to join us?"

"No thanks. I like to read the programme before the game starts."

Deke passed on, shaking hands. "Hi, nice to see ya again. Sefton Gorius at your service. Got your alley paved yet? No problem, give me a call any time. Office is always open."

Gilly had given his spare ticket at the door to a boy in a tattered parka who looked like he could not afford the admission. Now the boy sat down beside him, munching on a hot dog. His eyes watched Gilly suspiciously from under a Montréal Canadiens toque. They stood up together when "O Canada" began to blare through the sound system.

The Regina Pats were playing their arch enemies, the Flin Flon Bombers. At least the fans and the Bombers were arch enemies. From the first face-off the spectators howled and jeered every time a Bomber checked a Pat into the boards and they cheered lustily when an opponent was speared with a hockey stick or rammed into the goal post. For their part, the Bombers responded in kind, taking pleasure in titillating the crowd with their high-sticking and crosschecking. It was not malice so much as the performer's need to respond to an audience's expectations, in the way one wrestler must be cast as a villain and the other a saint. In Flin Flon, the following week, the roles would be reversed.

For the audience, the Pats could do no wrong. Led by the amazing Tuck, they skated and passed and checked like a precision instrument, rushing from one end of the rink to the other, dazzling the crowd with their moves. They did everything but score, which they couldn't do because of the Bomber goalie, a superhuman contortionist who was clearly headed for the pros. At the end of the first period, the game was a scoreless tie. The crowd trooped to the coffee counters, hoarse from shouting. Gilly met Deke shaking hands on the ramp.

"George! We were just coming to get you for a drink! How's the game goin'?"

"Great game, Deke."

"Reminds you of your youth, eh?"

"Sure does."

"Come on, I'll buy y'a snort."

In the Directors' Lounge, the party had been underway for an hour. Fred Twamley was there, grinning widely to see Gilly in his new coat. So were Doug Linton, Bart Fester and most of the rest of the boys. They were in animated discussion with the PR man who had been engaged by the city for a straight five percent off the top to publicize the new building campaign. He was the veteran of a dozen United Appeal Fund campaigns and was outlining the strategy for the evening's reception. There would be two groups of people there to hit: Important People and The Press. The Important People, a notoriously tight-fisted group, were not there to sign cheques, but to dazzle The Press. The Press was there to sell the campaign to the ordinary citizens of the city, who would pay for the new stadium. There were no ordinary citizens at the reception.

The second period was not as wild as the first, as the two teams settled in for hard play. The most skillful players began to dominate the game and the crowd's attention was rivetted on Danny Tuck. Tuck was a one man bullet of blurred motion, whirling and diving for the puck, leaping over flying body checks, laying perfect passes on his wingers' sticks while sliding between two defencemen. He was brilliant, though he was small. Gilly wondered how he would fare in the pro leagues, where brute force dominated the game.

Deke and Bart showed up behind him with five minutes left in the second period. Bart was lurching noticeably.

"Came to watch the game for a while," the Mayor said, acknowledging the awed looks of recognition from the citizens around. "What's 'a score?"

"Still nothing-nothing. Watch this kid, Deke. He's fantastic!"

"Who? Tuck? Yeah, he's our ace-in-the-hole. That boy's gonna build us a new hockey rink. Hope it's finished before he gets drafted by Montréal."

"Say, George," Bart began, "the boys were wonderin' if you'd like to join us later for a couple of hands of poker —"

The roar of the crowd drowned out his words. Styrofoam coffee cups flew in all directions. A three man Bomber breakaway had just scored the first goal against the Pat defence and because he had turned to listen to Fester, Gilly had missed it. There were only two minutes left in the period. Enraged, he stood up and began walking out. "To hell with it. Let's go have a drink."

The lounge was now crowded, as The Press and VIP's awaited the end of the game when free liquor would be served. Bart was at Gilly's elbow introducing him to various people.

"You ever get into hockey in a big way, George?" Vic Tesko asked. "I mean as an investment?"

"Just baseball."

"I hear there's big money being put up for expansion in the NHL. Six more teams."

"Is that so?"

"Sure. Look at the AFL. Wouldn't surprise me if there was another league set up sometime soon."

"There aren't enough good hockey players."

Vic and Doug and Fred laughed. "Money can buy hockey players anywhere, George! If you had enough money, you could buy Bobby Hull. You could buy Gordie Howe!"

"There isn't enough money in the world," Gilly retorted.

"Gordie Howe can not be bought."

"George, how can you *say* that? *You* know how it goes. It isn't a sport anymore, it's a business! Nobody goes out and learns hockey on a frozen duckpond with a horse turd for a puck. Kids learn to play at professional schools today. They're not so dumb anymore, either. First thing they learn is how to sign a contract."

"You said it, Vic! Kids are gettin' too dam' greedy! Just out for what they can get and to hell with the fans and the spirit of the game."

"What's 'a score?" Deke said, staggering toward them.

"One-nothing for Flin Flon," Gilly replied. "I think I'll go catch the last act."

"Don't forget. Big speech after the game!" Bart shouted.

The boy in the red and blue toque was waiting when Gilly sat down. "Good game, eh?" Gilly said.

The kid shrugged. "There was a fight last week," he said. "Lotsa blood."

The teams came out with spine-snapping force in the third period. The Pats rushed headlong down the ice time after time, led by their relentless little centre, Tuck, only to be stopped at the mouth of the goal. The excitement even spread back to the lounge; one by one the dignitaries trickled into the aisles to watch the game. Bart squeezed between Gilly and the boy.

"So what's 'a speech gonna be about, George?"

"You'll see."

"Now, 'at's not fair, George. I gotta do the introduction, y'know, and if things don't go just right at this goddam reception, all the shit comes down on me. So, if you could just give me some idea ——"

Gilly turned and glared at him. "The only thing which interests me right now is hockey. Maybe I'll talk about that."

A light glowed in Bart's bloodshot eyes. "At's *great*, George! Jut so long as I know. Hockey, eh?"

He lurched to his feet just as the crowd went wild again. Danny Tuck had scored the tying goal and Gilly had missed *it*, too. The boy who was not interested in the conversation, but whose view had been blocked by Bart Fester, shoved at him with both hands. Bart went toppling onto the heads of the yelling spectators below.

"What did you do that for?" Gilly said, trying not to laugh as they watched the Industrial Commissioner being kicked and punched all the way to the bottom. "You'd better disappear before he gets back."

Bart crawled back up the aisle and disappeared toward the lounge to lick his wounds, and Deke Gorius sat down in the boy's seat to watch the rest of the game. He fell asleep just as it ended, a one-one tie.

By the time they reached the lounge, Bart had spread the word that George Rizutto was going to establish a professional hockey team in Regina. The place was awash with alcohol and rumours. "George!" Bart said, limping up to him, "Come and meet some people."

Murray Lozinski, the Royal Bank manager, said, "I've been trying to talk to you since the luncheon, Mr. Rizutto. I don't know if you've set up a bank account in the city yet, or who you usually deal with, but I would consider it a great privilege to be able to put my staff at your disposal."

Gilly grinned his most sincere grin. "There's nothing I need right now, thanks."

"But there might be," Lozinski pointed out. "I heard you mention you were travelling short of cash. I keep a fund of five thousand dollars available for standby and we could put that at your disposal till your chequing account is transferred from uh, De Kalb."

"Well, I'll think about it."

"That's fantastic, Mr. Rizutto! We offer the best service in the city. Drop in and have a look at our vault sometime."

Bart broke in again with another person. "An old friend of yours, Mr. Rizutto. Premier Morgan."

Boss Morgan was even more pompous and self-assured than he'd been four and a half years before. He had every reason to be; he was Premier of the province. "I understand we've already met," he said, peering at Gilly through his thick lenses.

"Very briefly, at a political reception in uh, up north. You wouldn't remember me. You were in the Opposition then. How did you do it?"

Morgan looked around, then leaned forward to whisper. "Nothing to it. We out-socialized the Socialists. Everything bigger and better. Free drug plan. More highways. But don't worry. That's only for the public. But you and I know where the real power is. Right? That's why I'm interested in what you're going to say tonight."

A large man with a face like a slab of sirloin approached carrying a bottle of beer in one hand. "Hi, Boss. Gonna introduce me to the guest?"

Morgan grimaced. "Sure thing, Dan. George Rizutto, this is Dan Potz, Chief of Police for Regina."

The ice rattled sharply in Gilly's glass. He suddenly remembered who he was and who he wasn't, and the policemen knocking at Miss Blackwood's door. Had that only been two days ago?

"Well, Mr, Rizutto, what's my chances of getting in on the ground floor of this project?"

"I'm not sure, Chief."

"Well, I got a few thousand dollars salted away I'd like to spend in a good cause, as long as it brings home a profit. Good for your backers to know the Chief of Police is involved, eh?" He nudged Gilly.

"I imagine it would. They want to be assured Regina is a law-abiding community."

"You can bet on it, Mr. Rizutto. Your money couldn't come to a safer community. Don't believe what you might read in the newspaper about crime rates. I make the figures up myself."

"What figures?"

"The ones on the higher crime rates. It's the only way we can get a budget increase. Don't tell the Mayor or Fester, eh?"

Gilly shook his head.

"No crime, no pay rise, you follow me?"

"I certainly do. You mean you need criminals to keep the wheels of justice rolling."

"Well, we got all a those we need. Goddam town's fillin' up with halfbreeds and Indians. No respect for the law at all, out every night beating and screwing each other. We got 'em pretty well concentrated now in one area of the city, though."

"And how do you — control them?"

"Simple. They're movin' in from the countryside in swarms, you see? Regina's gonna be half Indian one a these days. Same as every other city in Western Canada. Welfare, see? That's what brings 'em in. The easy life. But all you gotta do is leave 'em be. If they don't kill each other fightin' over women and cheap wine, they'll drink themselves to death. Problem's solved."

Bart appeared with Vic Tesko and Fred Twamley.

"The moment's here, George. Reporters are champing at the bit. Microphone's over there."

Gilly turned to him, but the smile had faded from the millionaire's handsome face. He put an empty glass in Bart's hand. "You talk to them," he said. "I have to go."

"What? Hey, quit joking!"

Gilly walked out of the reception leaving the crowd stunned as the door slammed behind him. A taxi was waiting outside. "Take me to a strange place," he said.

"Town's fulla strange places, buddy. Whuddaya got in mind?"

"A bar. An Indian bar."

"Well, 'at's as weird as they come, okay. You sure you know what you're doing?"

"That's got nothin' to do with it."

The night flowed past him again, a nightmare of stinking beer parlours, teenage hookers, dying old men and women with blank eyes nodding off beside the jukeboxes — all of them running together and becoming one: the beer parlour in Meadow Lake. Would he ever reach the door and walk out of it again? As Gillman Savard, there was no hope. The dream of finding Maggie had been his only chance and now it was fading too. Gillman Savard might just as well cease to exist. George Rizutto had better odds for survival. At least he had money waiting for him at the bank.

* * * * *

12

Carney and the prison authorities had tried to persuade Gilly to return to Brochet, or at least Meadow Lake, and stop running from his past. But although he wanted to see Wilfred and the girls again, he knew he would only make his father angry and his mother cry. Besides, he preferred to go south

— as far as he could, which wasn't very far as it turned out.

Carney had found a job for him in Saskatoon, which was about halfway to Regina and a tenth of the distance to San Francisco. The job was at Motormack Trucking Company, where Carney had himself worked during the summers when he had studied at university. It was a probationary position, but it paid well and Gilly was promised time off in the fall to try out for the Saskatoon Hilltops football team.

Even Clint Malach had approved. Saskatoon was a favourite stamping ground of his; in fact, he would be there in six months when he was released from the Pen himself. He told Gilly to look for him at the Westbury Hotel.

Earl Jensen was waiting at the railway station, as Carney had said he would, pacing back and forth in the lobby. Jensen was a big, rugged man. He habitually ran his hand along a wide scar on the top of his head which glistened through his brushcut. Carney had described him as a "busy man," a self-made success at the age of thirty-four who was looking for new worlds to conquer. He believed in giving a fellow an even break.

"Mr. Jensen?" Gilly said, walking up to him.

"You're Savard. Got your bag? Come on, I'll take you around."

Jensen drove to the west end of the city where his trucking operation was located. It was a Sunday and the place was idle, but Jensen showed him the loading dock, the warehouse and the truck service bays. He had started trucking after his discharge from the Army in 1946, buying one truck and hiring a vacant garage. He had made a fortune in the post-war construction boom, and married into the city's largest automobile dealership. The firms merged. When Gilly arrived in the spring of 1953, Motormack had no rivals. Jensen ran the semis and a dozen vans out of his new depot. For his own transport, he drove a Volkswagen, one of the earliest models. He had brought it back from Europe after the war. Jensen had been impressed by the single-minded ambition of the German people who shook off defeat to rebuild their shattered country.

They drove to a rooming house on Avenue F, where Jensen had arranged Gilly's room and board for fifty dollars a month. The house was only five blocks from work. Gilly would begin at eight a.m. the next morning as a "swamper" on the loading dock. If he performed well, there would be a future for him at Motormack Trucking.

"Meanwhile," Jensen said, "what plans have you got for tonight?"

"Nothing. Guess I'll listen to *Amos 'n' Andy*."

"For your first night in town, I'll take you home for dinner and you can meet my wife. My foster daughter's there too. Don't get any bright ideas, though."

The Volkswagen sped across Broadway Bridge to the east side of the river, winding along the riverbank and past stately old houses where people stared at the whining little bug. On Temperance, the car pulled up in front of the grandest house Gilly had ever seen.

Mrs. Jensen met them at the door. She was wearing a chic evening dress and her hair was sculpted into golden perfection.

"Elizabeth, this is Gilly Savard, the kid I was telling you about. Brought him home for dinner."

"Bully for you." She turned to Gilly. "You're the one just out of jail?"

Gilly looked at Jensen for direction. "Yes," he said.

"Motormack Trucking. 'Give me your starving and your miserable and your homeless!'" She gestured grandly and staggered toward the kitchen. Gilly realized she was drunk.

"Where's Maggie?" Jensen asked.

His wife shrugged. "Fixing the salad."

"Liz, I wish you wouldn't do that."

"Do what?"

"Treat her like she was kitchen help."

"She *wanted* to do it, goddammit!"

"Okay, okay. Maggie!" he called. "Come out here. Meet our latest Motormack recruit!"

The living room was bigger than André Savard's house and the carpet alone would have covered Mme. Savard's garden. Gilly hid behind one of the wingback chairs as a slim, dark-haired girl stepped into the archway of the room.

"This is Margarete Steffen — our foster daughter from Germany. Gilly Savard. She came back with us last year, when we went on holiday."

The girl smiled a defensive, shy smile, which kept trying

to disappear. "I am pleased to meet you, Geelly. Already I haff heard much about you."

She extended her hand formally, but with an attitude of polite terror. He was afraid of touching her because she seemed so frightened of being hurt. Jensen put his arm around her and hugged her fondly; he escorted her to the piano in the corner of the room. She played some classical music which Gilly had never heard before. The piece was complicated and delicate and very hypnotic.

Jensen murmured, "Maggie's come through tough times, Gilly. We discovered her in a displaced persons camp in Koblenz. Her parents died in the war."

"Oh." Gilly couldn't think of anything appropriate to say. He wanted to reach out and gently touch her.

"This is too much," Elizabeth said, swaying as she left the room. "I better go open the wine."

There was an awkward moment of silence and Maggie said, "Prison must be a very strange place. Myself, I am fascinated by strange places. You will tell me about it, Geelly?"

"What — what kind of strange places?"

"Oh — prisons — camps — monuments — any place which has a story. I look at the — aa — charts ——?"

"Maps?" Gilly suggested.

"Yess, maps — and the world is full of wonderful strange places. You believe too, ya? — I see by your smile."

Jensen looked back and forth at the two youngsters. "Hey, take it easy, honey — or this galloot's going to fall in love with you! You know there mustn't be complications for your plans."

But it was too late. When the girl and her guardian turned and walked in laughter toward the dining room, Gilly could only shamble behind like a trained bear, hopelessly in love.

13

Bart Fester was in agony. Not only had he somehow offended Rizutto at last night's hockey game, but also everyone was holding him personally responsible: the Mayor, the Chief of Police, even the Premier. He ached from head to foot with the bruises he had got when that damned kid had pushed him ass-over-teakettle into the crowd. Now, if they didn't get professional hockey in Regina, he was as good as finished. To top it all off, another cold front was blowing in from the north. He sat at his desk trying to decide whether or not to phone the eccentric millionaire.

The whole crazy ball of wax really began to unravel when Fred Twamley phoned. "Hi Bart, how's she hangin'?"

"Straight down, Fred. Straight down. What's up?"

"Boy, that was some scene last night, eh? Good thing Vic got up and started talkin' off the top of his head like that. Got everybody calmed down. Weird guy, that Rizutto."

"I don't even wanna talk about it."

"Just thought I'd tell you about another crazy thing he did."

"Oh?"

"You remember yesterday when he bought those new clothes and left his old ones behind? I was looking at the shirt this morning. It was made in Prince Albert Penitentiary!"

"How do you know?"

"Label inside it, on the collar. You figure that's how he made all his money? Wearing jail-made shirts? Pretty odd, anyway."

"Odd is not the word. That guy's an out-and-out *nut!*"

"Well, just thought I'd call and give you the gossip."

"So long, Fred," Bart said, his mind already racing ahead to the next question: what the hell was going on? Maybe this guy was a screwball Rizutto, a cousin impersonating the real George Rizutto Jr. He knew too much to be an imposter.

He phoned Dan Potz. "Dan, it's Bart Fester."

"What the hell do *you* want?" the Chief growled.

"Just a couple of things. Can you check on our eccentric millionaire?"

"Like what?"

"Oh — make sure he's who he says he is. There's something that doesn't add up."

"Listen, Fester, if you do one more thing to bugger up this hockey deal, I'm going to have *you* investigated."

Bart interrupted and told the Chief of Police the story of the shirt. Potz said he would phone back. In the meantime, Bart called Frank Gelowitz at the hotel. "Frank, has our American import been running up a big expense bill?"

Frank checked. "No, nothing spectacular. Couple of meals, some drinks."

"Any long distance phone calls?"

"Let's see — a couple to De Kalb, Illinois. That's where he's from."

"Yeah, yeah, I know. Okay, thanks."

Well, that checked out anyway. All Bart could do now was wait and see what this Rizutto had up his sleeve. He drummed his fingers on the desk until he gave himself a headache. The telephone rang.

"Bart? Potz here."

"Forget it, Chief. I just checked the hotel. He's the real thing. He's been phoning home to De Kalb."

"Well, hold onto your chair, Fester. I've just been talking to Staff Sergeant Harry Swift of the RCMP. Our boys have been working with him for three days trying to track down a guy by the name of Gilly Savard. Are you sitting down? He matches Rizutto's description a hundred percent! A master con, with a record as long as your arm."

"My God! He's got a bank account set up with Murray at the Royal! What time is it?"

"Ten-fifteen. I'll send over a couple of cars right now."

Bart took off running; the Royal was right around the corner. He and Potz's squad cars and Harry Swift's 1950 English Prefect arrived simultaneously to witness the same spectacle: Gilly Savard walking out the door, stuffing four thousand dollars into the inside pocket of his new fur overcoat. There was a rented silver Lincoln waiting at the curb with a girl from Office Overload seated behind the steering wheel. Gilly took one look at the gathering crowd, smiled his mysterious smile and bowed in welcome.

14

Scanning the pages of *The Toronto Star* a few days later, a freelance filmmaker came across this item:

CON ARTIST
DUPES MAYOR

Regina (CP) — A bunco man with steel nerves and a brassy style pleaded guilty today to charges of fraud and false pretences and was sentenced to three years in prison.

Court was told that a former Saskatoon man had duped Mayor Sefton Gorius of Regina, Barton Fester, the city's Industrial Commissioner, and most of the city council with plans for a new commercial enterprise in Regina.

There was no loss of money reported.

The filmmaker had been looking for just such a story — something with substance and dramatic flair, something "television," which would make the producers sit up and blink. There was only one con artist with that style who would be likely to show up in Regina. He remembered his days as a cub reporter there, the slow circling-in to the city on Swift's wall map, and he reached for his telephone. Bart Fester had been one of his contacts on the City Hall beat.

Bart was naturally evasive on the telephone. "There's no news in this! Just a nut trying to get a few free lunches."

"Was his name Gillman Savard?"

"You know him?"

"I'd like the whole story — how he pulled it off, the names of all the people and so on."

"Is this for publication?"

"I want to do an item for CBC television."

"Television? Listen, we're already getting clobbered by the local media on this!"

"Look at the other side of it. It's publicity. You'll be on every TV screen in the country. You can do your promotion song-and-dance."

134

"You guys always edit that stuff out," Bart said petulantly. But he finally gave the filmmaker all the information he had. The story never did appear on television, but it started a thick file in the filmmaker's office. He had a hunch that some day Gillman Savard would be the inspiration for a great movie. He made a note to write to him at Kingston Penitentiary.

THREE
CALGARY

It was without a compeer among swindles. It was perfect, it was rounded, symmetrical, completely colossal.

Mark Twain,
Life on the Mississippi

1

While Gilly served slow time in Kingston Pentitentiary, he began a correspondence which later supplied most of the details of his story. The filmmaker wanted to do a full-length documentary on Gilly when he was released. However, by the spring of 1967, when Gilly was scheduled to get out of Kingston, the filmmaker had moved west again and had become a producer-director in Vancouver. He was a young man on his way to the top, the whiz kid of the communications industry, equally adept behind a camera or on the telephone. Canadian television had come of age with the celebration of Centennial Year. In Vancouver, his camera crew was recording every Centennial project in sight, with footage left over to document the flower children at English Bay. The young liberated middle-class was flocking to Canada's sunshine coast.

Gilly wrote to say that *he* was planning to travel to Vancouver so that his story could be made into a documentary film. The producer replied, politely postponing the project and Gilly's request for expenses until after the Nanaimo-Vancouver Bathtub Race — when the priorities for the season would be more clear. He promised to keep in touch, but in the bustle of Centennial madness, he forgot about the proposal.

So it was with some surprise that the producer received an envelope from Gilly in September with a B.C. postmark. Inside, there were two pieces of paper. One was a sheet of lined paper with the return address of #3914, P.O. Box 150, New Westminster, B.C. It said:

As you can see by the letterhead, I am still unsuccessful in my attempts to remain independent of this country's penal system. However, when the skating season begins, maybe I can pull a "Lucien Rivard" and get out to do the show that we talked about.

It now appears as though I will be behind bars for some time to come, though I am trying for a transfer to William Head, a minimum security institution on Vancouver Island. In the meantime, you might like to visit me here and carry out some of the interviews you planned. If you want to travel from Vancouver, get in touch with my C.O. (Classifications Officer) and she will set up an appointment.

Are you still a Saskatchewan Roughriders' fan? It may look *at the moment* like they will terrorize the opposition. But my Calgary Stampeders will eventually come through. You might like to put a little money on the outcome of the league, the way we did last year. It'll give me a sporting chance to win some of my money back.

Sincerely,
Gillman W. Savard.

The other piece of paper was a clipping from the front page of the July 27 edition of *The Kamloops Sentinel*:

APARTMENT PROMOTER ARRESTED

Gillman F. Savard, the man who represented himself as a wealthy building contractor in Kamloops last week, was sentenced to four years imprisonment Monday on several charges of fraud.

Savard, whose home town was given by police

as Brochet, Sask., was exposed when a tracer from *The Kamloops Sentinel* revealed that the B.C. Better Business Bureau had never heard of the firm Savard claimed to represent.

He was apprehended by the RCMP in the luxury suite he had taken at the Mountainview Motel and charged with the offences.

Last week, Savard announced at a press conference that he was planning to build a million dollar apartment block near the proposed site of Cariboo College. He had already deposited a fraudulent $45,000.00 cheque in the Royal Bank and had begun drawing on the account.

Other charges resulted from a bad cheque to the advertising department of *The Kamloops Sentinel* and a charge of public mischief transferred by the Calgary RCMP.

When asked why he had committed the crimes, Savard told the judge he had run out of money and felt that it was time for him to return to prison again as he had spent most of his adult life behind bars. The judge obliged him.

The producer asked his secretary to arrange an interview. He was curious to see if the con man had changed since he had first seen him in that Regina courtroom. Two weeks later, he drove inland along the Fraser River, twelve miles to New Westminster. He was escorted to a room with glass windows, at one of which Gilly soon appeared. They sat on each side of the glass partition and spoke through a telephone.

The producer noticed that Gilly's black hair had grown perceptibly lighter in colour. There was a slight salting of white at the temples which made him look even more distinguished. He appeared out of character in the khaki prison uniform.

"Well," Gilly grinned. "Ten bucks says the Roughriders won't make the playoffs."

"Ten bucks, it is. As long as you don't forget you still owe me a fiver from last season."

"Yeah — well, I would have paid you if I'd made it to

Vancouver. As you can see, I'm a few miles shy. I was going to do the great trans-Canada train ride, before the opportunity disappeared forever."

"I didn't think people travelled by train anymore. Not clear across the country."

"It was a personal Centennial project," Gilly smiled. "I've been thinking about it for a long time. Had all the places marked on my map."

"Something obviously went wrong."

"Yeah. Everything was fine till I got on the train in Toronto."

* * * * *

2

Sitting in Kingston Penitentiary after the debacle in Regina, Gilly thought a lot about Maggie and his failed search. Faith and stubbornness clearly had their limits. But without the image of her waiting, what meaning did his life have? Was it, as Clint Malach said, all an empty con game?

Certainly the world had conspired against them, almost from the beginning, when he had sat tongue-tied and foolish in the Jensen dining room as the meal proceeded to its tense conclusion. Maggie had tried to make tactful conversation about Gilly's life in prison, while Elizabeth Jensen gradually faded into a boozy coma. Finally, even Maggie fell silent and Jensen drove him back to his boarding house across the river.

This was the last time Gilly was invited to his employer's home, but Jensen could not be accused of snobbery. He simply wanted to see his protégé assume the role he had prepared for her in the new world. Jensen was a decent boss, friendly and anxious to see Gilly succeed. By the end of May, Gilly was promoted from the loading dock and put in charge of the office delivery van. He received a raise in salary to $8.00 a day.

Through Dumbell Carter, one of the drivers, Gilly was able to find a local rugby club which was looking for players. The Assassins were a motley band of ex-Britons who used rugby as an excuse to get away from their wives on Saturday afternoons and drink with the gang. They played in rags and running shoes and were chronically short-handed. Gilly, as a "colonial," was lumped in with a couple of Irish forwards and a New Zealander. They were allowed to play, but generally they were excluded from social life off the field. Gilly confirmed their low opinions of Canadians; he took little interest in their boasts of practical jokes and infidelities. He had memorized no raunchy drinking songs. He was usually treated with more respect by members of the opposite side, whether it was a team of touring Welshmen or a rugby gang from Winnipeg. By the middle of summer, Gilly played regularly at fullback and scored most of his team's points with the penalty goals he could kick from almost any distance.

By the end of summer, rugby ceased to interest Gilly very much. He dreamed of Maggie Steffen and the way her long dark hair bobbed above her shoulder blades; it was so different from the fashion of short "permed" hair. Her pale delicate face and dark eyes shone at him through a sentimental halo. He schemed of ways to see her again, constantly driving the delivery truck past Jensen's house for a glimpse of her.

They did meet again, by romantic coincidence, one Sunday in June when Gilly was running through the park along the west riverbank. He did this for hours on Sundays when the sun sparkled through the tall elms and the air rose from the flower beds in waves of pure oxygen. He would lope for miles and for many hours along the grassy paths, and would have done so on this day had he not collided suddenly with a bicycle going in the opposite direction. The collision sent the cyclist flying into a lilac shrub in a blur of ankle-length skirt. As she struggled from the bush, Gilly realized to his horror that he had knocked down the girl he adored. He curbed his impulse to flee the scene and plucked her bicycle free from the branches.

"Aa! You are Geellman!" she cried.

"Yes. Yes, I am. I — I'm sorry I —"

"Never mind," she laughed. "Is good joke. I don't usually watch people running in zis park. Now I will keep my eyes — grated?"

"Peeled."

"But my poor bicycle. Is it fractured?"

Blushing bright red below his dark crewcut, Gilly pulled the bicycle upright and studied it.

"Were you planning anything especial?"

'No, no, just running," he explained, giving his legs a couple of illustrative pumps. "I like to run."

She smiled a heart-melting smile and he stood transfixed. "Would you go in my direction for some distance?"

He nodded, his voice gone. Together, they rambled through the park, past the bridges and the towered Bessborough Hotel which looked over the river like a medieval castle. Maggie's bicycle was an expensive English racing model, with the top bar removed to accommodate her long skirt. He trotted beside her, entranced, until they reached the foot of University Bridge which crossed the river in a series of looping arches. On the east side of the bridge were the greystone buildings of the university.

"This way!" Maggie cried, whizzing up the half mile of sloping incline. As they neared the top, she slipped her machine into top gear and, with a saucy wave of the hand, disappeared into the maze of green avenues. For a moment Gilly stood gazing at the exclusive houses. She had disappeared from sight. Late for supper and dejected, he trotted back across the bridge to his boarding house on Avenue F. He spent the rest of the night in front of his landlady's radio. It was the best night of the week — Edgar Bergen and *Amos 'n' Andy* — but Gilly couldn't listen. In his imagination, all he could see was the flutter of Maggie's slim hand as she disappeared among the mansions on Temperance Street.

It would have been unwise, he knew, to ask Earl Jensen about her. She had a special significance to his boss that Gilly recognized, but did not understand. Jensen often spoke of her, but she was in some untouchable realm across the river, one that his workers did not invade lightly.

Gilly began haunting the parks along the riverbank on Sundays and after work. Driving his truck, he scanned the streets looking for a purple racing bike. Then, in July, while loping along Spadina Crescent, he saw her bike. She was nearly a mile ahead, past the dam, but there was no mistaking the long green skirt and the flying hair. He sped over the grass, leaping bushes and ploughing through flower beds, but she disappeared from sight. He re-doubled his efforts, taking a diagonal route to intercept her, and came hurtling out of the greenery directly into her path, once again knocking down the bicycle and sending his dream rolling along the ground in a cloud of dust.

This time, however, he had prepared some lines of conversation.

"Hi!" he said, lifting her onto the path with one hand. "Fancy meeting you here!"

"Aah," she said with a shy sideways smile that he immediately committed to memory. "Want to go for another run?"

Gilly blushed. "If we go across the bridge, you'll have to slow down."

"But if I did, you would follow me home, and zat is not appropriate. I must disappear — like Zinderella and ze Magic Pumpkin."

"Let's go a different way then. Along the river. We've got the rest of the afternoon!"

She smiled at him. "You don't like challenges, Geelly? When you play your football games, are you zurrendering before the match begins?"

Gilly resisted this dangerous invitation. Instead, they strolled along the path discussing the hot dry weather which shimmered around them. Gilly walked with his arms across his chest, clutching at his armpits to cover his sweaty smell. "Would you like to go somewhere?" he said.

"I know, Geelly! Why don't we go to the hotel for a lemonade?"

"The Bess?" He pointed in surprise at the Gothic turrets climbing toward the sun. "We can't go in there!"

"Who tells you we can't? Come on."

They parked her bicycle at the door of the hotel. She took Gilly's arm and they stepped past the startled doorman. Gilly was so electrified by the touch of her fingers that he didn't even notice when the lemonade and hot buttered tea-cakes arrived. She was telling him about her trip from Europe with the Jensens on the *S.S. Queen Elizabeth*.

"Why did you leave?" he asked curiously.

She looked at him, confused. "There was nossing. My family was dead. The city was bombed. No one could help me."

"No jobs?"

"But I — you see, I have no training. That is, I knew English and French from school, but — unless you were a prostitute —"

"Were there many uh —?"

"Armies of zem. It was the only way for sousands of girls."

They agreed to meet the following Sunday in the park. But the days passed like years and Gilly began to suffer the fever of the stricken. Hot flushes would send him suddenly reeling across the Motormack loading dock, moaning, "Maggie, Maggie," still trying to hide his affliction from the curious truckers. The bottom would fall out of his stomach without warning, like a sudden ascent in an elevator, when he wondered if she might not show up again. He avoided Jensen, knowing he would blush and tremble if Maggie's name was mentioned. He knew he would be fired instantly if his boss ever found out.

As the product of a household with no privacy, Gilly was not ignorant of the grammar of sex. He had watched the senior students at Meadow Lake grappling in the trees behind the baseball diamond. And the exaggerated accounts of Crab Campbell and Clint Malach had given him some idea of sexual adventures, but he could not associate Maggie with the tension he felt in his loins.

In that Saturday's rugby game, Gilly played his position like a spastic, dropping easy catches and punting short dribbling kicks which the opposition accepted as the gifts they were. The Englishmen refused to talk to him after the game and he went home by himself counting the hours until he would see her again.

At eight o'clock Sunday morning, he was galloping from one end of the park to the other, trying to relieve his anxiety. The clock in front of the newspaper office indicated five hours until the appointed time.. He veered between cold despair that he would never see her again and wild leaps of ecstasy as he imagined he saw her purple bicycle coming down the path. He was plunged into gloom again if it were a couple of boys pedalling past on their way fishing.

When two o'clock came and she had not arrived, Gilly

was hysterical. He dashed from one path to another, criss-crossing the park, looping around the hotel, running back past the clock. By three p.m., he knew she would not come, but he could not leave. He was still running up and down the paths when the streetlamps were turned on at ten o'clock, though he was exhausted and his feet were blistered. He ran once more to the bridge, looking across it to the east. For a long time, he contemplated the cool dark river sliding along below him. He walked home thinking Crab and Clint might be right. Maybe it was true that women were bitches, that they were evil sirens who broke one's heart. But he knew he would be back running in the park the next day. And the next.

* * * * *

3

Gilly had taken the bus from Kingston to catch the midnight train from Union Station. For once, with three years of prison savings, he was going to travel in style: drawing room, full meal service and all tips covered. He planned to sit in the glass-bubble dome car and watch the country roll by from Toronto to Vancouver and the warm Pacific. There would be a new beginning *there*, even if the movie came to nothing.

At the station, he had his shoes polished at the brass-and-marble shoeshine stand. People bustled everywhere, charged with the electricity of travelling to new and different places. It was the end of June and school was out. Chased by exasperated parents, children were running in all directions.

He climbed onto the end car of the train, where the porter showed him to his bedroom. He set the "GOV'T. OF CANADA" club bag on the bed and flashed him a wide grin. Gilly strolled the corridor, through the half-a-dozen Pullman cars which were being made up into berths, and into the bar car. He had just sat down to taste a glass of beer when he heard Clint Malach's familiar voice crackle in his ear. "How ya doin', Gilly, my boy? All set to take the world by storm?"

"Jesus!" Gilly leapt to his feet. "Where'd you come

from?"

"Oh, I been waitin' for ya, Gilly. Been doin' perty good since I left Regina. And you? How was dirty old Kingston?"

"Just what I expected. Rougher than P.A. Rotten hockey team."

"You all ready to dazzle the world with your brilliant talent?"

"I'm not looking for a job, if that's what you mean. I'm headed for Vancouver."

"So I heard. So I heard."

The train eased gently out of the station, a tunnel wall sliding past the windows as they watched. The skyline of Toronto burst abruptly into view, a golden array of lights against the midnight sky. Gilly suddenly recalled Crab Campbell and his stories of the fabulous cities. The train picked up speed, clicking westward over the rails, as he watched the glow of the lights fade behind.

"Still in the Vitalife business, Clint?"

"Naa. That ended up a real drag. Not my bag."

"Got caught?"

"To hell, I got caught! There was nothing illegal with that con shot!" He glowered into his beer. "Got me for something else."

"Same old luck."

"A liquor rap, while I was entertaining a lady Vitalifer at Waskesiu. Then a lot of old bum raps caught up with me. Two years in Stoney Mountain."

"Are you going to tell me why we are both on the same train travelling west?"

Malach's lined face rearranged itself into a grin. "I got a business proposition for ya."

"I don't want to know about it."

"When are you gonna grow up, Gilly my boy? I tried to do you a favour last time and you wouldn't listen! So you went and pulled down three years — for what? For nothin'! You shouldn't listen to yourself, ya know that?"

"I got a chance to do something different now. A movie."

Malach stared at him in disgust. "You're gonna make a movie? As a goddam con man? You better get yourself certified!"

"So, what's your scam?"

148

"I knew you'd come around!"

"I'm curious, that's all."

"Okay. What's the biggest thing going on right now?"

"Mini-skirts?"

"No, but you're close."

"Expo '67?"

"You're getting hot. *The Centennial Celebration* — right? Millions of people across the country, singing their hearts out with 'O Canada' and waving maple leaf flags, eh? And this is just the start of it! You watch the wave of patriotism that follows! It'll be the greatest gimmick to hit the public since they invented tits!"

"So what are you promoting — flags?"

"All of it! Flags! Maple leaf wallets, maple leaf jackets, maple leaf kitchen sinks! Stuffed Mountie dolls! Beadwork beavers! Gilly, we are gonna make a *bundle*!"

"Sounds kinda silly to me."

"Well, you sleep on it for a day or two. We got all kinds of time before we get to Calgary."

"I'm not going to Calgary. I'm going to Vancouver."

Malach grinned and ordered another round. That night, Gilly lay in his bunk drinking beer, watching the countryside roll past in the moonlight. They were only two hours out of Toronto and already they were in the wilderness. He fell asleep before Sudbury, where a Montréal section joined the train. The jolt woke him up and he couldn't sleep for a long time. He was thinking about Clint Malach and the flags.

In the morning, Lake Superior flashed in and out of sight, among the rock falls along the track. Gilly quickly got up and walked to the dining car, where the waiters swayed along the aisle with trays of oatmeal porridge, juice and coffee balanced on their fingertips. He sat down at a vacant table, admiring the starched white linen tablecloth and the slender silver vase which sprouted a fresh rose. Life — for a passing few seconds — was perfect. At that moment, Malach appeared looking rumpled and snarly.

"What's wrong with you? Sleeping in a daycoach?"

"I'm in a roomette! You know what a roomette is?"

Gilly shook his head and ordered another cup of black coffee.

"It's a ladies' can with a bed on top of it! Don't ever try

to sleep in one after drinking eight beers. God. I nearly killed myself."

They spent the morning in the dome car watching moose browse in the clearings along the track on one side, while on the other side, the waves of Lake Superior crashed against the rocks.

"You see these towns we're going through, Gilly? Notice all the Centennial signs? All over the country! Every little place has its own Centennial project. Look! Even in Schreiber, fer Crissakes!"

Gilly wondered what was happening in Brochet. He could see his mother making a Centennial quilt the way she had knitted Victory socks during the war.

"Well — what's so special about Calgary?"

"In Calgary, my boy, is the Calgary *Stampede*! It opens Monday. I'm setting up a Centennial Booth there and we're going to give the public a chance to buy this stuff. You and me."

"Who's providing this stuff?"

"I got backers, don't worry. Smart fellas. They got booths at all the big fairs. C.N.E., Expo. You and me handle the western circuit."

"Why me?"

Malach gazed at him with a fond contempt. "I knew you would ask that! Same old story, Gilly. All I want you to do is stand there and look handsome. I'll do the talking. But I got a spiel you can learn. Now just lay back and enjoy the scenery. Hey, lemme have a look at your map."

Gilly listened through Fort William and Kenora as Malach raved about the key chains and the maple leaf coffee mugs. In Winnipeg, they got off the train when it halted in the station. It was here, Malach said, that Gilly would meet one of his backers. He would be joining them on the train for the rest of the journey. They strolled into the cavernous lobby which fronted the station like a cathedral. A small, ferret-like man in a striped business suit was loitering near a pay phone.

"There he is. Hey, Pepsi!" Malach ran over and grasped the man's hand. "Pepsi, this is the guy I told ya about — Gilly Savard."

Pepsi was perhaps five feet four in elevator shoes. He had a wide grin, full of corn-coloured teeth, and a pencil

150

moustache under a flattened nose. "Let's get on the goddam train," he said. "There's a cop eyeing me."

Across the lobby a crewcut young man in a sports shirt was peeking at them through the curtain of a photo machine.

"Okay," Malach said. "I got ya a roomette next to mine. You bring the Ookpiks?"

They hurried back to the train, although it was not due to leave for half an hour. As Malach and Pepsi disappeared toward the bar car, Gilly went to his bedroom and lay down. He watched the sun set over the maze of tracks in Winnipeg's massive railway yards as the train pulled out, carrying them west.

Malach and Pepsi showed up at his room an hour later with a bottle of whiskey. Gilly had been studying the vast prairie which was scudding past in the moonlight, marvelling at the way it all receded until nothing was left but the great expanse of space between him and the distant stars.

"Gilly, you gotta see this! It's gonna put us in Rio de Janeiro. Show him, Pepsi!"

The little man reached into his jacket pocket and extracted a brown scrap of fur. He turned it over to demonstrate a pair of eyes sewn onto it and two hands, one of which waved a tiny maple leaf flag.

"This," Malach exclaimed, "is an Ookpik!" It had been designed by a sweatshop in Hamtramck, Michigan, and looked like a cross between a cute Eskimo and a stoned owl. It wholesaled for $4.00 a hundred and sold over the counter for $4.00 apiece. And it was completely legal. Pepsi had sales permits, licences, invoices — all the paperwork.

He had a number of other hot items, too, like tiny corked bottles of Ottawa air and fake coins of prominent Canadians. Then Pepsi proudly revealed the deluxe item, a Sooperkik. This was an Ookpik cut from a mink pelt and adorned with fourteen-carat gold eyes. It retailed for $56.00.

"Who would pay $56.00 for *that*?" Gilly asked indignantly.

Pepsi and Clint just laughed and put it away, patting the Sooperkik's furry little head. They went back to the bar car to celebrate as Gilly tried to get some sleep. But as the train rolled closer to Regina through the night, he kept seeing Maggie's shy sideways smile.

Maggie flashed her smile at him the following Sunday in the riverbank park beside the bandshell, waiting for him to run past as though the previous Sunday had never occurred. "Where haf you been, Geelly?" she said coyly.

To calm his anguish, she explained that the Jensens had invited her on a surprise drive to Pike Lake for a picnic. She had tried to argue, but could not stay behind without exposing their secret. She could not telephone him either because she didn't know the number of his rooming house.

"It's okay," Gilly said. "I wasn't worried."

"But we must not let that happen again, Geelly. I was so frantic, sinking of you here in the park. I tried to throw a message to you with my mind. We must tell them."

"Tell who?"

"Tell the Jensens that we — see each other."

"No, no, we can't. Jensen is my boss! And his wife — she's not used to — people like me."

"People like you?"

"You know. She's — educated."

Maggie laughed. "No, Geelly. Education *frees* people from class distinctions! Besides, zis is not Europe! You are a classless society in America, Geelly!"

"I suppose," he said glumly, pushing her bicycle along as they walked toward the hotel.

"Anyway, we must do *some*thing. It is absurd for us to meet in this park like athletes."

"What do you want to do?"

"You must come to the house and escort me out some-where. Perhaps we go to a play. Or a movie."

"I'm going to get a car pretty soon," he said. "As soon as I save five hundred bucks. Then we could go to a drive-in! Or a ride out in the country. Maybe even take a trip to Regina!"

"What is Regina?"

"I've never been there, but it's really neat. A guy I know used to tell me about it. It ain't very far. It's got a lake in the centre of it."

"Like Geneva," she sighed.

Over tea cakes, she told him of her dreams of travel around the world: to Paris, Rio de Janeiro, Hollywood,

Athens — all the glamorous cities in the world. Before the war, she had been to London with her parents and had seen Buckingham Palace and Tower Bridge. "Have you ever wanted to travel, Geelly?"

He told Maggie about his maps and about his plans to see all the cities and towns he had memorized. She promised to show him Elizabeth Jensen's big atlas, which contained every city and village in every country of the world. Together, they would tour them all — all those faraway places with the strange sounding names that they sang about on the radio.

The following Sunday, Maggie announced that their first date together would be to attend a performance of the Canadian Players in September. The touring company was presenting "Scenes from Shakespeare." Maggie had been reading the plays in English and pressed a copy of *Othello* into Gilly's hands.

"I'll try to read it," he said gazing at the book doubtfully. Pennistone had been a Shakespeare enthusiast, too, but Gilly had never advanced far in his appreciation of *A Midsummer Night's Dream*.

"I told Earl and Elizabeth we were going to the performance," she said. "It is approved."

"What did he say?"

"Well — he was upset."

"He doesn't think I should be going out with you."

"Yes, zat is true. He will get over it. He is not such an aristocrat himself."

But Jensen did not get over it. His attitude grew hostile and churlish; in all of Gilly's work, faults were now found. He had become a troubleshooter, delivering messages, supplies or men from one location to another. He had earned this position of trust. But he wanted to drive one of the big rigs.

On the Friday evening of their date, Gilly walked over the bridge and along the drive, knowing that there would be trouble. His feet munched through a carpet of dead leaves. He was wearing a new blue serge suit with padded shoulders and six-inch lapels and had splurged on a rich green tie with yellow hand-painted flowers and a large white "G" in the centre. A handkerchief blossomed from the right breast

153

pocket of his suit. He tapped the brass knocker on the door.

Jensen flung the door open. "Well, hello there! Do step in. *Maggie!*" he called. "Your boyfriend is here."

"I'm not her boyfriend," Gilly said nervously. "Yet."

"Where'd you get the tie?" Jensen said. "Paint it yourself?"

"No. They had a whole rack of them at Eaton's, with different letters. I got 'G' for Gillman."

"So I see."

"Well, I think it's charming," Elizabeth Jensen said, breezing into the living room. "Can I get you a drink, Gillman?"

"No thanks. We have to get going to the show. Starts in half an hour."

"Well, I hope you have a good time. It isn't often we get worthwhile theatre in Saskatoon. But of course, *we* aren't going."

"Don't you like Shakespeare, Mrs. Jensen?"

"Earl finds it boring. Don't you, Earl?"

A silence fell which was measured by the deep ticking of a clock in the hallway. Gilly gazed around the room. The Jensens maintained their silence. Once, when he glanced over at Mrs. Jensen, he was startled to discover her staring at his crotch. There was a deeply shocked expression on her face. Gilly's eyes flickered cautiously downward. He had forgotten to button up his fly. It was not only open, but gaping wide, revealing himself to the entire gathering.

Gilly's training as a fast-thinking scrum-half paid off; he surged to his feet and ran to the leaded Tudor window which looked out over the Jensens' spacious lawn. "Will you look at *that*?" he cried, pointing toward the yard in a transparent ploy to focus attention elsewhere. The Jensens looked out the casement to see what he was pointing at.

"My God!" Mrs. Jensen cried, reeling back in shock.

Gilly looked then where his finger was pointing. Against the sunset, a pair of dogs was silhouetted, a female Cocker Spaniel and a huge black Labrador, copulating in ecstatic fury in the middle of Jensen's manicured lawn.

Maggie rescued him at that moment by sweeping into the room. She looked radiant, twirling about in a bright yellow taffeta dress.

"Come, Geelly! We must go or we'll be late."

'You *did* say you were going to a play, didn't you?"

Jensen said.

"Yes, of course. It's at the university theatre. Why?"

"Just be sure you have her back by ten o'clock, Savard, or there'll be trouble."

Maggie sighed as they hurried down the street. "That man! He is as jealous as a lover. Or a father. Imagine — ten o'clock! He has no right to say things to me in that rude way."

"He said it to me."

"I hope he's not going to be difficult," Maggie sighed again. "Tell me, did you read about the noble Moor?"

Gilly admitted he hadn't understood much of it. And at the play, he wondered why Maggie preferred this silly play-acting to the real thing at the movies. The lines were right over his head. But it was wrong to blame Shakespeare with a girl beside him so enchanting, so unbearably sweet, that he could not take his eyes from her all evening. He sat with his muscles tightening like springs and sweated like a squeezed sponge. She hardly noticed him, so deeply was she being transported to ecstasy by the ranting actors.

After the performance, Maggie raved about the superb poetry and the catharsis in classical tragedy, none of which Gilly heard. He was staring into her dancing eyes.

"Geelly!" she cried. "It is decided. I will become an actress! A great actress! Don't you feel a similar call?"

"Aw, I could never get up in front of a bunch of people like that."

"Zen you shall be my manager! You will manage me to become the toast of New York and Berlin."

She chattered on as they walked home along the leaf-shrouded sidewalks. Gilly's mind whirled with doubts. What would he do when they got to the front door? Would she want to kiss? Did he know how? Gilly cursed himself for his lack of practice. At the last corner before the house, she stopped and looked up at him with an expectant smile. Her lips were poised, her eyes closed in shy expectation. Unmistakeably, she was inviting a kiss. It was the moment of truth.

"You wanna kiss?" Gilly stammered.

Her smile spread making it hard for her to keep her lips puckered. She nodded.

155

"Right *now*?" he wanted to know.

She opened her eyes and, still smiling, took him by the hand. When they reached the house and it was already too late, she turned and kissed him on his lips right in front of Earl Jensen who was watching from the front window.

"Goodnight, Geellman," she said, smiling her shy sideways smile.

He staggered down the steps to the street where he turned and waved once. Then he galloped back toward the bridge, halting occasionally to hug himself joyfully and leap into the air.

* * * * *

5

When the train rumbled into Regina at five a.m., Gilly was still tossing in his bed, wrestling with a vision which would not fade. He quickly got dressed and walked into the station. It was only a twenty minute stop, but there was time to go and look up her name in the telephone directory to see if somehow she had shown up again. Maybe he would get off the train and never get back on.

As he climbed the steps from the undergound passage to the station, he saw the young policeman from Winnipeg disappear into the building ahead of him. Gilly ran to the entrance and watched through the glass door as he marched up to a burly man who was lounging against the ticket counter and began an animated conversation with him. It was Staff Sergeant Harry Swift.

Gilly tiptoed back down the stairs. Fleeing to the train, he locked his door, threw himself back in bed and covered himself with blankets like a frightened child. Sleep was an impossibility; he was living a nightmare that was torturous enough in waking. As the train wheels clacked across the prairie to Calgary, he stared from the window with red, weary eyes, knowing that whatever happened in the next week, he was fated to have another tangle with the Law. All his resources would be called upon to survive this new test and if he wanted to come out of it whole, he would be wise to make all his moves with care. His life was like a train running down the tracks, a fired bullet over which he had no control or power. The only thing to do was hang in there and hope for the best — like the morning he had stood waiting at the door of the Saskatoon Bus Depot and watched the clock creeping toward nine o'clock. The night before, he and Maggie had lain awake for hours, planning their escape. They had decided finally against buying a car and going to Regina. They would pool their resources and go to Hollywood where Maggie would become a famous movie actress and where Earl Jensen would never find them. His sick jealousy and his threats would be left behind forever.

Gilly shifted the club bag at his feet, trying to hide the "GOV'T. OF CANADA" gilt lettering in case someone in the bus station thought he had stolen it. He had bought it at an early-opening second-hand store that morning for a dollar, leaving $147.00 more in his pocket. He was chilled from the walk through the rain and had to keep wiping his nose.

When the loudspeaker announced the boarding of the bus, he began to panic. Should he buy their tickets and get on, waiting for Maggie on the bus? Did he dare phone the house and see if she had left? Maybe Jensen had caught her sneaking in through the window of her room the night before. Maybe she had made up the whole fantasy. Maybe this was just another of his bright vivid nightmares.

As the second hand swept past 8:59 and began its inevitable revolution toward nine o'clock, Gilly knew *something* had gone wrong. He sat down on the bench in the station, hearing the motor of their bus to the faraway places cough into life and back out of the bay.

"Okay, Savard. Stand up!"

Earl Jensen towered above him, his handsome face twisted in rage. "Stand up, goddammit!"

When Gilly stood up, Jensen smacked him in the jaw, spinning him along the bench. Instantly, a crowd formed to watch the fight.

"I caught her sneaking into the house this morning. I knew she'd been out with you. It didn't take long to drag the truth out of her."

"Where is she?" Gilly said, trying to get up from the floor.

"*I'm* looking after her and she won't be seeing you again,

I'll make sure of that! She's *mine*, Savard — my ward! I'm not going to hand her over to some halfbreed scum!" He pulled a cheque out of his shirt pocket and flung it at Gilly. "That's whatever pay you've got coming. I don't want to see you around again. Is that clear? My advice is to head back to wherever you came from. Don't bother going back to your room, either. You forgot to tell your landlady you had skipped out — so I told her for you."

Gilly watched him stomp out the door to his wife's Monarch which was parked at the curb. In the back, Maggie was crying and fighting with Elizabeth Jensen, trying to open the door and jump out of the car. Gilly tried to run after the car, but it accelerated and was gone.

The first snow of the year began to fall as he trudged down First Avenue, trying frantically to think out his options. He couldn't leave the city without Maggie. But did he have a choice? Where could he go for help? Who would believe Jensen was not just a loving guardian? Why didn't Elizabeth Jensen see her husband's unhealthy obsession and do something? Could he turn to *her* for help? Certainly no one at the truck depot would dare to help him now.

Then Gilly remembered Clint Malach and the Westbury Hotel. He crossed below the underpass and went along Twentieth Street to a row of seedy hotels and pawnshops. He asked the desk clerk in the lobby of the Westbury if he knew where Clint Malach might be found.

"Um," the man said, not looking up from his newspaper.

"I'd like to get in touch with him."

"Who are you?"

"Name's Savard. We knew each other in P.A."

"Beer parlour's open at eleven. Probably catch him then."

Malach drifted in at noon, wearing a wide-shouldered "Zoot" suit and a big fedora, grinning his wrinkled grin and looking as brash as ever. "Gilly, my boy! How's life treatin' ya?"

"I got a problem, Clint."

"You look like it! Whad she do, throw ya out inna street?"

He brayed with laughter as Gilly told him the story, finding none of it surprising. "No problem at all, old buddy. I'll have a couple of my boys check it out right away. We'll get word to the dame and before ya know it, you'll be ridin' off into the sunset."

"But we have to find out whether it's illegal! What he's doing, I mean. And if we can get into trouble?"

Malach looked at him pityingly. "Gilly, my boy, I woulda thought you'd picked up more smarts by now, the length of time you been out. Just leave it to me, will ya? In the meantime, you stay here and warm yourself up with a couple of draft. I gotta make a phone call."

When Malach returned, he told Gilly about his scheme to bring three-dimensional movies to the city. All he needed was the backing of *one* movie house, but the bastards were scared of trying anything new. Television had just arrived on the scene and they were all frightened silly of losing money. All he needed was a trained 3-D camera operator, like the guy from the States he had met in P.A., to show them the thing worked. If Gilly could just pick up the lingo of that guy from California, they would all be rolling in money. Then there would be no problem with this Jensen creep. Money solved everything.

Two days later, Malach walked into the Westbury beer parlour with the news. "De Kalb, Illinois," he said.

"What's that?"

"That's where he sent the girl of your dreams, my boy. A girl's boarding school in the States. Royal Oak College, it's called. Seems like he's determined to put her out of your reach."

"I'll go and get her!"

"Not so hasty, Gilly my boy. How are you going to get across the border? Have you got a visa? Not with a criminal record, you don't. They ask questions, you know."

"I'll worry about that when I get there."

"We need somebody here to run this 3-D equipment, Gilly. Lotsa money in it for you and it's suppose ta be real easy to learn."

But Gilly was already gone out the door. The only attraction in his life was 1,300 miles to the southeast, in another country and across a dozen colours of the atlas. There was nothing to keep him in Saskatoon.

6

"What's wrong with you?" Pepsi asked when Malach pushed Gilly, white-faced and tense, into the taxi from the Calgary train station.

"Maybe he's not cut out for long train rides."

"Okay, now here's the drill. We'll go to the hotel and check in, then head over to the Stampede Grounds and make sure the stuff got here. Then we can start getting the booth stocked today."

The taxi took them to the Ace Hotel, just off the Centre Street Bridge, in the old Chinatown district. Gilly rebelled. "Why do we have to stay in a dump like this if we're each clearing a thousand a week?"

Pepsi flashed a grin of yellow teeth. "It's because of the fuzz, Savard. Might be okay for you and your joe-college charm to mix with the highrollers, but the rest of us attract cops."

Gilly remembered the young Mountie on the train and was mollified. Maybe the police were after *these* guys after all, and not him. "Okay," he said. "But as soon as I draw some pay, I'm moving into a decent place."

"Anti-social sunnuvabitch, ain't he?" Pepsi grinned. "Now, whaddaya say we go and have a look at all the chuckwaggins and cow shit?"

From the gate of the west end of the grounds, the Stampede midway appeared like a futuristic city under construction. Crews tore around in tractors and trucks, installing water and electricity to service the strange metropolis. Along the centre of the midway, shops and booths were being thrown up with incredible speed: casinos, sideshows and hamburger joints. They walked past fire stations and toilets and ambulance posts, banks of digger machines, carny games and girly shows. The Fun House stood at one end, an enormous clown's head which nodded in laughter, mocking the scene. Behind it they could see the steel webs of the airplane rides and the ferris wheels. Workers and shills and bright-eyed schoolboys climbed and sweated and strained to have it all in place for the next morning when the great Stampede began, when a hundred thousand people would burst through the gates eager to buy a few hours of escape from their mundane lives.

Pepsi's Centennial Booth was a pitchman's dream. They could see it a hundred yards down the midway, an enormous multifaced glass box shining in the sun like a diamond, surmounted by a bank of flagpoles waving red and white Canadian flags. Loudspeakers crowned the roof, surrounded by high-beam searchlights to keep the jewel glittering long into the night.

The truck from Detroit was being unloaded, the boxes stacked in the centre of the booth. The three men had the shelves filled and everything in place by six o'clock.

"Me and Malach are gonna get a hamburger and go over the pitch for a while, Savard. I want you to go and impress some people." Pepsi handed Gilly an engraved invitation which invited the manager of the Centennial Booth, Stampede Licence #316, to the crowning of the Stampede Queen at seven p.m. in the Glenwood Club. It was for selected exhibitors and Stampede officials.

"Why don't you go?" Gilly said, hoping to get out and explore the city.

"Quit asking stupid questions, Savard. Just go and look patriotic. You might even enjoy it. Meet a few heavies."

Gilly certainly enjoyed the iced champagne and sculptured mounds of caviar. Wearing a name tag that said "Gillman H. Savard, Director, Centennial Promotions Commission," it was not long before Gilly found himself in earnest conversation with one of the heavies, C. Francis Goodman, a top executive of the world's wealthiest oil company and a director of the Stampede. Among dozens of other corporate directorates, Francis Goodman also sat on the board of the Calgary Stampeders football club, a fact which ensured Gilly's attention. This man had free tickets to all the home games.

"Fantastic show, eh?" Goodman observed.

"Very impressive."

"The Queen is coming up next. Wait till you lay eyes on *this* hunk of flesh, Gillman!"

"You know who it is already?"

"Well, not officially — but the Queen was picked weeks ago. We have to keep it a secret till the grand moment. There she is now."

161

The future Stampede Queen was a stunning redhead of eighteen who was doing her best to pretend she didn't know the outcome. But her smile couldn't stop condescending to the two also-rans who flanked her.

"How do they pick them?" Gilly said.

"Usual thing. Intelligence, good looks, measurements, charm. It was pretty close this year, but Julie there had the inside track — her uncle's a Liberal senator. But Sherry is the best in bed."

Sherry was a black-haired beauty with a siren smile and the subtlety of a Stampede bronco. She was ignoring the Queen-to-be and attracting her own, much larger, circle of admiring men. The third girl was a vacant blonde who Goodman said was a niece of one of the Stampede directors.

"When is the first football game this year?" Gilly said finally.

"Well, let's see — there's an exhibition game in about two weeks. Are you a Calgary fan?"

"Is the Pope Catholic?" Gilly grinned. "I know the Stampeder play-book better than your quarterback does."

"Oh? You go to a lot of games?"

"Let's say I'm a distant fan. I've probably seen every Stampeder game televised."

"Really? Did you used to play football or something?"

"Here and there. Not professionally. Played English rugby for a while."

"Hey, how'd you like to come out and watch a Stampeder practice on Wednesday night?"

Gilly's face lit up in boyish excitement, though he half expected to see the prize taken back. "I wouldn't mind. Does it cost anything?"

Goodman laughed. "Not when you're with a club director. I'll introduce you to the boys. In the meantime, you can do me a favour."

"Oh?"

"Not a big one. We need an escort for one of the Stampede Princesses."

"One of *them*? Right now? Which one?"

"Sherry. Not tonight, though. At the parade tomorrow. You get to ride in a Caddy convertible through the city."

"I don't get it. Why me?"

"Well, I was supposed to do it myself but — she's a little sore about losing the contest."

A swell of applause filled the ballroom as the judges mounted the platform. The three girls followed with dazzling smiles, as though still eagerly awaiting the results. The little blonde burst fetchingly into tears when she was announced as the Second Princess. Sherry flashed a wide brilliant smile and hugged the winner when she was acclaimed First Princess. Then she hugged the judges, completely stealing the show from Julie, the Queen, who could only manage a modest acknowledgement.

"Okay," Gilly said. "But I have to check with my partners just to be sure they don't need me in the morning."

"I'll send a car around to pick you up. Where you staying?"

"I don't uh, have a place yet. What's a good hotel?"

"Calgary Inn, if you can get a room. Didn't you make a reservation?"

"Uh no . . ."

"Let me look after that for you," Goodman said magnanimously. "The Inn has a block of rooms they're holding for the Stampede. Just give them my name. Now come and meet your Princess."

Gilly excused himself to go to the washroom before the introduction. While standing at the urinal, he became aware of another man standing before the porcelain on his right. Gilly glanced at him and his bladder nearly seized up. It was the cop from Winnipeg. He must have followed him to the reception.

Turning hastily to escape, Gilly fumbled his dribbling cock back into his fly and headed or the door. The policeman backed away from the urinal, stepping ponderously into Gilly's path.

"Hey — watch it, eh?"

"Sorry — I'm in a hurry —" Gilly murmured.

"Wait a minute. Aren't you Savard?"

"Um, yeah."

"Constable Summerville. C.I.D. I'm working undercover with Staff Sergeant Swift of Regina. Just a sec. He gave me something for you."

He took an envelope from inside his jacket and put it in Gilly's hand.

"What is it?" Gilly said cautiously.

"Three hundred and fifty dollars cash. Expenses for a week's work, at fifty bucks a day."

"For me?"

Summerville nodded. "We want you to keep us informed on what your friends are up to. Clint Malach and Pepsi Vaccarino."

"They're not up to anything. It's legit as hell! What's wrong with you guys?"

"If they're clean, then it's easy money for you, right? All you gotta do is keep us in touch."

"I'm not a stoolie. You're wasting your time," Gilly said, heading for the door. He stopped. "All I have to do is tell you everything we do?"

"That's the arrangement."

"Make it another fifty a day to cover my hotel and you've got a deal. Then you can reach me at the Calgary Inn from now on. I'll be there tonight, but I don't want to be disturbed."

He left the detective in the washroom and entered the luxurious ballroom with its shimmering cut glass and crystal. Goodman was whispering in Sherry's ear. Gilly smiled and waved, then hurried toward them. At least he would not be going back to the Ace Hotel to face Pepsi's sinister grin and the endless exulting about all the money they were making.

* * * * *

7

Crossing the U.S. border into Minnesota, Gilly felt a weight drop from his shoulders, as though he had left history behind him forever. To avoid the customs authorities, he had driven a stolen car, a black '49 Ford, across the border on a dirt road just east of Emerson, Manitoba.

Although the highway stretched ahead for hundreds of miles, Gilly knew he would find her. This time he would plan their escape and it would be perfect. No one would trace them. As he sped along U.S. Highway 2, east of Crookston, the landscape changed from the vast flatlands of the Canadian prairies to the mixed-farm country of the midwest U.S. He drove for two days, through a thousand square miles of corn and soybean, through Bemidji and St. Cloud, Minneapolis and Madison. He plunged into America's heartland, where the autumn air seemed to shimmer with prosperity. The Burma-Shave signs and the Schlitz taverns welcomed him to a land of liberty that he recognized from magazines. Everyone talked in a real American twang, like the radio heroes of his youth. When he arrived in De Kalb, he was cresting on a new flame of confidence which was only slightly dampened by the reception in the drugstore where he asked for the Royal Oak Collge.

"You mind my askin' why you wanta know?" the clerk said, her eyes taking in his dusty clothes and unwashed facc.

"I gotta package I'm supposed to deliver to the office."

"We-e-lll. If you jus' take that first road north across the crick, you'll find it smack-dab on the other side. Ivy and stuff crawlin' all over it. Can't miss." She stared suspiciously after him as he ran out and jumped back into his Ford.

Gilly easily recognized the college from two blocks away, a mock Victorian confection, like a wedding cake gonc crazy. He kncw he could not just walk into the office and ask for Maggie, however. They had probably been warned about him.

There was a little malt shop called Hory's across the street from the main gate of the school. Inside, a couple of girls in stiff navy-blue uniforms were idling at the counter trying to persuade the soda jerk to put some money in the jukebox. They wanted to hear "How Much Is That Doggie in the Window?" Gilly studied the comic books until they left, then sauntered over to the soda fountain. "You Hory?"

"I'm Bud."

"I got a message I'm supposed to deliver to a girl at the school, Bud," Gilly said. "Guess you must know most of them, eh?"

"Most of 'em." Bud shrugged elaborately.

"This girl is a German girl. That is, she talks with a funny accent, you know?"

"There's a whole slew of 'em like that."

"She probably orders lemonade."

Bud's freckled face broke into a wide grin. "Maggie!"

165

"Right! You know her?"

"Naw — well, just the name. She don't talk much. But — lemonade, y'know?"

"Does she come in often?"

"Just Sundays. That's how I know her. Not many of 'em come in Sundays."

"Can I get inside there to see her?"

"No way. That place is like Alcatraz."

It was Wednesday. Gilly decided to execute his plan. He would find a job and earn some money for their escape. It shouldn't be difficult, he knew, in a town as wealthy as De Kalb obviously was. The school was surrounded by several columned old mansions, grander than anything he had seen, even in Saskatoon. A block down the street, he could see the biggest and most ornate mansion, a huge brownstone house controlling an acre of lawn, surrounded by service buildings.

"Who lives there?" Gilly pointed Bud toward the edifice.

"That's Rizutto's, mister. But they don't take in roomers, if you're looking for a place to live."

Gilly thanked him and strolled down the street. An old man was out on the Rizutto lawn, raking oak leaves into piles.

"Nope. I do all the gardenin' myself," the old man said, taking in Gilly's appearance at a glance. "But if yer interested, I think the boss is looking for a couple of hands out at the stables."

"Where's the stables?"

"Out in Kingston, about fifteen miles down that road. You tell 'em I sent ya."

Gilly drove down the road in a daze of self-congratulation. He was going to his first job in the Land of Opportunity. The head groom took one look at Gilly and said, "A Canuck, huh?" He hired him on the spot: twenty dollars a week and a bunk in the hostel, no questions asked about a work permit. He could have Sundays off and the cost of his stable boy's uniform would be deducted from his wages.

On Sunday, he borrowed all the money he could from the groom, bathed and put on his best clothes. Consuming one lemonade after another, he waited at the malt shop under Bud's curious gaze. Then he saw her. She was walking across the street to Hory's, her shy smile glowing above her drab uniform.

She did not see him when she stepped through the door. As the doorbell's tinkle echoed in the room, her eyes glanced around the room at knee level. They stopped at Gilly's polished black Oxfords, hesitated, then widened in surprise as they took in the pair of familiar tweed pants, his red-and-yellow jacket and his steady grin. She dropped the book in her hand and ran to him, laughing, as he stood up to hug her. Bud, the soda jerk, stared trying to figure out what was going on.

They walked out into the cold sunny afternoon, telling their incoherent tales of despair and hope, parables of the enormity of time and space.

"I've got a job here, earning money for our trip," Gilly said. "Get ready as soon as you can. We can take off again on our journey to faraway places."

"How soon must we leave, Geelly? In three weeks, I start my Christmas exams."

"Well, I imagine Jensen will find out I'm here pretty soon. We shouldn't wait around too long."

"Earl said if I got into trouble here, he would send me back to Germany," she said, the tears filling her eyes. "I don't want to go back, Geelly. Maybe we should wait, ya?"

"It's too late now to do anything else. I'm getting everything organized. All we have to do is stay out of sight for a while. Don't you want to go to Hollywood?"

"Sometimes I think we should have gone to Regina, like you said the first time. Perhaps we are seeking too much."

"Next Sunday — just be ready to go. I'll wait for you here at the malt shop."

He walked her back to the school at six o'clock, when she was due to re-enter its grim exterior. The gate was almost identical to the one at the front of the P.A. Pen.

"I must go in now, Geelly. I see you next Sunday. You have your maps?"

"I don't need 'em anymore. Got the route memorized."

"No one can memorize a map," Maggie laughed. "I will go in now, before they come looking." They kissed again and she ran through the gate.

Gilly walked anxiously back to his car. Maybe they should have just gone, driven away while they had the chance. When they were separated, bad things happened. They must never be separated again.

* * * * *

8

Clint Malach was yelling from somewhere and there was pounding on a door. "Savard! I know yer in there! Wake up!"

Gilly staggered to the door and Malach burst in, tearing his hair and making terrible faces.

"You idiot!"

"I didn't get a chance to tell you, I changed hotels last night."

"Yeah, you forgot! It took me all morning just to find out where you were! I had to get that Goodman sunnavabitch out of bed at seven o'clock."

"Serves him right. Sit down and have a drink."

Gilly gestured at the half-full bottle of Southern Comfort on the dresser. Malach drank straight from the bottle.

"What's the problem?" Gilly said, getting dressed.

"What's the *problem*? You up and disappeared! We thought you'd split! We have to be ready for the big extravaganza! The gates open in two hours."

"Yeah, well, I won't be able to make it. I've been invited to ride in the parade with one of the Princesses."

Malach looked around the dishevelled room, at the empty glasses by the bottle, then back at Gilly. "You better talk to Pepsi about that," he growled. "He's already super pissed off."

"Well, go calm him down. I have to be at the parade route in half an hour. I'm gonna need Wednesday night off, too. I'm going to a football practice."

The heat outside was withering, at least ninety degrees Fahrenheit. Thousands of people jammed the streets under umbrellas and newspaper hats, waiting for the big parade. It was already due to start when he arrived. Sherry was perched atop the back seat of the convertible, bouncing with impatience, while the driver revved the engine, both of them anxiously looking around for Gilly.

He climbed into the car, eyes closed against the awful glare of the red leather in the broiling sun. The car swerved into its place in the parade and Sherry began waving dramatically.

"Where were you, you son of a bitch?" she hissed between her smiling lips.

"Slept in. It's been a long time since I spent an evening with a Princess."

"Bad enough I have a last minute replacement, but then he comes late!"

"That's not what you said last night."

They turned the first corner of the route and the crowd roared at the sight of the Princess, her white sunsuit and warm brown flesh dazzling their eyes.

"Just remember, big boy, this is *my day* and you better not do anything to fuck it up. If there was any justice, I'd be up there in the Lincoln and you'd be riding back here with that bitch!" The Queen was several cars ahead waving to an even greater swell of applause.

"Aw, Sher!" the driver said. "Quit bein' a poor loser."

"And you shut up or I'll tell your wife on you!"

After the first mile of parade route, they reached the tall petroleum buildings of downtown Calgary, where the crowds multiplied by the thousands. Gilly made a tentative wave or two at the crowd. They waved and yelled back. As he reached over and confiscated the driver's white cowboy hat, his hangover faded into the bright morning air. Everyone in sight was wearing cowboy hats, even the parading Blackfoot Indians and the Pincher Creek Junior Kinsmen Band and Fancy Marching Corps. Western costume was the style, from the Mounties to the firemen and clowns, and among half the politicians of Alberta. With a white ten gallon hat in his hand, Gilly could outwave them all.

"Who is that guy?" people yelled as the car passed.

"Tommy Hunter!"

"Naw, Tommy Hunter was last year! He had pimples!"

"Hoss Cartwright! It's Hoss Cartwright!"

"Don't be a knucklehead. Hoss is fat!"

Sherry kicked him in the back with a dainty silver slipper. "Keep still, you bastard!" she fumed, not missing a wave. She rolled her buttocks back on the seat, for her gold lamé panties to glitter in the sun. "It's *me* they want to see!"

169

As the parade rolled on, Gilly had to keep curbing his enthusiasm while the Princess worked at maintaining hers. When they arrived at the Stampede Grounds, Gilly stepped out of the car to go to work. "Thanks for the ride. What are you doing the rest of the week?"

"Get lost, creep."

He waved one last time and was swept away by the crowd streaming toward the gates. Inside the grounds, the big ferris wheels turned their first revolutions of the day. The Roll-o-Planes and the Octopus began to spin. As Gilly strolled by the Foot-Long Red-Hots and The Living Head and the weight-guessers, the amplified grating voices of the midway barkers crackled through the heat. As he passed The Fun House, he could see the Centennial Booth ahead, flashing like a diamond in the sun. Already, he could hear Malach's voice.

"Ladies and gentlemen, we now invite you to take part in the event of a lifetime, the one hundredth anniversary of the Confederation of this great country. This is our year of nationhood and pride. This is the year of *national celebration*!

"Now, we give *you* the opportunity to take part. If you saw the Centennial Train — if you saw the voyageurs paddling across the nation's waterways — if you *too* want to contribute to this great extravaganza of national pride — then enter our pavilion! Examine our display of national arts and crafts! This is no crude midway come-on, ladies and gentlemen! No hard sell and no soft sell. But an eye-dazzling display of beautiful art objects — which can be purchased, if you wish."

By noon, Gilly realized what a superb gimmick Clint Malach and his backers had stumbled onto. He could not fill the shelves with stock fast enough for each succeeding wave of grabbing hands. Malach stopped them cold in their streak along the midway. As Pepsi had predicted, the hottest items were the Ookpiks and the Sooperkiks. Exhausted, they sat around the booth that night munching on cold Stampede burgers while the lights went out along the midway. Pepsi had gone and placed a long distance call to the States for another consignment of goods to be shipped air express.

"I hear you went out and had yourself a good time last night, Savard."

"I tried."

"Where ya stayin' now?"

"Calgary Inn. Downtown."

"Just as long as we can count on you being here when you're supposed to be."

"I'll be here. Except Wednesday night. I want to see a football practice."

"A *what*?"

"He's a sports nut, Pepsi. The Stampeders are a big thing for him."

"Nothin' doin'. We need him here. I never heard of anythin' so stupid."

"It's okay, kid. You'll get another chance," Malach said. "You just keep givin' 'em that big smile the way ya did today. You notice that, Pepsi?"

"Yeah. Okay, let's get some rest. And if ya get anymore a that Princess treatment, Savard, send some of it our way, will ya?"

By Wednesday, however, the air shipment hadn't arrived and they were nearly out of stock. Pepsi swore heartily at the loss of revenue, but he gave Gilly the night off.

Gilly was just leaving the Stampede Grounds gates when Constable Summerville slipped discreetly out of the shadows, his close-cropped head gleaming with reflected neon. "What's the word?" he said conspiratorially.

"Well, we sold all the Sooperkiks, all the Ookpiks and nearly everything else. A few ashtrays left. Lots of bottled air."

"Bottled what?"

"Air from Parliament Hill."

"I'm not sure how useful this is, Savard."

'It's what you asked for, isn't it? Say, what's your first name, anyway?"

"Donald."

"Okay, Donald. You tell me what you want to know and I'll try to provide an answer. You got my hotel money?"

Summerville took another envelope from his pocket. "We're not really sure what's going on. But whatever it is, it's big. Your friend Pepsi has powerful connections."

"You bet it's big! We pulled in over fifty thousand in two days. But that's *legitimate*, Donald — so I still don't know what you want. By the way, does the expense money include meals?"

"It certainly does."

"Fifty lousy bucks a day?"

"Listen Savard, it's more than I get. And you just told me you're making thousands!"

"Well — I haven't got paid yet. Where's Swift, anyway?"

"He'll be here tomorrow. He'll probably want to talk to you."

"Yeah," Gilly said without enthusiasm. "Are you driving past McMahon Stadium by any chance?"

Summerville drove Gilly to the football field where the team was practising. Goodman met him at the gate and escorted him inside the empty stadium. "Coach doesn't encourage visitors," he said, "so we'll just stand over here out of the way."

They watched the players being pushed through calisthenics and field drills. The coach then sent the defensive and offensive squads off with his assistants and began supervising the new place-kicker. The kicker was a rookie who had difficulty finding the range of the goalpost.

"Look at that jerk," Goodman scoffed. "Can't put it through from ten yards out. I could do better myself."

"So could I," Gilly said. "From thirty yards."

"It isn't as easy as it looks, you know. Those guys are under a lot of pressure."

Gilly laughed. "I can boot a football through those uprights from forty yards out on the dead run."

Goodman gazed at Gilly thoughtfully, his eyes travelling up from his boots to his broad shoulders. "Where did you learn to do that?"

"In the uh, service. Playing rugby."

Francis Goodman immediately walked down to the field and spoke in urgent tones to the coach. It was worth a try; with the kicker they had, the Stampeders would be the league doormats in 1967. The coach was dubious, but told Goodman to bring his boy along on Friday and they would have a look at him. It wasn't a promise, but it was enough to plant the seed of an idea which sprouted and grew for the rest of the week inside Gilly's head.

9

After six days of slogging wheelbarrows full of horse manure out of the Rizutto riding stables, Gilly had worked up a lot of enthusiasm for the escape. On Sunday morning at five, he folded his red and white stable boy's uniform into his leather bag, raided the bunkhouse kitchen for all the food he could carry and drove into De Kalb. He parked the car at the rear of the malt shop and stretched out under a seat blanket to wait in the freezing darkness. By ten, she still had not come.

Gilly walked into the malt shop and confronted Bud. "You remember I was in the other day, looking for that girl?"

"Yeah," the boy said shiftily, looking across the street, and Gilly knew something had gone wrong. He grabbed Bud by his bow-tie. "Have you seen her since Sunday?"

"No."

Gilly punched him in the mouth. *"What do you know about her?"*

"She's in the detention unit."

"The what?"

"Detention! It's where they put runaways and trouble-makers."

"You mean she's in a *cell*?"

Gilly hustled the soda jerk outside to the car and smacked him several times across the face. "Did you tell them I was talking to her?"

"They — they came and asked. I'm supposed to."

Gilly took a step backward and kicked him in the testicles. As the youth bent over yelling, he clouted him twice more across the head to shut him up. "Now come and show me where she is, before I break your neck."

"I don't know where the room is. I never been inside."

"You know where the office is?"

"Yeah."

"Let's go." Pushing Bud ahead and slapping him across the back of the head, Gilly walked through the front gate. "You're going to tell them they made a mistake. You are going to say, this guy is a relative of Jensen's in Saskatoon. That's all you have to say."

"They won't listen to me."

"They will if you look desperate enough. Just remember I'll be waiting out here." Gilly punched him through the door marked "Office." He listened outside until Bud began whining and crying, then gave up in disgust. He was burning bridges anyway, so he might as well go out in a blaze of glory. He walked down the hallway until he saw a young girl beside a water fountain, staring at him.

"Where's the detention unit?" he asked.

She looked at him boldly. "Have you come to take Maggie?"

"Where is the goddam detention unit?"

She pointed upward.

"Can you take me?"

"Are you going to run away and get married?" the girl asked as they rushed down the hall. "I can help you."

"How?"

"There's a way out the back door."

Gilly looked at her again and saw a tiny, blonde girl with knowing eyes and an eager face. She was no more than thirteen. Too young to be a friend of Maggie's, but obviously a friend. "Can you drive a car?" he said.

"Can I!"

"There's an old Ford parked in the alley by the malt shop. Bring it around to the back entrance."

She took him upstairs to the senior residence and ran to get the car. The place was swarming with girls in various states of Sunday morning dress. They shrieked prettily as he walked past, giggling and making him blush. There was a door at the end of the hall with a wire grid on the window and a large Yale lock.

"Where's the key?"

"Lonnie's got a copy. Lonnie!"

One of the seniors ran forward with the key and opened the door. The room was full of mattresses bolted to the walls. There was a small bed and table in one corner where Maggie sat, staring in disbelief as he stepped inside and said, "Where's your bag?"

She pointed upstairs to another floor, her eyes filling with tears. "They took it."

"Never mind. Let's go."

She ran behind him, barefoot in her nightdress, as the girls clamoured their goodbyes. When they reached the hall on the ground floor, a posse from the office galloped toward them in full cry, Bud trailing behind them.

"Stand back!" Gilly roared, pointing his finger at them. "I've got a gun!"

The school administration retreated screaming down the hall. Gilly and Maggie turned down the stairs to the basement, running down a dark concrete corridor, past the gymnasium to the service entrance. The car was waiting there with the young girl at the wheel. She jumped out, bouncing with excitement.

"Geelly, we shouldn't!"

"I know, I know," he said. "But we're not making the same mistake twice. And we're finally on our way."

They jumped in and Gilly roared the car out the driveway, to the highway leading west. As the sun warmed the day, their spirits rose. Maggie began to sing the song they had learned during the summer in Saskatoon:

Those faraway places with strange-sounding names
Faraway over the sea.
Those faraway places with them strange-sounding
    names,
Are calling, calling me.

The west beckoned them with its golden glow and Maggie curled against him in her nightgown. "Come on, Geelly, sing."

Going to China or maybe Siam.
I want to see for myself,
Those faraway places I've been reading about,
In a book that I took from a shelf.

"Are we going to Hollywood?" she said.

Gilly shrugged. "Maybe. Maybe San Francisco — the Golden City with the Golden Gate."

They call me a dreamer, well maybe I am.
But I know that I'm yearning to see

Those faraway places with the strange-sounding names
That are calling, calling me.

* * * * *

10

On Thursday, the second shipment from Hamtramck had
arrived and by Friday, it was nearly sold out. Pepsi and
Malach were going crazy; the more they sold, the wilder
they got, forseeing the lost thousands on Saturday, the
biggest day of all. Gilly had no problem getting Friday night
off to attend the football practice.

First, Gilly had to sign a waiver on injury claims, witnessed
by Francis Goodman. Then, to the amusement of the other
players, they went to the equipment room and he was suited
up.

"Here's the new kicker, boys!" one laughed. "Take a good
look at him, 'cuz he won't be here long!"

The coach put the team through warm-ups, then took
Gilly down to the goalposts. The players gathered to watch.
He placed the ball on a tee at the twenty-five yard line and
gestured. Gilly paced off a few steps back of the ball, then
launched into three long strides and a sideways instep kick
that lofted the ball into a long spiralling drive. It whistled
through the uprights.

"Hmph!" the coach said, and put the ball on the thirty-
five yard line. Gilly repeated the performance and did it
again at the forty-five yard line.

"Okay, that's enough," the coach said. "You never played
professional ball before, eh?"

"No."

"What else can you do?"

"Well, the rules are different in rugby — but I can tackle.
And I can take a hit."

The coach called out, "Harris! Parslow! Pajakowski!"
Three of the most brutal tacklers in the game ran forward.
"This guy's going to try a couple of position field goals.
Rattle him."

They set up in field goal formation. The centre snapped
the ball to Gilly. The tacklers charged. He dropped the ball

to the ground with a twist, driving his boot into it at the same instant. The ball soared over the heads of the rushing tacklers and through the goalpost.

"What the hell was *that*?" the coach yelled.

"Dropkick."

"Is it legal?"

"Yeah, in Canadian rules. As long as it touches the ground."

Before anyone else could talk to Gilly, Goodman and the coach hustled him to the equipment room to get his signature on an option. On Sunday, he would be dressed for the first exhibition game of the season against the Saskatchewan Roughriders. He would be on the bench, their secret weapon. Gilly left the stadium as if he were in a dream.

* * * * *

11

All the way through Rock Falls and Wheatland, they sang, through Mechanicsville, Cedar Rapids and Fort Dodge. In Correctionville, they stopped to buy food and an outfit for Maggie. Five miles out of town, crossing the east fork of the Little Sioux River, the Ford's overworked engine threw a connecting rod and ground to a halt.

Gilly was moved to curse. It was night on the plains and bitterly cold. There were no lights to be seen in any direction. He was shivering in his leather jacket and Maggie did not even have a coat. Any second now, the highway patrol would swoop down on them to investigate the stalled car. Gilly said nonchalantly, "The hell with it. It's too cold to sit around here. Let's head for warmer weather."

"What do you mean?"

"We'll catch a ride into Sioux City, get a night's rest and then we'll head southwest. Whaddaya say?"

"I say yes — wherever the road takes us."

They pushed the car into the ditch. Maggie wrapped herself in the seat blanket while he re-packed his bag with food and clothing. It wasn't long before a farmer drove by, heading for a night's fun in Sioux City. He dropped them off at a cheap hotel which he knew.

It was the first time they had been in bed together. Gilly

177

was appallingly ignorant of the relationship between anatomy and passion — but Maggie was patient and he was zealous. They finally fell asleep at four a.m. They were still in a coma of spent ecstasy when the chambermaid flung the door open at noon, check-out time, and threw them out.

They walked the streets toward the edge of town, not noticing the dark clouds building in the sky as they cavorted in childish foolery and sang their song.

"Where now, Geelly?"

"South for a ways — we'll look for a little sunshine."

It was slow progress hitchhiking because they had to run and hide in the ditch each time they thought a police car was approaching. But before evening, they had reached Omaha and the sun broke through the clouds once more.

"See?" Gilly said. "Sunshine's back. Now we head west, to the blue Pacific."

They had no money for a room, so they travelled on the back highways, sleeping in cars when they got a chance and singing their way through Weeping Water and Lincoln and Gothenburg and North Platte and Ogallala. Approaching Cheyenne, the mountains rose ahead of them like a barrier and they turned south again, through Greeley and Denver.

In the cold streets of Denver, Santa Claus decorations glittered everywhere and the carolling voices of Christmas surrounded them. They suddenly remembered their homes, thousands of miles away.

"It's getting too cold for hitchhiking," Gilly said. "Why don't we stay here for a while? I could find a job and earn some money." Maggie nodded silently. She had been sick for two days.

"We'll be in California by New Year's," he said.

Gilly found a job washing cars in a hotel garage, as hordes of skiers flocked to Colorado for the season. Maggie stayed in the rooming house and nursed her fever. The winter solstice passed, when the mountain-shrouded city was enveloped in twenty hours of darkness. Gilly worked evenings for the tips and scrounged through Salvation Army thrift stores in the mornings acquiring the heavy winter clothes they would need for the final trek through the mountains.

12

On Saturday, the sun was hotter than ever and the mobs poured into the Stampede Grounds. Malach and Pepsi were hysterical from frustration. They had sold out of the Sooper-kiks the night before. Pepsi had rush-ordered another load of merchandise, which could not possibly arrive in time. They would tear down that night and the next day, before moving on to Edmonton's Klondike Days.

Pepsi ordered Gilly to go and enjoy the chuckwagon races.

The chuckwagon races were the most exciting sporting event Gilly had ever seen, with all their dust and sweat and raw fury, as the cowboys flung themselves and their horses around the figure-eight course in a storm of smashing wagons and raucous curses. Yet the gut-busting display was so poorly attended compared to the tawdry hucksterism of the midway that Gilly grew depressed while he watched. The rodeo riders fought their saddle broncs and Brahma bulls in a fantastic display of raw courage — and for what? A few dollars a day — less than he made in a hour in the glass Centennial Booth. In Montréal, millions of dollars are being spent on the candy floss contract at Expo '67.

Having time to spare after the rodeo, Gilly wandered out of the exhibition grounds into the city. Traffic choked the streets, six cars wide in all directions. The drivers grew short-tempered in the heat, cursing each other and their children crying in the back seats. He strolled away from the traffic along Second Street, crossing the tiny Elbow River a mile above its junction with the swift Bow. He paused to watch the slow summer water trickling below, glistening in the sun. Upstream, under the First Street bridge, lay a tiny island, an oasis of trees and grass, just beyond the cacophony of cars and trucks. A young man and woman were stretched on the grass there, basking in the sun and stroking each other sensuously — isolated from the turmoil surrounding them, like he and Maggie had been, segregated from the busy world in their passion.

A car screeched to a stop on the road behind him. He turned to see a Pontiac with Constable Summerville sitting at the wheel. Framed in the passenger's open window was the square unsmiling face of Staff Sergeant Harry Swift.

"I hear you've taken up football," Swift said. "I always thought you were bullshitting us with that rugby stuff."

"What do you want?"

"I came to get your report."

"I told your chauffeur last time. We're selling beaded moccasins and Ookpiks like crazy. Closing the place up tonight. Pepsi's operation is legal, I tell you."

"Get in," Swift said, opening the back door of the sedan. "Okay, Don, let's take Gilly for a little drive."

The car wheeled north across the river and out of the city. To the west, Gilly could see the sharp, snowy peaks of the Rocky Mountains, glistening along the horizon like a row of bright teeth.

"Where are we going?"

"You always liked strange places, didn't you, Savard? Well, we're going to see Spy Hill jail."

"You got nothing on me, Swift. This is psychological torture."

Summerville pulled the car into the parking lot of a big factory-like building sprawled among the Calgary foothills.

"You're in deep trouble, Savard, unless you come up with some answers. Pepsi Vaccarino is a front man for the Montréal Mafia and they don't mess around with two-bit souvenir stands. It's a front for something else. Bogus money, drugs, I don't know. It's a national set-up. If you don't believe me, there's a guy in jail here that will confirm it."

"Take me home, will you? I got a party tonight. You have no reason to hold me."

Swift reached into his pocket and removed his notebook. "Do you know there's a guy in Regina who has a three-year-old cheque in your name? Charges still pending."

"You can't do this."

"I only have one set of rules to play with, Gilly. Now do you want to go and play football tomorrow or not?"

"Well, I'll see what I can find out. You hafta give me time."

"Till tomorrow morning."

They dropped him back at the Stampede Grounds where the crowds milled through the gates more frantically than ever. The Centennial Booth had been stripped clean of merchandise and Malach and Pepsi were finishing off a bottle of scotch. They were both blind drunk. Princess Sherry was there to see if Gilly would take her to the Stampede wind-up party. His two partners were trying to sweet talk her into spending a night at the Ace Hotel. It was ridiculous, he thought. These two idiots weren't gangsters. They didn't have to be when they could play a legal con game on this scale. He rescued Sherry from their clutches.

The wind-up party was held in the Crowfoot Room of the Calgary Inn. Everyone from Calgary society was in attendance. Francis Goodman was there with Bert Parslow, one of the football players Gilly had met the day before. Parslow was a Black from South Carolina, a defensive end who had been imported for the new season, and was being hailed in the press as the shiftiest defensive player in the league. He had been a shade too small for the NFL, where he had bounced from one team to another for a couple of years looking for a regular position.

"Hey, man," he said, grabbing Gilly's arm. "That's some talented toe you got there. 'Zat right you never played football before?"

"Not pro."

"Well, I'll tell you, buddy, you sure gonna teach these stubble-jumpers somethin' about field position, if you can do that in a game. Come over here and let me buy you a drink."

Parslow pulled him to the bar, leaving Goodman with the girl. "Only thing I can't figure out is why you want to do it."

"I *always* wanted to play football."

"Yeah, man, I dig it, but Goodman tells me you got a big government job, pullin' down a regular salary. Why do you want to run around in a numbered sweater gettin' your brains bashed out?"

"I like football. I dreamed about it all my life. Never had the chance till now."

Parslow looked at him in amazement. "A *true amateur*, huh? Well, man, I never thought I'd live to see the day. What do you think you're gettin' into?"

"I don't know. But I think I'll enjoy it."

Parslow's dark eyes smouldered with contempt. "Yeah, man, I useta have ideas like that when I was playin' college ball, but I'm tellin' ya, you'll soon lose 'em. Ya gotta to survive."

"Why?"

"Because it isn't a *game* anymore, no more'n any other sport. When people do it for money, it's a *business* — which is why Goodman is in it. It's *big* business, man! And it's all fodder for the idiot box. To sell beer and cigarettes. I don't know a single player who isn't in it for the bread! So where does that leave you?"

"I don't know," Gilly said, removing Parslow's hand from his jacket. He felt tired, as if the weight of the crushing week had suddenly fallen on top of him. Everyone wanted to know where he was going. Francis Goodman was waiting for a reply. So was Sherry. In a corner of the room, Constable Donald Summerville nursed a glass of ginger ale and waited from a discreet distance.

Gilly had to get out. He excused himself, mumbling about the washroom, then slipped down the hall and into the street.

A cloud of dust lay over the city like a heated shroud. But above it, he could see stars blinking through the haze. He began walking in no particular direction. He wanted to get away from the noise, but Calgary stretched on forever. He crossed the river and turned up 14th Street, past the Jubilee Auditorium. Below, in the city, he could see the pinball colours of the Stampede winking and turning and flashing in a last frenzy of distraction. He began walking faster.

The big empty shell of McMahon Stadium loomed out of the darkness. Workmen were working late there, putting the last touches of paint on the gates before the season-opener. Gilly walked in. A couple of high floodlights illuminated the lush green turf. An old man and a boy were chalking the grid across its surface; it looked like a net holding down the grass. He began to trot around the edge of the field on the cinder track, his head back, gazing at the stars which wheeled overhead. Around and around he jogged, waiting for the answers to come. He could sense Clint and Swift and Sherry and his mother and Pepsi and Parslow in the grandstand, waiting for them, too.

The goalposts clicked past again and again as he circled the field, like the questions snapping in his brain. When would he stop? Who was he doing this for? If he could not break free from the waiting stares, was he doomed to run the treadmill forever? If he stayed to win his fame and fortune on the gridiron, would he be crushed like a fly? Should he go to Vancouver to tell his story to the filmmaker? He was still running when the morning light began to glow in the east. He ran out of the stadium into the hushed silence of the city lying dazed in the ghostly light after a week-long debauch.

He ran towards the saw-toothed palisade of western mountains. He would tell his story, explain himself to the world. But there was one last duty to fulfill before he disappeared beyond the wall of the Rockies. A telephone booth appeared at the side of the road in front of him, just as the sun squinted over the horizon. He dialed the number Swift had written for him on a piece of paper.

"Swift?" he said when the detective finally answered. "I finally figured it out. They're peddling dope. There's two caps of heroin in every one of those fancy fur owls they call Sooperkiks. They're shipped up from the States. Wait till they get set up in Edmonton and then go in and take the place apart."

"Got it! Great work, Savard. Where are you going to be?"

"Me? I'm going East. Had enough of this crap. Maybe I'll go and have a look at the Centennial Flame on Parliament Hill before it gets turned out. Maybe take in Expo."

"Okay, thanks for everything. Stay out of trouble, eh?"

"You said it, Sarge." Gilly hung up and began his long run through the mountains.

* * * * *

13

On New Year's Day, 1954, Gilly and Maggie ascended the eastern face of the Rockies in the cab of an oil-tanker, crawling upward yard by painful yard, crossing the Continental Divide as the driver yodelled, "Ceegareets and whiskey and wild, wild women," roaring through Rabbit Ears Pass and Strawberry Daniels Pass, plunging out of the mountains to the Great Salt Desert and the Mormon city that stretched in front of them like Babylon.

They crossed the Bonneville Flats in the back of a farm

pick-up truck. Maggie had grown sicker and was vomiting over the side. They passed through Battle Mountain and Lovelock, rattling into Reno. Beyond, they could see the Sierras and beyond the mountains, they knew, was the land of dreams.

Finding a room in Reno was not difficult; there were hundreds of rooming houses, most of them catering to the divorce industry. There were none of the awkward questions about their marital status they had been lying about during their travels. Many miles back they had decided they would get married in Reno. Maggie rested in the rooming house while Gilly ventured forth to find the required licence for their marriage.

At the licence bureau, he was informed that medical examinations would be required for both of them. He was brusquely handed a mimeographed list of medical practitioners in the city. It took some time before Gilly could find a doctor who made house calls — he felt that Maggie was too ill to sit waiting in a clinic — but a Dr. Grant Perry finally agreed to visit their rooming house that evening.

Dr. Perry was a former insurance doctor from Omaha who was attracted to the more lucrative side of medical practice and moved to Reno as a professional abortionist. He recognized Maggie's problem immediately. "Fifty dollars," he said to Gilly, taking him aside. "A hundred if I do it here."

"Do what?"

"Perform the abortion, of course."

"You don't understand. We want to get married. I told you that."

"Married? What did you need *me* for?"

"Because we need medical certificates."

Grumbling with disappointment, Dr. Perry collected the ten dollar fees for the medical forms and stalked out while the prospective father informed his future bride of her condition. They had barely discussed the significance of the new factor when two Reno police detectives broke into the room with a warrant for Gilly's arrest. He was sought on six counts of theft, two of assault and illegal entry at the border. There was a charge of car theft outstanding from Canada. They would be allowed five minutes together, then Maggie was to be removed and flown back to Canada.

There was not much they could do in five minutes, except cling to each other in silent tears amid their collapsed dreams. There would be no future for a long, long time. Gilly would spend years in American jails and would be deported finally to serve a further sentence in Canada. They could not imagine what fate awaited Maggie. But as the police came and parted them, she cried, "Regina! We will meet in Regina!" Then she was gone.

FOUR
TORONTO

I have not rendered anyone unhappy; I have not plundered the widow; I have not turned anyone adrift penniless on the world; I have merely availed myself of superfluous cash.

Nikolai Gogol,
Dead Souls

1

In October of 1970, there were few tranquil harbours in the raging sea of Canadian politics. The kidnapping of Cross and Laporte, the "insurrection" of the FLQ, the October Crisis and the War Measures Act — all combined to shatter the renowned Canadian smugness forever, only three years after the magic of Centennial Year and Expo '67.

One such quiet harbour was the institution of William Head Jail located at the southwestern corner of this vast country. It lay on the extreme southern tip of Vancouver Island overlooking the Strait of Juan de Fuca and, in former years, it had been a quarantine station serving the West Coast ports. Thousands of immigrants from the Orient had been placed in isolation there for varying periods of time — depending more on their political health than on their medical health — before entering the country. In more recent times, it had been converted to a minimum security prison.

William Head was actually the name of the peninsula on which the prison was located. A barbed wire and cindercrete barrier separated it from the rest of the Island. In fact, it was the vast Pacific Ocean which formed the walls of Gilly Savard's latest prison. After years of trying to reach the Pacific, he now spent his days gazing out at the sea turning this irony over and over in his head.

Life was considerably more tolerable at William Head than it was at his previous places of confinement. Although the climate tended to be damp, it was perfect for playing rugby; as in England, the game could be played all winter long. At the age of thirty-seven, however, he was slowing down and was relegated to the position of fullback where his precision at kicking goals was still admired. But his interest in sports had not waned.

In fact, the only reason Gilly was seeking an early parole to his scheduled release date of 1972 was because of the football season. The Calgary Stampeders looked like contenders for the championship for the first time in twenty years. Gilly had been betting all season on his favourite team and this had created much interest within the jail. After trouncing the Saskatchewan Roughriders 30 to 0 in the first match of the game, the Stamps had fallen into a slough of misfortune and bad timing. Gilly was counting on the comeback of quarterback Jerry Keeling and the famous Roughrider jinx to win back his money before the end of the season.

* * * * *

2

Another isolated centre of calmness in October, 1970, was the Toronto office of Media Masters Ltd., not far from the corner of Bloor and Bay Streets. Gilly's friend, the television producer from Vancouver, had been recruited by the federal Liberal Party two years previously to develop Pierre Elliott Trudeau's image as a titillating swinger and sell it to the starstruck Canadian public. He had succeeded, and his triumph had resulted in a television media consulting firm with a particular preference for politics. His success had been so great that he had attracted the attention of both the Democratic and Republican parties in the U.S. At this time, he was negotiating discreetly with both for the approaching 1972 election, an election in which President Richard Nixon would once again be seeking power.

Late one Friday afternoon that October, a letter arrived on the filmmaker's desk with a postmark from Metchosin,

B.C. It was a letter from Gilly Savard which began:

> Greetings from the West!
>
> Congratulations on your continuing success. Unfortunately, my movements have been restricted again, but I hope to see you soon. The purpose of my writing now is for you to help me get parole before the end of my term. The hearings come up again soon and if you would be good enough to be a reference on my behalf, I am sure it would help. What I would like to do is to get out in time to travel east for the Grey Cup game which is being held in Toronto this year. If it can be managed, then we could make arrangements to produce that film we talked about a few years back. It seems to me that the story of my life would be instructive to many people, especially young ones, and this would be a good reason for my parole. If you agree, please write to the Corrections Officer here at William Head. As soon as I am released, I will travel east and we can plan the project. I will travel at the time of the Grey Cup game, in late November, and that way kill two birds with one stone.
>
> In the meantime, maybe you'd like to make a five dollar bet on the outcome of Saturday's first semi-final game between Calgary and Saskatchewan? If you are still a Saskatchewan believer, you will no doubt be prepared to accept even odds. They did finish the season at the top of the league so stand a good chance against the mighty Stamps. Is it a bet?
>
> Sincerely,
Gilly Savard

The media consultant put the letter on the glass top of his desk and gazed at it for a moment. He let his eyes wander toward the window which looked over the metropolis from the building's fortieth floor. He had nearly forgotten about Gilly Savard. He was already past the creative phase of his life when he could indulge in such quixotic projects. Savard's story, while interesting, was only the story of one man — and a loser at that. The filmmaker's ambition now was to influence an entire nation, to find the point of leverage to change the world. Surely, however, he could invest a few minutes to help Gilly out of jail in view of the assistance Savard's story had been to him during his climb to the top. And, to say the least, the Roughriders looked like a sure bet in the western final. He called his secretary into the inner office.

"Take a letter to the administration at William Head," he began.

* * * * *

3

On a Saturday afternoon some three weeks later, Gilly watched the first game of the western final with his friend Cassidy in the prison's television lounge. Jim Cassidy was a likeable young tough from Vancouver who had been halted momentarily in his pursuit of a life of crime. He wasn't too bright, but he had the shoulders of a first class prop forward and usually played with Gilly on the first fifteen. Moreover, he had played football in high school and was an avid fan. He too had bet on Saskatchewan all season and now held over $50.00 worth of Gilly's tobacco ration. This was despite the fact that the Roughriders had been without their star runningback George Reed for most of the season. Reed had now returned to the line-up.

Gilly's faith, however, was unshakeable and he placed another $5.00's worth of tobacco on his heroes. Several dozen convicts had crowded into the lounge to watch the game. Three minutes after the opening kick-off, with Calgary ready to march down the field and score, Gilly was called from the lounge by his Corrections Officer. The parole board was meeting in another wing and would be considering his application. It was important that he be there to answer any questions.

"Couldn't I go after the game is over? They'll be checking at least twenty applications."

"Well," the officer said. "It's in your interest to be there."

Gilly waited outside the conference room for three hours

before they called him in to tell him his application had been rejected. Despite his three year record of good behaviour, he was considered too unstable to risk sending into the outside world. Moreover, his reason for leaving, to allow a dramatization of his life, could end up an embarrassment to everyone — including himself.

The game was long over when Gilly wandered back to his wing of the prison. He went to his cell, a small room measuring eight by twelve feet, to consider his options. Cassidy was waiting there for him.

"Hey man — what happened? Ja *get* it?"

Gilly shook his head.

"Jeez, that's a drag. Hey, this'll cheer y'up. Stampeders won: 28-11." He handed Gilly several bales of tobacco.

"Thanks."

"So what're ya gonna do now?"

"I dunno. Two years to go."

"Yeah, it's a fuckin' drag, man. You think about what I toljuh, eh?"

It was Cassidy's ambition to leave the jail as soon as possible. He had rigged up an escape and wanted Gilly's partnership in the plan. It depended on moving across the Island's rugged territory, for which Gilly's map-reading ability was essential.

"When's the next game?" Gilly said. It was a best-of-three series between the two teams.

"Wednesday. In Calgary."

"Calgary?" Gilly said, his eyes lighting up. "Calgary's only eight hundred miles away, isn't it?"

"I dunno. You're the expert with maps."

That night they made their escape preparations while the rest of the inmates partied on fermented potatoes and plums.

* * * * *

4

Sunday dawned bright and sunny. The two men waited until low tide was due and the afternoon volleyball game was well underway in the exercise yard. Then they slipped away to the west shore of the peninsula. No one noticed as they clambered over the rough boulders along the waterline toward the chainlink security fence that ran into the sea. When they reached the fence, they removed their clothing and stowed it in the cloth bags that they were carrying. Then, holding their bundles over their heads, they waded into the water and struck out swimming around the fence at the point where it disappeared below the sea.

By dusk, they had reached Pedder Bay Marina by walking across the adjacent peninsula. The marina was really a small commercial dock for fishing boats with a sign that said, "Motor Launches for Rent." Gilly and Cassidy walked toward the small office, the hoods of their khaki parkas covering their faces.

The operator stepped out onto the dock, regarding them suspiciously. "Can I help you?"

"Any boats available?"

"Sure. All of 'em. Goin' fishing?" He looked pointedly at their lack of fishing gear.

"I'll tell you what it is, cap'n," Cassidy began. "We walked all the way from Colwood. We just gotta get to Sooke before eight o'clock or my ole lady's gonna kill me."

"Zatso?"

"How much for a boat to get us to Sooke?"

"I usually rent by the hour. How would you get it back?"

"Bring it back in the morning. We'll rent it off ya for five bucks."

"Yeah, I'd need a deposit, though."

"I'll leave ya my watch," Cassidy said, pulling his watch off his wrist. "It's a hunnert-and-twenty dollar Bulova. Please, ya gotta help me out. My ole lady's gonna freak out for sure."

The two men jumped into the nearest boat and cranked the engine into action before the marina operator could object. He watched them disappear into the darkness on the bay and turned to examine the watch. It had stopped at two o'clock.

The fugitives reached the fishing village of Sooke without difficulty and tied the dinghy up among the fishing trawlers at the dock. Then they ran for the road that looped up the west side of the Island.

"How long before they come after us, do you reckon?"

Gilly asked.

"Till bed check anyways. As soon as they see we split, they'll close the road from William Head into Victoria. Where's 'a map?"

Gilly pulled the Island map from his pocket and spread it out under a streetlight. "See?" he pointed. "The road goes up here to Point No Point, then through Jordan River to Port Renfrew. If what you say is true, nobody travels it this time of year except loggers. At Renfrew, we cut across the middle of the Island — there. We won't be anywhere *near* Victoria or the Lower Island. We can catch a ferry to the Mainland from Nanaimo. *If* we can get there by morning."

"Far-out!" Cassidy laughed and slapped him on the back. "We're on our way!"

Just then, a huge logging truck roared out of the darkness. They stuck out their thumbs as it rumbled past showering them with dust and gravel. The big trucks never stop. Still, they had to try. They were luckier with a beaten-up sedan that clattered to a stop beside them twenty minutes later. It was a hippie driving to Port Renfrew for reasons he declined to discuss. However, he did share several joints of marijuana with them which he rolled from a huge bag he kept stashed in a door panel.

When they arrived at Port Renfrew, it was near midnight and a heavy rain had begun to fall. At the edge of town, they found a truckers' all-night restaurant which was open. A loaded truck was idling beside the gas pumps. Inside, the place looked deserted, but after a moment, a waitress staggered out of the kitchen tacking her hair together.

"Coffee?" she said.

"Yeah, coffee. Where's the guy who belongs to the truck?"

"Siggy!" she called toward the kitchen. "Couple a guys wanta see ya!" She turned back to them. "Nothing to eat?"

"Let's have some eggs," Gilly said. They had about two dollars between them.

The truck driver appeared hastily pulling on his clothes. "What is it?" he said irritably.

"You going over the mountains tonight to the east side?"

"The San Juan River Road? At night? You gotta be jokin'!"

"How come?"

"Well, it's *snowin'* up there tonight! I'll be lucky to get through in the morning. You wanta ride or somethin'?"

"Yeah," Cassidy said. "Whadda we do now — wait?"

"Suit yourselves. You guys play cribbage?"

"Sure."

"Then you guys play crib. I bin waitin' two weeks to see Pauline here. Let us know if somebody comes in."

The waitress gave them some toast and eggs and disappeared into the kitchen behind their pilot to freedom. They sat down to wait the night, hoping that the news would not reach this far north for at least a few hours.

* * * * *

5

Morning found them hunched in the cab of a huge White truck pulling ten tons of logged fir up the high mountain range that split Vancouver Island in two. The higher they ascended, the deeper the snow was piled on the road and the more the driver cursed. But as there was no place on the tight hairpin bends to stop, let alone turn, there was no going back. They roared through depths of wet snow as though it was water. Then came the descent, a stomach-churning plummet down the east face at forty miles an hour, heeling through bends in the road, leaving them behind in a haze of slush, gears gnashing all the way. At the bottom, the grinning trucker released his two passengers. He left them in a state of shock at the village of Shawnigan Lake and the truck roared off toward the Mill Bay ferry.

Gilly and Cassidy were headed in the opposite direction, north toward Nanaimo, and their luck held with them to the extent they were able to flag down a delivery van. It was travelling the highway toward the ferry terminal at Departure Bay. There, a hitch developed in their headlong flight when the van stopped opposite the ticket window.

"Here's the money for me and the vehicle," the driver said. "These guys are only riding with me."

At this point, the escapees didn't have even ten cents. "I don't suppose you'd accept a cheque?" Cassidy suggested hopefully.

The ticket agent shook his head emphatically. "Two bucks apiece."

"Here," Gilly said. "Put it on my credit card." He offered the plastic card to the open window, playing it like a trump ace.

"Credit card?" the agent said suspiciously.

"American Express," Gilly replied, with all the authority of an actor in a television commercial. The agent rang up the charges. "On second thought," Gilly said, "make it for twenty dollars. I have to buy some things on the boat."

The *Queen of Esquimalt* was waiting at the dock as they drove down to load. Thanking the driver, the refugees ran up to the dining lounge and ordered two trays of breakfast apiece. They gorged themselves as the Island coastline began to fade behind them in the morning sunshine.

"What next, man?" Cassidy mumbled, rubbing crumbs of toast from his lips with a napkin. Gilly was reading the morning *Province*.

"I don't know. We'll have to see what kind of reception we get in Vancouver. It's been too easy this far. I don't think they've put out the alarm yet."

"Maybe they didn't notice we were gone till this morning, eh? Still searching the compound, I bet."

"Just have to wait and see."

"You still thinkin' of tryna get to Calgary?" Cassidy said.

"Why, do you want to go along?"

"Naw, Vancouver's my hangout. I know this little pool hall on East Broadway we could knock off easy for a couple hundred bucks. Then we could find some chickies and have ourselves a blast. Eh? Whaddaya say, man?"

"No heists. I wouldn't mind gettin' a hotel, though. I'm ready to sleep for a week. The bench in that café was murder."

"How we gonna do that?"

"What's the best place in town?"

Cassidy shrugged. "Bayshore, I giss. Down by the Yacht Club on the harbour. But that's *posh*, man! We don't stand a chance, gettin' in there."

Gilly tore a page out of the newspaper and slid it across the table to Cassidy. "Look at this." It was a photograph of Howard Hughes, the American billionaire. The article was headlined, "Howard Hughes Evades Press, Leaves Las Vegas Hotel."

"So what?" Cassidy said, but Gilly only smiled enigmatically. The smile lingered on his lips when their taxi pulled up to the marquee at the luxurious Bayshore Inn. Cassidy, having been coached on the way from the bus terminal, jumped smartly out of the cab and snapped his fingers at a uniformed doorman.

"Quick, you — a wheelchair!"

"A what, sir?" In his parka and jeans, Cassidy did not look much like a Bayshore guest.

"Buddy," he snapped, "the man sitting in this taxi is *Howard Hughes*! We're just checking in. Now, are you gonna get us a wheelchair — or not?"

The doorman ran to the telephone at the door and ordered a wheelchair brought to the entrance.

"*Hurry up*," Cassidy added, advancing on him, "before the TV cameras get here from the airport!"

A pair of bellboys ran out of the door with a wheelchair and rolled it to the taxi. With much solicitude, Cassidy helped Gilly slide into the chair and covered his head with a blanket from the seat. Then he pushed the chair at top speed toward the totel. The doorman flung open the glass door.

As the apparition went past, Gilly lifted a corner of the blanket. Then he pushed the chair at top speed toward the hotel. The doorman flung open the glass door.

"Thank you, sir," the doorman said, bowing deeply.

The desk clerk watched with awe, hesitating for perhaps the first time in his career as the blanket-covered wheelchair approached the counter with its retinue of bellboys. Gilly lifted the blanket again as the chair rolled to a stop.

"When our bags arrive from the airport, I want them sent up to our room *immediately*. Understood?"

"Yes, sir. Um, what room was that, sir?"

"You incompetent *fool*!" Gilly hissed furiously. "Did you not reserve the penthouse for us?"

"Yes, sir — of course, sir, the penthouse. Bellboy, take Mr. Hu——"

"*Shut your mouth!*" Gilly yelled. "Do you want the reporters down here? Somebody take the key from this idiot before he alerts the whole city!"

With a hostile glare, Cassidy extended his hand for the key. The perspiring clerk dropped it into his hand and Gilly dropped the blanket over his face again. "Warn the staff that no one is to come into our suite without permission! No calls! And if any of the media discover I'm here, we'll buy the hotel and dismiss the entire staff. Is that clear?"

"Yes, sir," the desk clerk said. The bellboys nodded in unison. Cassidy rolled the wheelchair into the elevator.

In their penthouse suite, one of the most opulent in the city, Gilly and Cassidy cavorted for several minutes, leaping onto the beds and sofas, turning on every television set, air conditioner and bed vibrator they could find.

"Hey, how about some food?" Cassidy yelled.

"You just had breakfast two hours ago."

"It's awready suppertime. Order us a couple of steaks from room service."

No sooner had Gilly begun to order a sumptuous meal than Cassidy turned up the volume of the television set and yelled, "Hey, listen to this!"

"And from the Island," the news announcer smiled, "more information on the spectacular breakout from William Head prison at Metchosin."

"Forget the dessert," Gilly said to room service. "We'll order it later."

"Victoria and Esquimalt police are conducting an intensive search for two convicts who escaped from the minimum security jail sometime on Sunday night. As their disappearance was not discovered until late this morning, it is speculated they had outside help in their breakout. One of the pair, Gillman R. Savard, is a notorious confidence artist. His accomplice, James Cassidy, has a long record of violent crime, including both armed robbery and assault, and is considered dangerous. Both are reported to have underworld connections. Vancouver and Lower Mainland police, meanwhile, have been alerted to watch for the pair as they may try to cross to the Mainland. Checks are being made at all airports and ferry terminals."

"Wonder why they missed us last night?" Gilly said.

Cassidy shrugged and switched off the TV. "Somebody musta done us a favour, I guess. Hey, now we gotta get us some decent threads to wear. Can you do that by phone, too? I'm gonna grab a sauna bath before the food comes up."

Their feast was the sort that convicts and soldiers fantasize about during long hours of solitude. The two men ate surrounded by an array of meats on silver trays, gleaming crystal wine glasses and ice buckets of champagne, and mounds of salad at their fingertips. In the middle of dinner, a delivery boy showed up with the suits that Gilly had ordered from the exclusive clothing store downstairs. Gilly gave him some numbers to write down on the invoices and the boy bowed his way out of the room.

When they had quaffed the last of the wine, donned their new clothes and stuffed their prison garb into one of the overhead lighting panels, Cassidy turned to Gilly in high expectation. "Now are we gonna find us some broads?"

"Not yet. First we have to move to a new hotel."

"*Huh?*"

"Too much heat here. We have to go."

"Whaddya mean — *heat*?"

Gilly pointed out the window toward the street twenty floors below. In front of the hotel, a pair of CBC television trucks were parked surrounded by lights and a group of reporters.

"Oh," Cassidy said, and they began looking for the service exit from the hotel. Once past the newshounds, they hurried up Georgia Street toward the centre of the city. In their new clothes, they had no difficulty booking into the elegant — though much more conservative — Hotel Vancouver. Its turn-of-the-century ambience, Gilly said, was more suited to their taste. Cassidy thought it was too stuffy, but as long as it would impress the women, he didn't care. He led Gilly down Granville Street where hookers and pimps lined the sidewalks and every hotel offered service to the sexually deprived. Gilly scorned it all.

Eventually, they found themselves at the door of the Arts Club on Seymour Street. On Monday night, it was relatively quiet, but inside they could hear laughing voices. Cigarette smoke and the sound of clinking glasses drifted through the door. They entered behind a group of people who had obviously come from a play somewhere in the city.

"Wow, look at all 'a chicks! — and the fags! Hey, what kinda place is this, anyway?" Cassidy stood in wonder just inside the door.

"It's a theatre club. You know — showbiz and the like. Biggest con game of all. Hi there!" Gilly saluted a couple of young women who paused in their dramatic progress toward the bar.

"Well, hi," said one, painted rather gaudily. "I'm Pam. You're new here, aren't you?"

Gilly smiled his most dazzling smile. "Just arrived in town."

"This is Rosemary," Pam said, presenting her plainer companion. "Who's he?"

"Cassidy. He's the extrovert."

In no time at all, all four were having such a good time drinking Grand Marnier and laughing away the world's absurdities that they decided to retire to their room at the Hotel Vancouver where drinks could be put on a tab. Gilly was running low on cash again.

Outside the door of the Club, a man suddenly appeared out of the shadows and spoke to Pam. Gilly was sober enough to take in his somewhat sinister appearance, noting in particular his long hair and several strands of beads about his neck. So he wasn't surprised when a violent knock came on the door of their hotel suite about an hour later, a hammering loud enough to rattle the wine bottles on the bedside tables.

"Who the hell is that?" Pam cried.

Cassidy sat up, his face gone white.

"Rosemary, come outa there!" a man's voice cried outside the door. "I know you're in there!"

"It's my husband, Bill," Rosemary said in horror. "I'd know his voice anywhere."

Gilly laughed.

"Pam!" a second man's voice bellowed. "Lemme in before I smash the door down!"

"That's Ronnie!" Pam yelped.

The two women rushed about in a panic throwing their clothes on. Cassidy leaped to the window in hope of finding an exit.

Gilly laughed again. "James, I think we should call the cops and have these gatecrashers removed before they cause a disturbance!"

"The *cops*? Are you nuts?"

"*Please*, you guys," Pam moaned. "They'll kill us if they find us in here with you guys." Her plea was punctuated by even louder hammering on the door.

"Come on outa there, you little slut, or I'll break every bone in your boyfriend's body!"

Cassidy's rugged face broke into a wide grin as he realized what game they were now playing. "Sound's tough, don't he?"

Gilly crossed to the telephone and dialled a number. "Hello, front desk? Yes, we have a slight problem here. A couple of deadbeats outside the door of our suite are making a racket. Right. Exactly. Would you mind? Thanks a lot."

The two girls looked at one another, a new panic in their eyes. Pam ventured to the rattling door. "Ronnie — can you hear me? *Cut it out for a minnit, will ya?* The house dicks are coming up! You guys better take a walk. You hear me?"

The hammering continued for a minute, then stopped abruptly. There was a sound of scuffling outside, then silence. Gilly opened the door and saw a pair of uniformed security guards escorting the two hustlers down the hall to the elevator.

A house detective in a three-piece suit was standing at the door trying to peer in past Gilly's arm. "Sorry about the disturbance, sir. Everything all right?"

"Yes, yes — we're all fine now."

"I'll need some information, sir, to press charges."

"Oh, don't bother with charges. No harm done at all. Just a couple of harmless drunks."

"Yes, sir," the detective said reluctantly. "If you say so, sir."

"Goodnight," Gilly said. To his surprise, Pam and Rosemary looked relieved when he stepped back into the room. Gilly lifted a bottle and poured glasses of wine all around. "To a quiet evening, at last," he said, raising his glass. They all toasted the evening.

6

The aftermath of the two fugitives' soirée had to be seen in the cold light of dawn for it to achieve the full effect: a room full of empty glasses and bottles, scattered clothing, ashtrays heaped with cigarette butts, overturned furniture as far as the eye could see. This was what greeted Gilly's red-slitted eyes as his consciousness responded to a heavy, slow knocking at the door.

"Cassidy!" he rasped. "Answer the door. The boyfriends are back."

Cassidy stumbled out of bed and standing in his underwear, swung open the door. It was not the two hustlers. It was two other men: a large hulking brute whose fist was raised to knock again and a little flashily-dressed runt with bright yellow teeth.

"Pepsi Vaccarino!" Gilly moaned. He slid beneath the covers of the bed.

"Where is that bastard Savard?" he heard the Mafioso's voice snarl. The next thing he knew, the bed tilted up on one side and he and Rosemary rolled onto the carpeted floor.

"Get those broads outa here," Pepsi said to Cassidy. The girls needed no further invitation. They ran for their clothes. It was the first time in his life that Gilly had ever seen women dress so fast.

"You gotta be outa your fuckin' mind, Savard," Pepsi said, standing over Gilly. "Passin' cheques in the centre of Vancouver! The cops are turnin' the place upside down looking for ya! Every exit to the city has got two roadblocks on it."

Suddenly, Gilly made sense of the whole puzzle: their too-easy escape from jail, Cassidy's acquiescence. The young tough was sulking in a corner, avoiding Gilly's eyes. "You phoned him last night, didn't you? You arranged for our roll calls in jail Sunday night!"

"Everybody needs a little help from their friends, eh, Savard?" Pepsi winked at Gilly and gestured at him to start dressing.

"Well, it was very nice of you guys and all — but now that we've had our little party, I think it's time for me to start

rambling back to the old homestead at William Head. Say —
I don't suppose you could give me a hand getting back *in*?"

"Ha ha. We got a few unfinished business details to settle
first, don't we, Savard?"

"Huh? That Centennial business, you mean? I thought we
came out even on that. Don't tell me you guys finally ran out
of bottled air!"

"You've forgotten the little encounter we had with the
law after you left, huh?" Pepsi grinned evilly. His partner
removed a pistol from the inner folds of his jacket. Cassidy
began to edge toward the door.

"Put the gun away, Shithead," Pepsi said. "We're in real
estate now, Savard. What do you know about real estate?"

"Nothing. Nothing at all."

"Come on, you must know something!"

"I know it's getting to be worth a lot of money. A lot of
speculation is going on. And the mob is moving in."

"That's right, Savard. You got good ears. The mob *is*
moving in. As a matter of fact, my friends are moving out
of the heavy trades and into real estate. Cleaning up the
old act."

"I know, don't tell me. It's all legal. So what's the hard-
ware for then?"

"Shithead here's my employment officer. I thought I'd
need help persuading you to come back east and work with
us. We'll give you a little hole to cool out in for a while, then
set you up as a real estate agent."

"Ha! When I recover from my broken legs?"

"*Gilly*, we're not sore about what happened at the Stampede! That was kid's stuff. Water under the bridge. Oh sure,
I was pissed off at the time. Them Mounties tore all our
Sooperkiks apart lookin' fer smack or somethin'. But you
wouldn't do nuthin' like that again, would you?"

"No."

"We went to a lot of trouble getting you all this phoney
I.D. See? Fred Tchitchikov." He handed Gilly an assortment
of papers and cards. "With these, you'll be in the clear."

Gilly flicked through them. "Where's Clint Malach?"

Shithead laughed a hearty laugh. Pepsi said, "He spent a
few months working for us in Montréal. At "Man and His
World" — one of the hamburger concessions. But he lost the

204

will to co-operate. Fell offa the Gyratron."

"I see. Does this mean I won't get to see the football game tomorrow in Calgary?"

This caused great gales of laughter which Gilly himself joined. Vaccarino put his arm around Gilly's shoulder and the group moved out the door, like any group of convention-eering tourists. Down the elevator and past the desk, Pepsi chattered away about real estate. As they moved into the lobby, Gilly spied a tobacco store that he had noticed on the way in, the Fortunato Tobacco Shoppe. "Hang on. I have to get some smokes."

Pepsi's muscleman stuck out a beefy hand and stopped him.

"Let him get the smokes," Pepsi said. "You go with him. We'll wait here."

Gilly walked into the store and bought his cigarettes. As he remembered, the shop had another door opening onto the street. Outside, he could see crowds of people bustling past in the noonhour sunshine. He turned back to the lobby and Shithead preceded him through the door. In a flash, Gilly wheeled in the opposite direction and sped out the other door onto the street. He sprinted around the corner onto Georgia Street and ran down the sidewalk, knocking pedes-trians out of the way, not stopping for the red lights.

Running toward the bus terminal, Gilly saw the place was virtually surrounded by police. He veered north to Pender Street and jogged through Chinatown where the crowded streets gave him a feeling of cover. Around Main Street, he turned sharply into a sporting goods store and emerged a few minutes later in the guise of a serious jogger, wearing a purple and gold sweatsuit, with a pair of sunglasses for good measure. In his hand was a new Adidas bag con-taining his three hundred dollar suit.

Thus attired, Gilly could begin to appreciate the sunshine of the fine November day. His spirits lifted as he jogged along Hastings Street past Empire Stadium. His face creased with a grin as he chugged along Sperling past Burnaby Lake. Trotting down the hill by the New Westminster Penitentiary, he gave an involuntary chuckle and waved to the guards patrolling the ramparts of the grim fortress. But his good humour almost died in his throat as he loped up the western slope of Patullo Bridge to the rise at the centre. At the eastern end of the bridge, a pair of police cars formed a road-block and a line of traffic snaked back to where he stood. There was no turning back now. He jogged down the slope and past the roadblock. The sweating policemen did not even notice him, so preoccupied were they with the honking queue of traffic. Gilly laughed so hard that he had to stop by the roadside ditch and rest from the exertion.

He was clear. Beyond the bridge, the highway was bor-dered by open countryside. He was in his own element once again. He made a brief foray into a clump of alders beside the road and re-emerged a few minutes later costumed in his good suit. Checking the map of British Columbia in his pocket, he noted that there was a Canadian Air Force base at Chilliwack about a hundred miles to the east. He announced this as his destination to the next driver who offered him a ride.

On his arrival at Chilliwack, he was quickly able to locate an officer who dabbled in real estate on the side, Flying Officer Art Burkitt. In fact, most of the officers stationed at Chilliwack dabbled in real estate, but the commissionaire at the gate reckoned that Burkitt was the most successful. He rarely flew anymore. He had moved into the public relations branch of the Armed Services where he could find accom-modation for newly transferred personnel. The commission-aire was able to direct Gilly to the Hole-in-the-Wall Club where F.O. Burkitt would be sure to be found. This was a men's only club located in a large cave in a mountainside between Chilliwack and Abbotsford that served as the unofficial officer's mess for the airbase.

By two o'clock the next morning, after a few rum and Cokes, several hands of bullshit poker and many exchanges of anecdotes, Burkitt was in possession of a cheque for ten thousand dollars and Gilly held a first option to purchase a collapsing condominium on the outskirts of Chilliwack — as well as the promise of a seat on an Armed Forces C-130 flying in six hours time to Penhold, Alberta. As a parting gesture of good faith, Burkitt took him to the base and found him a place to sleep on the aircraft.

7

On Wednesday, Gilly flew for the first time in his life. As the plane took off, his stomach seemed to stay behind, but this discomfort was soon forgotten as he watched the snow-capped peaks of the Coast Mountains descend to the level of his feet. Mount Garibaldi — as he identified it on his map — crossed into view from the northwest. He could see Harrison Lake stretching north from the ribbon of the Fraser River. As the plane climbed toward the sun, the mountains dropped below like a bed of jagged rocks, split into rifts by the Fraser Canyon which ran from Hope to Hell's Gate. The aircraft droned over the plateaus of the Okanagan, then the mountain ranges of the Monashees, the Selkirks and the Purcells, before finally soaring over the peaks of the mighty Rocky Mountains, like a runner clearing one last savage hurdle. Immediately, the bright checkered fields of the high Alberta plains flashed into view and Gilly felt the plane descend again.

Like most modern journeys, his great leap had been accomplished in good time. It was only two o'clock in the afternoon when he unfastened his seat belt and thanked the air crew. But from Penhold, only eighty miles from Calgary, it was hard to move. There were no buses until seven o'clock, far too late to make it to the game. Gilly was forced to walk to the highway and begin hitchhiking once again. A cold November wind was blowing across the prairie and he knew he was underdressed for the climate, but he persevered until a farm pick-up truck appeared and stopped beside him.

"How far ya goin', mister?"

"Calgary. I have to get to the football game."

The farmer stared at Gilly in disbelief. "Football game? I'm only goin' into Innisfail."

"That's fine. Anything's a help. The game starts at eight," Gilly explained.

"Okay, jump in."

"Thanks. It's a really important game. I have to get there."

"Real dedicated fan, aincha? Never could figger out why you people sit around freezin' yer asses off, watchin' grown men kick a pigskin around. You go to all the games, I s'pose?"

"No, it's my first one," Gilly admitted.

"Zatso?" the farmer said, then lapsed into meditative silence for the rest of the way to Innisfail.

It took Gilly three more rides to reach Calgary. Finally, he was dropped at the Stampeders' ticket office, just off 8th Avenue, miles away from the stadium. When he rushed into the office, the clock showed 7:45. At the counter, a girl was counting money and ticket stubs.

"Quick. A ticket for tonight's game. On the fifty yard line, if you have one."

The girl glanced at him in pity. "I'm sorry, sir. The seats for tonight's game have been sold out for two days. It's the playoffs, eh?"

"Nothing?"

"You might go to the stadium and see if anybody is selling tickets outside the gate. There's a few scalpers."

"Can I change somewhere?"

"Pardon?"

"I want to change — put on my running outfit."

The girl stared at him without blinking as he whisked off his suit and put on his jogging costume, then sprinted out of the office. He'd never make it there on time, he knew, but he could still catch most of the game. This time, at least, he knew the way. He pounded through downtown Calgary like an express train. He was a mile from McMahon Stadium when he heard the roar of the crowd. As the arena hove into view, he imagined his red and white football warriors battling on the turf. He steamed up to the main entrance where a crowd milled around still seeking entry.

Suddenly, a pair of yellow teeth flashed in the glare of the mercury vapour lamps above the gate. Gilly ducked behind a car. As he peered around the car's fender, he could see Pepsi's head swivelling back and forth examining the faces in the crowd. Gilly turned around and sprinted to a second entrance on the far side of the stadium.

Approaching cautiously, he was not surprised to see Cassidy lurking in the shadows, also scanning the late arrivals. Gilly slipped by him, hiding behind a passing car, and proceeded to the only remaining entrance, the press and special passes gate, which was on the back side of the stadium. It looked unused, but just inside the gate he could see Shithead's bulky silhouette waiting for his prey. Once again, Gilly retreated, this time to a parking lot across the street. Common sense told him to abandon his quest and get out of the city while he still had a chance. It was bad enough the police were looking for him, but Pepsi Vaccarino and his crew were *dedicated*. From inside the stadium, he could hear the whistle blow to end the first quarter. The crowd roared. Perhaps, he thought, he could outwait them. Surely, they wouldn't stand in the cold breeze for the whole game waiting for him. He crawled into an unlocked car and put his suit on over his jogging outfit.

An hour later, Shithead was still there in the falling snow, clapping his hands together and glancing at his watch. Gilly cursed him under his breath. It wasn't warm in the car either, but at least he was out of the wind. It was probably three quarter time. The next time Gilly looked up, the muscleman had disappeared from the gate. Seizing his chance, Gilly jumped out of the car and flitted in through the press entrance.

Shouldering his way through the jammed crowd, he tried to find a place to watch the game. He looked up at the score-board which said: Calgary − 3; Sask. − 4. There were only thirty-nine seconds remaining in the final quarter. A mighty cheer went up from the crowd and he plunged toward the sidelines of the field to see what was happening.

The Stampeders held the ball on the twelve yard line deep inside Roughrider territory. It was first down so they would have three chances to score. They had the series sewn up! Keeling took the ball from the centre and faded back to pass. Parslow was in the clear. One completion and the game was in the bag. Suddenly, Keeling's protection disappeared and the Saskatchewan defence poured through the gap. He was hit by three men. The football squirted into the air and came down in the arms of a green and white player, Number 36, Saskatchewan's all-star tackle, big Ed McQuarters. Like a diesel truck, he barrelled eighty-seven yards down the field for a touchdown while the crowd screamed in anguish.

Gilly stood in shock as the score flashed on the board: Calgary − 3; Sask. − 11. The fans began to file toward the exit in a dead silence. The series was tied at one game apiece. The teams would move to Regina for a game on Saturday −

the 21st of November — that would determine the western final. Gilly turned and slumped out of the stadium. His odyssey seemed to be endless.

* * * * *

8

It was Friday before the bus rolled into Prince Albert and Gilly stepped off into the scenes of his youth. The cold northwest wind had continued to blow and brought with it a two inch snowfall which covered the ground. But now, Gilly was prepared. He had stopped overnight in Meadow Lake to buy a snowmobile suit, a bulky zippered coverall that made him look like an astronaut. Its bright gold colour stood out sharply against the grey of downtown Prince Albert.

Following his uncle's directions, he made his way up the southern slope of the city to the Sacred Heart Senior Citizens Home. There, a nun met him at the entrance. She escorted him down a long corridor lined with crucifixes and icons to a room in the interior. The home was a converted public school and its dark halls reverberated with echoes from the past. Here and there, clusters of old people — many in wheelchairs — waited for death to catch up to them. The nun stopped at a door.

"She probably won't recognize you, Mr. Savard."

Gilly shrugged. The nun pushed the door open. Mme. Savard was seated across the tiny bare room in front of the window. She had the same expression of endless patience on her face that Gilly had seen on the faces of the old people in the hall. Although her hair had turned white, Mme. Savard appeared neither frail nor feeble.

"Hi, Mama," Gilly said.

"Is that you, Gillman?"

He ran forward and embraced her as tears came to his eyes.

"Why are you wearing those funny overalls?" she said when he stepped back to take another look at her.

"It's a snowmobile suit, Ma. To keep out the cold. I'm going to a football game in Regina."

"Football?"

"Yeah — it's a long story. How's everybody at home?"

"Everybody?"

"Well, they told me Papa was dead, but — the others."

"Oh, the girls are married. Wilfred became a priest."

"Did he?" There was a silence, then Gilly grinned. "That's great, Ma. One of us finally made it for you."

Mme. Savard turned back to the window, her eyes suddenly sad again. "His parish is St. Laurent, you know — across the river from Batoche. Where the grotto shrine is."

"That's nice. I'll try to look him up on the way down. The thing is, though, I'm in kind of a hurry. . . ."

"You were always in a hurry, Gillman. Always running. Where are you hurrying to now?"

"I told you, Ma. It's the final game in the western series! And the Stampeders are going to go all the way! They're going to win the Grey Cup!"

Mme. Savard did not reply. She continued to gaze out the window. Reflected in the glass, he could see a tear roll down her cheek. Beside her on the wall stood a crucifix and suspended below it were her rosary beads.

"Ma?" Gilly said, but she would not reply.

* * * * *

9

The filmmaker had a choice. He could watch the western final on CBC or catch the Green Bay-Chicago game on one of the American channels. He would ordinarily have watched the American game, but his interest in the Calgary-Saskatchewan series had been piqued by Gilly's bet. On the other hand, the news that Savard had escaped from jail and was a fugitive somewhere on the West Coast made the bet irrelevant. With a sigh, he turned to the CBC. He would watch at least the first quarter, till the Packers kicked off.

The screen of his colour television set contradicted him. Regina's Taylor Field was in *black and white*. "Yes, folks," the commentator said, "the scene here is incredible! The temperature is a mere three degrees above zero!"

"And that's Fahrenheit, Dave!" a second commentator added.

211

"Right, Don. That's — let's see, nearly twenty below zero Celsius, for those of you into metric conversion and — get this — the wind is blowing at thirty-five m.p.h. out of the northwest!"

"Which makes a chill factor of thirty degrees below zero, Dave."

"Well, you can see what the field looks like on the long shot behind the goalposts here — like some Arctic wasteland. Definitely not a day to be playing football!"

As the filmmaker watched, the cameras panned around the stands and the colour reappeared on his set. He could hardly believe it. The stands were packed with fans! They were there in tens of thousands, huddling under blankets and down-filled sleeping bags, wearing great-coats and fur parkas and carrying portable heaters and thermos bottles. This raised the level of interest considerably. This was more than a mere sports contest, it was going to be a spectacle of human endurance! He settled down to watch.

From the opening kick-off, he could see that the idea of playing a *real* game was ridiculous. The ball flew through the air and was fumbled not only by the first receiver, but also by the next three players who touched the bouncing bladder. One of the Stampeders finally managed to smother it in a snowdrift on the sidelines. For nearly two hours, the filmmaker watched a comedy of dropped passes, multiple fumbles and players skidding in the snow. Periodically, the cameras would cut to the sidelines and show one of the unfortunate quarterbacks thawing his fingers in a fur muff, a red nose glowing through the driven snow. In a perverse way, it was actually exciting! With less than a minute left in the game, Saskatchewan was leading 14 to 12.

"Well, Don, this hometown crowd at Taylor Field is just going wild! What a game, eh? No telling which way it's going to go as we head into the final minute."

"Well, Dave, Saskatchewan has the ball so all they have to do is hang in there for three more plays and it'll be all sewn up."

"You have to hand it to these fans though, Don — they're sticking it out, rooting for their team. I feel sorry for the folks who travelled from Calgary, though. Look at that fellow down there on the fifty yard line."

The cameras picked out a fan sitting in the crowd in a bright gold snowmobile suit waving a pennant that read, "Go Stamps!"

"Hang on, Don — there's another fumble in the Saskatchewan backfield and — yes, Calgary has recovered! Wayne Harris grabbed that football and ran it all the way down to the Roughrider ten yard line!"

The camera belatedly picked up the pile of players on the Saskatchewan ten yard line.

"Well, that makes for a whole new ball game! We'd better wait and see what the Stampeder coach is going to come up with. They've just been handed a fantastic opportunity."

"Yes, Dave — provided they can hold onto the ball!"

On the next play, the Stampeder halfback fumbled the ball on the Saskatchewan four yard line. The stadium erupted in hysterical delight. The cameras flashed to the scoreboard to show that there were thirty seconds left in the game. Even the commentators were silent.

The Roughriders ran the ball twice in an effort to eat up time, but it was all they could do just to keep possession. They were forced to punt with seconds left in the game. The Calgary receiver ran the ball back to the twenty-six yard line. The clock showed one second.

"Wow, what a finish! Well, if you were in the coach's shoes, what would you call, Don?"

"There's only one call in this situation, Dave — a field goal attempt. They're only two points behind and if they can make it from this distance against the wind — that would give them the game and the trip to Toronto for the Grey Cup! Unfortunately, Calgary's kicking has been very poor this season, so they *could* surprise us with a forward pass in a touchdown effort."

"Wait a minute, Don. Someone has run onto the field! That Calgary fan in the snowmobile suit! He's trying to reach the Calgary bench!"

"Ha ha — a fan offering his services! Well, he couldn't do worse than what they've had the rest of the season. Too late, though — one of Regina's finest is escorting him out. It looks like he'll spend the rest of the game outside the gate."

"That's what you get for trying to be helpful, I guess. Well, there's the kick and — it's *good*! How about that!

Thirty-five yards into the teeth of the howling gale! And there goes the gun! Well, that's it, folks. Calgary 15; Saskachewan 14! And now a word from our sponsors."

* * * * *

10

"Grey Cup Special — Calgary to Toronto!" read the banner emblazoned across the front of the C.P.R. Canadian as it rolled into the Regina station. Football fans leaned from the platform doors waving pennants and whiskey bottles, just getting warmed up for their two day party across the country. Gilly waved a welcoming salute at the gleaming aluminum cars sliding by. A grin stretched across his face and a white Stetson hat crowned his dark hair. He wore a thick blanket coat of red plaid and his feet were encased in $150.00 cowboy boots. His left hand held a suitcase containing his snowmobile suit and half a case of beer. Just as he was about to step onto the train, a hand shot out of the crowd and grasped the arm of his coat.

"You'll have to wait for another year to see the Grey Cup, Savard!" a familiar voice growled. Gilly's eyes followed the arm to a set of stern shoulders, and a face that looked terribly familiar. Staff Sergeant Harry Swift was triumphant at last. Behind him was the Chief of Police of Regina, Dan Potz, scowling vengefully.

"You've got the wrong guy," Gilly said hopelessly. "I'm just a football fan."

Swift shook his head. "That's not what your friends in Calgary say. Besides, I got this little handful of paper you've been trailing across Western Canada." He offered him a handful of useless cheques that Gilly had issued in the last few days, as well as some that looked suspiciously like relics from his last visit to Regina.

"*Aboooord!*" the conductor called behind them as the train slid away on its long journey fifteen hundred miles to the east.

"Listen, Staff — you've got to give me a break on this! These are all small cheques. If you charge me, they'll send me back to the P.A. Pen. The mob is after me! I'll never come out alive!"

"You should have thought of that before you split from William Head, Savard. I'm getting tired of chasing you down. I wouldn't be surprised if they gave you the 'bitch'."

"Swift — *please*." The "bitch" was a charge of habitual criminal behaviour, an archaic procedure which meant automatic life imprisonment. It was normally applied against violent psychopaths.

"We're going to get you good this time, Savard," Chief Potz growled. "You'll be lucky to be out of solitary by this time next year."

* * * * *

11

On Grey Cup Day, the media consultant lounged in his sumptuous Jarvis Street apartment, one hand gripping a crystal glass of Ne Plus Ultra and the other fondling the curves of his latest girlfriend, a blonde by the name of either Sheila or Shirley that he had met at a singles club the night before. They were watching his twenty-four inch colour television set. The national Bacchanal was in progress.

Fans in western costumes danced and caroused through the streets of Toronto, leaping about on colourful parade floats. Cowboys on gaily decorated horses lassoed pretty girls on the sidewalks. It was a celebration to defy the coming winter solstice, a dance for the descent of Persephone into the underworld. An announcer suddenly appeared on the screen.

"We'll return in a few minutes to our live coverage of the Grey Cup Parade coming to you from downtown Toronto. And of course, stay tuned for live action from C.N.E. Stadium due to begin at two o'clock. Here is the CBC News."

A newsreader appeared. "The FLQ cell which kidnapped British diplomat James Cross and held him hostage for six weeks in a Montréal apartment has negotiated an escape from the country. The members fled this morning to Cuba on an Armed Forces plane after negotiating safe passage to the Montréal airport."

The screen showed the kidnappers climbing into a taxi

with a couple of suitcases. One of them, a woman, clutched a large television set which she was taking with her in her exile. The film cut abruptly to a shot of the taxi racing across the city, behind police cruisers, and arriving at the airport. The terrorists carried the television set from the taxi onto the airplane.

The newsreader continued, "American bombing of Cambodia continued today with a massive bombardment of Viet Cong and Khmer Rouge positions despite President Richard Nixon's public denial that the American Air Force was involved. An estimated ten million tons of explosives have been dropped on the country this month, more than was dropped on Japan during World War II."

"And in Northern Ireland, the provisional wing of the Irish Republican Army today vowed to carry out a Holy War against the British, punctuating its demands with hit-and-run bombings of several Protestant pubs in Belfast. Seven were left dead — five of them Catholics — and more than two dozen were injured." Ambulance attendants were shown on the screen carrying the wounded away.

"In Western Canada, one of the country's best-known confidence men, Gillman N. Savard, was found hanging in his cell at Prince Albert Penitentiary yesterday morning."

"*What?*" The media consultant leaped to his feet, his Scotch whiskey and his girl flung in either direction. He stared at the screen in shock.

"Prison officials said that Savard, recently the object of a countrywide manhunt after his escape from a B.C. prison, had apparently committed suicide. He was sent to Prince Albert this week as a habitual criminal after court hearings in Regina."

"What *is* it, sweetie?" the girl whimpered.

"Gilly Savard! That guy I told you about. The con man! I had a bet with him on this game!"

"Huh?"

"And in the world of sports," the newsreader continued, "the Montréal Canadiens today reported the signing to their club for the coming season of star junior, Guy Lafleur.

The consultant went across the room to the mahogany liquor cabinet and poured himself another glass of scotch. He drank it all down.

The television announcer smiled brightly. "And in Toronto, of course, today is Grey Cup Day, as the best in the east and west, the Calgary Stampeders and Ottawa Roughriders, fight it out for national supremacy. We return to the parade in progress."

As the parade reappeared on the screen, rolling into the gates of the C.N.E. Stadium, the consultant poured yet another glass of scotch. He took the bottle and his glass and returned to the sofa to stare in disbelief at his television set. Marching bands and cheerleaders followed the floats and cowboys. The stands of the stadium swarmed with ecstatic celebrants. Miss Grey Cup circled the field in a grey Lincoln convertible, waving and throwing kisses to the crowd. Several scenes from past Grey Cup games were shown, famous scenes that were run every year, of players who were magically allowed to retain their former glory.

A trumpet fanfare announced the latest gladiators, who trotted onto the field to be introduced in close-ups on the television screen. As the strains of "O Canada" began over the loudspeakers, the crowd stood up and Prime Minister Pierre Elliott Trudeau was escorted onto the field by two Mounties. With a wave to the crowd, he performed the ceremonial kick-off. The cameras switched to a Molson's beer commercial. Now somewhat glassy-eyed, the consultant continued to stare at the screen. The game got underway.

The filmmaker could not comprehend what was happening. He had sent his recommendation for Gilly's parole. He should have been at the game watching his favourite team in action. And now, he was dead. What had happened? Could he have killed himself in despair because he would never be able to leave jail again? Had the Mafia got him inside the Pen?

"Harkness comes up to the ball and gets a *good* kick away. It is taken by Parslow who gets under it at the ten yard line. He dipsy-doodles and *drives* for about twelve yards before he's finally brought down by Diefenbaker. Oh-oh, a flag on the play, the first penalty of the game is coming up — who is it, Don — Calgary?"

"It's Calgary, Dave."

"To Calgary, for clipping. That will take the ball back to the eleven yard line and a whole new situation."

This was the moment for a cigarette commercial, a pause

217

in the ritual of good and evil which was unfolding as living room entertainment across the nation. In a million homes, citizens lit up cigarettes and prepared to scream for blood.

"Well, a *tough* second down decision for Russ Jackson, with second and twenty-six to go following that penalty to Lamarsh. The halfback Kierans has been carried off the field, which *definitely* leaves them shorthanded going into the wind! Do you agree, Don?"

"I definitely concur, Dave, but Ottawa's problem with the deep defensive secondaries is going to have to be resolved before they can ——"

"Thank you, Don, and now back to the live action. Lang centres the ball and ——"

As the media consultant watched, stupified, the camera panned around the stadium. For a moment, the spectators became the spectacle. They waved and shouted for the camera. The camera zoomed in on a face in the crowd — a man waving a white Stetson hat. Beside him was a woman who flashed a shy sideways smile. The camera panned back to the action on the field.

"It's her!" the consultant shrieked. "That's the girl! They're both there!" He fell to his knees in front of his television set.

"What the hell is going on?" his girlfriend demanded to know.

"They didn't get him! I tell you, he's *there*!"

He stared at the machine, hoping its eye would return to the stands and explain the mystery. Was it just an hallucination? Or had the con man somehow switched his identity, escaped the prison and found the girl? Had he managed the ultimate con of all? Had he cheated death?

There was no answer from the machine. The game went on and on.

TALONBOOKS — FICTION IN PRINT 1979

Songs My Mother Taught Me — Audrey Thomas
Blown Figures — Audrey Thomas
Hungry Hills — George Ryga
Theme for Diverse Instruments — Jane Rule
Mrs. Blood — Audrey Thomas
Night Desk — George Ryga
Ballad of a Stonepicker — George Ryga
Dürer's Angel — Marie-Claire Blais
A Short Sad Book — George Bowering
Desert of the Heart — Jane Rule
The School-Marm Tree — Howard O'Hagan
The Woman Who Got on at Jasper Station
     & Other Stories — Howard O'Hagan
Wilderness Men — Howard O'Hagan
Latakia — Audrey Thomas
The Con Man — Ken Mitchell
Prisoner of Desire — britt hagarty